Worlds Unseen

LITTLE DOZEN PRESS

Worlds Unseen

Published by Little Dozen Press
Stevensville, Ontario, Canada
www.littledozen.com

Cover artwork by Deborah Thomson, copyright 2008
Cover design by Mercy Hope, copyright 2015

ISBN: 978-0-9739591-8-5

Worlds Unseen

The Seventh World Trilogy
Book One

Rachel Starr Thomson

Table of Contents

Prologue

THE HOUSE WAS FULL OF THE LITTLE NOISES OF LIFE. A bright fire crackled in the hearth, and over it the contents of a small iron pot hissed and bubbled. Mary's rocking chair creaked as her deft fingers wove a world in cross-stitch, visions of sunset and starlight. A mourning dove, tucked away in a nest in the corner of the stone window ledge, cooed softly.

Mary did not look up when a shadow fell across the picture in her hand. Through her eyelashes she saw a tall, dark-cloaked form with a gleaming knife in its hand. For a tenth of a second Mary's fingers faltered; she regained herself, and continued to sew. She bent her head closer to the cross-stitch and her chestnut hair fell over her shoulder.

"So you've come," she said, her voice perfectly level.

The cloaked figure's voice dripped with venom. "You expected me?"

The creak of the rocking chair filled the momentary silence, and the fire crackled. The pot was near to boiling over.

"I knew you would keep your promise," Mary said. "Though you have been much longer than I expected. And even now you are waiting."

The tall figure sneered. "Where is your fool of a husband?"

Mary said faintly, "He is coming."

Outside, the cooing of the dove had ceased. A man was

whistling as he came up the path to the cottage. His tune died out, choked by sudden fear, and his footsteps hastened to an urgent pace.

The cloaked figure raised the knife in the air. Mary lifted her head suddenly, and her blue eyes pierced through the black cloak to the woman beneath it, momentarily halting the hate-filled advance.

"Take care, woman," Mary said, "lest the power you seek to control someday overpower *you*."

The door of the house opened with the striking of wood against stone as John Davies rushed into the danger he sensed all around him.

The pot boiled over.

* * *

The cloaked woman hurried down the hill. She turned to look at the cottage once more, watching as the flames reduced even the stones to ash. She laughed wildly, her laughter swirling into the smoke-filled wind. The green hills around seemed to mourn as the heat and smoke blurred their ancient sides into wavering, uncertain mirages. High in the hills, a hawk cried.

The woman turned and strode along the path that led to the town. In the distance she heard a sheepdog barking, and her eyes narrowed as she pictured the small figure who was even now making her way to the ruined house.

It would be so easy to kill her, too. The woman's fingers clenched the handle of the knife, slippery with blood, that was now hidden beneath the black folds of her cloak. But no. The master would be angry. The girl was nothing and he did not want needless killing. It was not wise—it was better to let the ignorant live in fear. So he said.

She spat. Master Skraetock was a fool. True, at times she sounded just like him, speaking of wisdom for the sake of the future. Only now, with the stench of the kill hidden under her cloak and the wind carrying ashes up to the heavens, with the power of the Covenant Flame running wild in her veins, she did not care about wisdom.

She could hear the girl's footsteps on the hard earth, as the dog barked around her heels. Her fingers gripped the knife tighter . . . and relaxed. The rush of the Covenant Flame was beginning to die. She felt it slip away. She wished to kill if only to bring it back; but wisdom came with the going of it. She would obey. The girl would live.

For now.

1

A Shadowed Past

THE WAR IS OVER, and the King has gone from our land. Gone with him are the faithful children of men, and now only I am left! I alone remain to sing the Song of the Burning Light over this bloodstained ground. The Earth Brethren are gone; I know not where. It seems they are vanquished who once made all men tremble with fear before the strength of wolf and wind and water, of growing thing and of fire. They are gone, and never more shall I hear their battle cries all around me. My heart quakes to think of them conquered, yet how could it be otherwise? Their power was shattered in grief when the King's heart was pierced by the treachery of his beloved ones. Surely the anguish of his heart-breaking must shake this world so that nothing can stand untouched.

And the Shearim, the merry ones, the Fairest of Creation: they too are gone. They whom no one could kill have destroyed themselves that the children of men might be protected from their own wickedness. With the life-force which once danced in their eyes the Shearim have woven a Veil, a barrier between the Blackness and men. Yet my heart tells me that even the Veil cannot last forever. One day it will grow weak and tear, and the Shearim will pass out of the world forever. How the stars weep for us!

But now my blood grows hot within me and visions pass before my eyes, and I, the Poet, I, the Prophet, will speak! The Blackness will not reign victorious always. In the end the hearts of men will yearn again for their King, and he shall come! Hear, all you heavens. Listen to me, all you earth! Rejoice, for he will come again!

Yet quietly will it begin. His reign shall not be taken up first on the Throne of Men, but in their Hearts: in the hearts of small things, of insignificant things, of forgotten things. In their hearts shall be kindled the Love of the Ages, and they shall sing the Song of the Burning Light!

And he shall come.

* * *

The air was just beginning to take on a metallic chill when Maggie passed the Orphan House.

Its tall wrought iron gates frowned down on her and striped her face with shadows where they blocked the orange light of the windows. Creepers, brown with the coming of winter, wound their way up the red, soot-covered brick walls. The windows were barred and tightly shut. One, on the ground floor, had been cranked open, though bars crossed it. Maggie could hear the clanging and shouts coming from that window, and though she was too far away to feel it, she could imagine the oppressive heat drifting out into the evening. It was the kitchen, a room made hellish by the constant activity of twenty ovens. In the winter the window would be kept shut to keep the icy wind from blowing in and the expensive heat from drifting out. But not yet.

Maggie picked up her pace instinctively, as she always did before the glaring visage of the House. Had she been caught outside those walls as a child she would have been locked in the cupboard, or worse. Now, there was no one to shout her name, no one to threaten her and slap her and tell her not to try running away again. It had been years since the Orphan House had held her prisoner, yet the tyranny of the place still held some sway over her soul. So she walked faster.

From the kitchen came the harsh shrieking of a matron in a foul mood, and in the yard a dog sent up a dismal howl. The cold seemed to cling to Maggie, seeping through her heavy brown overcoat. She pulled it closer to her and shivered. It was a cold evening in an autumn that had thus far been unusually warm. A dragon-headed iron train screamed over a bridge in the distance. An elderly man with a decorated sword hanging from his belt nodded to her as he sauntered past.

The Orphan House behind her, Maggie turned down a residential street lined with old houses that were crammed in next to each other like books on a shelf. The street dead-ended in an iron fence that closed in a large property: a stately old house with yellow paint that was peeling and a flower garden that bloomed like the sun in summer. In the quickly fading light, the old house looked somewhat mournful. Most of its flowers had already succumbed to the frost. In an upstairs window a candle was burning, and a stout shape moved around the room in what looked like a waltz. Maggie smiled.

She turned from the view of the yellow house and ascended the creaking steps of her own home, the last on the bookshelf street, a slim, two-story brick house with peeling blue shutters at the windows. Maggie sighed when she thought of the hours she and Patricia had put into painting them just last summer, while Mrs. Cook, the owner of the house, puttered around in the kitchen baking cookies to feed "her girls" when they finished.

Maggie twisted the brass doorknob and pushed the door open. It protested loudly, and Maggie made a mental note to oil the hinges soon. If Pat had been home, surely the door would have been attended to earlier. She always noticed such things.

A bright fire was burning cheerfully in the fireplace, casting its glow over the small room. A painting of a river in the country hung over the mantle, which was covered in little glass figurines, newly dusted and glowing proudly in the firelight. On the wall, tucked in the shadows of the fireplace bricks, a slim sword hung on a hook. Pat had insisted on leaving it with them—how she expected either Maggie or Mrs. Cook to use it was a mystery.

Maggie collapsed into a high-backed stuffed chair near the fire without taking off her coat or boots. She closed her eyes and let all of her muscles relax, while the heat folded around her like a cocoon.

A loud, cheery voice interrupted her near slumber.

"Well, then," Eva Cook exclaimed, her ample form filling the doorway to the kitchen and blocking most of the light from that part of the house. "You're home. Did you get the parcel?"

Maggie sighed with the effort of pulling her body back into action. She reached a red-gloved hand inside her coat and pulled out a small packet wrapped in brown paper. She started to get up, but Mrs. Cook stopped her.

"No, dear," she said, "Don't you move. I know a tired body when I see one. Was it a really long walk?"

Maggie nodded. "Not too long, really, but I am tired. I always want to go to sleep after being out in the cold."

"Winter's coming after all," Mrs. Cook commented, "though I had hoped we would cheat it this year." She disappeared into the kitchen for a moment, and the light from the homey room came streaming back. She reappeared bearing a saucer and tea cup, steaming with hot tea.

"Here, dear," Mrs. Cook said. "Drink this."

Maggie took the cup and saucer and let the steam from the bittersweet drink warm her face. She took a sip and leaned back again with a smile.

"Thank you," she said. "But you don't need to fuss over me. You'd think I'd been gone as long as Pat."

Mrs. Cook didn't seem to notice Maggie's teasing tone. "I'm just taking care of you, Maggie Sheffield. You know as well as I do that you're not the strongest bird in the sky. One of these days you'll catch pneumonia, and I'll fuss then. How's your cold?"

Maggie chuckled. "Much better, with your tea steaming all the congestion out of me. It's been years since I was really sick. You needn't worry."

"I'm not worried," Mrs. Cook said with a sniff. She caught sight of Maggie grinning at her and said, "Not about the likes of you."

Maggie dipped her little finger in her tea, stirring it idly. "Something's missing from the tea," she said.

"Linlae leaf," Mrs. Cook said. "I ran out and was too busy to cut more."

Maggie set her tea aside and pushed herself out of her chair before Mrs. Cook could protest. "I'll get it," she said. She walked lightly to her guardian's side and stood on her tiptoes to kiss the tall old woman's cheek on her way out.

Mrs. Cook watched her march out the front door with a smile. She was so different from the old days, this girl. Eva could remember the days when even a hint of sharpness in her voice would send the little orphan into a fit of shivering, anxious fear. Maggie had been so small and skinny then, her auburn hair tangled and dirty.

"You don't want that one," the man from the Orphan House had said. "She's no good for nothin'—too weak, and ugly besides."

Mrs. Cook had seen through the dirt and grime to a child who desperately needed freedom. Margaret Sheffield was precisely the child she wanted.

She remembered clearly the first few days, when Maggie learned what it was like to be clean and well-fed and loved. She had accepted everything warily, as though she expected to wake up any moment and find the dream turned into a nightmare. Her greatest fear in those days had been that Patricia Black, herself an orphan, might prove to be an enemy. Pat, in true form, had taken the scared little thing under her wing.

Pat had cried the day that Maggie was sent off to Cryneth to live with John and Mary Davies, old friends of the Cooks'. Eva had cried, too, but she knew it was best. The mountains and Mary's songs were what Maggie needed to heal.

Even now, Mrs. Cook had to fight back tears at the thought of the way those years in Cryneth had ended. She remembered how Maggie had appeared on her back doorstep, half dead and nearly unrecognizable. She remembered how Pat had run for the doctor at the Orphan House. She remembered the doctor's words.

"She were never a well one. I don't see how she's made it this far, with all that smoke in her lungs. If I was you, Mrs. Cook, I'd be looking for a nice burial plot."

But Maggie had recovered. Her hands and arms were forever scarred from the burns. She never told anyone exactly what had happened, although they found out later that John and Mary had been killed in a fire. Maggie had been seen digging through the still-smoldering ashes for some remnant of the happiest days of her life. The villagers had tried to help her but she had run away.

Somehow, Maggie had found happiness again. Somehow, she had put it behind her. And every time Mrs. Cook saw the young woman smile, she thanked the stars for the power that had brought Maggie all the way back to her doorstep in Londren, and home.

* * *

The linlae tree grew between the house and the iron fence. It hugged the wall like a vine, its silvery bark and the last of its light green leaves beautiful against the soot-smudged brick. Maggie smiled as she reached up into the thin branches, pulling them down so that twigs and leaves brushed her face and baptized her with the scent of life. The leaves rustled as she searched for a good bunch to clip. The warm autumn had been good to the hardy little tree; it was still green in the face of coming winter. Maggie started to hum to herself when a sound made its way to her ears. She frowned, releasing the branches so that they jerked away and quivered above her.

There it was again. Something was moving in the dark shadows behind the house. Maggie peered down the alley, but she could see nothing. *A cat,* she thought. *It must be a cat.*

She shook off the uneasy feeling that had settled on her and finished clipping a branch. As she took a step toward home, something in the alley clattered. She turned, her heart leaping in her throat.

What was back there?

She turned to leave when the sound of a deep, racking cough sent shivers up her spine. That was no cat.

Maggie turned back around and walked quickly, deliberately, toward the safety of the front door. Pat, she thought, would have been in the alley by now, forcing a full confession from whoever was skulking in the shadows. Pity the fellow caught by *her* fierce questions. But Maggie was not Pat, and Pat was far away in Cryneth. She kept walking.

"Maggie Sheffield?" It was a trembling voice, old, and strangely familiar. It was deep with illness.

Maggie turned slowly to see a small, hunched old man step out from the shadows. He stood silhouetted against the fence, and Maggie could not see his face or his features. He stretched out a hand toward her. It was shaking.

"Maggie?" he asked again. He took a step forward and Maggie realized that he was about to fall. She dropped the leafy twigs in her hand and rushed forward, grabbing the old man's arm to steady him. He looked up at her with weary, gray eyes.

"Thank ye, Maggie," he said.

She knew who he was. The relief of recognition flooded her. Those gray eyes had regarded her kindly when she was a child in the Orphan House, and once they had watched her from the safety of the little house in Cryneth. In the Orphan House he had brought presents for the children once or twice a year—mittens and scarves, pieces of candy, sometimes even dolls for the girls and trains for the boys. She hadn't known why he had come to the Davies' in Cryneth. Evidently they were old friends. She had never known his full name—the children called him Old Dan.

She certainly had no idea what he was doing here now, hiding in an alley behind her home.

He began to cough again, and nearly doubled over with the effort. Maggie clutched at him, wishing she could somehow transfer strength from her body into his. He sounded as if he might never stop coughing. But the fit did come to an end, and he leaned against her, exhausted. She was alarmed at how thin and light he was.

"Come," she said, guiding him. "I live here, just a few more steps. We'll take good care of you."

Maggie helped him up the steps and opened the door. The hinges squeaked out an announcement of her return.

Mrs. Cook appeared from the kitchen, already talking. "I was beginning to wonder if you'd run away out there. Heavens, Maggie, what took you so—" she stopped in mid-sentence.

"Heavens," she breathed.

Maggie helped the weak old man into the high-backed chair near the fire. He nearly fell into it. Maggie removed his threadbare gloves and began rubbing his fingers between her own hands. She wanted to say something, but his eyes were closed and so she kept her mouth shut. When his hands felt a bit warmer, she took the muddy boots from his feet and set them near the fire to dry while she wrapped him in a blanket snatched from the arms of Mrs. Cook's rocking chair.

The lady of the house emerged from the depths of the kitchen with a washtub full of hot water.

"Come on, Maggie," she said. "In with his feet."

Mrs. Cook pressed a hand against the old man's wrinkled forehead. "Fever," she muttered. "Maggie, get another blanket from the cupboard upstairs. A thick one. Make that two. He's shivering."

Maggie rushed up the stairs, taking them two at a time, and threw open the cupboard at the end of the narrow hallway. She grabbed two thick blankets and flew back downstairs with them.

Mrs. Cook was stoking the fire, while the kettle shrieked its readiness in the kitchen.

"Get the tea, would you, dear?" Mrs. Cook asked in a tone of voice that made it clear she was not asking.

Maggie went into the whitewashed kitchen where the copper kettle rattled on the surface of the wood stove. She snatched it off and poured the water into a white teapot.

She reentered the living room with Mrs. Cook's largest tea cup and saucer, as well as two more just in case, and ducked back into the kitchen to fetch the teapot. When she came back out, Old Dan's eyes were open and Mrs. Cook seemed strangely agitated.

Maggie shifted her feet and licked her lips uncomfortably, feeling that she had missed something important.

"This is Old Dan." She felt like a child saying the name,

which was not really much of a name at all. "He's a friend."

"We know each other," Mrs. Cook said stiffly.

Maggie's eyebrows raised a good half-inch. "You do?" she asked incredulously.

"Evie and I are old friends," Old Dan said weakly, with a tinge of humour in his voice.

Mrs. Cook stood abruptly and started up the stairs. She turned when she was halfway up.

"I don't want him going up and down stairs in his condition," she said. "We'll fix up the guest room."

Maggie nodded. Silently, she picked up the bucket of coal that lay beside the fire and took a box of matches from the mantle. She felt Old Dan's eyes watching her, but she couldn't bring herself to say anything. Mrs. Cook had seemed almost angry.

She took the coal and matches to a small, cold room just off of the living room. It had a fireplace of its own, and she knelt down to prepare the room for its new occupant. Soon she had a fire blazing, and the lonely little room seemed cheered. Starched white curtains hung by its windows, overlooking a single bed. Mrs. Cook entered the room and started to make the bed with flannel sheets and a large feather blanket and pillows. A tiny bedside table held a gas lamp and an old book with gold writing on its cover. It had been years, Maggie thought, since the room had been occupied. She didn't recognize the book—perhaps a friend of Pat's had left it.

Before long, the room had been transformed. The lonely chill gave way before the warmth of the fire and the glow of the oil lamp that spilled onto the deep green blankets. Mrs. Cook stood with her hands on her hips and looked the room over with a satisfied nod. Maggie slipped out the door to get Old Dan.

He was sitting totally still except for the slight shaking of his hands. His eyes were open and he was staring into the fire, seemingly lost in thought. He didn't hear Maggie's approach.

She reached out a hand and laid it on his arm. He jumped slightly, then reached up his own gnarled hand and covered hers.

"I'm sorry," Maggie said. "I didn't mean to startle you."

He patted her hand. "No harm done, m'dear."

"Your room's ready," she explained, and took his arm to help him up. He stood with a struggle, and leaned on her as they walked to the room.

"It's not much," Maggie said.

Old Dan chuckled, and the effort made him fight to catch his breath again before speaking. "Don't forget I'm an old alley-dweller," he said with a twinkle in his eye. "The emperor's palace couldn't be any nicer."

He started to laugh again and set off a fit of coughing. Maggie lowered him onto the bed. She cast a concerned look at Mrs. Cook, who had a man's nightshirt draped over her arm.

"He'll be all right," Mrs. Cook said. "Go off to bed, Maggie. I'll watch after our guest. Get!"

Maggie left the room reluctantly. As she climbed the stairs to her own room, a flood of weariness washed over her. She had forgotten how tired she was.

* * *

The voices drifted up the stairs, rising and falling through the cracks in the floor into Maggie's room. She turned over in her sleep, pulling her quilt closer to her ears.

The voices sharpened, and Maggie awoke. For a moment she thought she had been dreaming, but then she heard them again. The conversation downstairs had grown heated.

She knew it was none of her business, but curiosity got the better of her groggy mind. She swung her feet out of bed, feeling the shock of cold when they touched the hardwood floor. The floorboards creaked as she lit the lamp beside her bed and pulled a robe on over her nightgown. Picking up the lamp, she stepped out into the hall. The voices had quieted.

Maggie stepped lightly down the stairs and through the living room to the spare room. The light was on, leaking through the slight crack where the door was not quite shut.

Maggie peered in through the crack. Mrs. Cook had moved her rocking chair to the bedside. Maggie could see her each time she rocked forward. Her eyes were swollen.

"You shouldn't have come here, Daniel," Mrs. Cook said, a hardness in her voice that Maggie had never heard before.

"I'm sorry, Evie," Old Dan's voice answered. "Perhaps you're right." He coughed painfully. "Truth is, I was afraid out there. I've never been so cold. I've never been afraid to die, before, but now... Well, I didn't think ye would turn me away."

Mrs. Cook's voice sounded as though she might lose control and start crying again. "No, Daniel, don't talk nonsense. Of course it was better that you come here than stay out there with such a—such a sickness." Her voice lowered, but Maggie still caught the words. "If only Maggie didn't know you."

"I didn't know she was here," Old Dan said.

The rocking chair leaned forward with a forceful creak. "Promise me you won't talk to her about anything more than the weather, Daniel Seaton. No talk of the old days. I don't want Maggie tangled up with the council."

"There is no council," Daniel's voice said. "Or have you forgotten? There's naught left now but you and me and the others, all scattered and hiding—and dead, some of us. The council is finished."

"And may it stay that way," Mrs. Cook said. There was silence for a moment, and then Daniel spoke again.

"Have you forgotten, Evie? Have you forgotten the way it was, in the old days? Surely you canna hate its memory so much."

"It was all a game back then," Mrs. Cook said. "We were children playing with fire."

There was a heavy sigh from the bed. "'Twas a glorious fire," Old Dan said. "But dangerous, yes."

"I want Maggie kept far away from it," Mrs. Cook said. "It was bad enough that she was there when Mary—"

"I know," Old Dan said. "Evie, there's somethin' I need to be tellin' ye."

There was an expectant silence, and Old Dan spoke again. His voice was barely a whisper this time, and Maggie was not sure if she had heard him right.

"I saw her," he said.

The rocking chair leaned forward, and Maggie could see Mrs. Cook's face. It had drained of colour. Maggie felt suddenly cold—the cold came from within, as though childhood fears had passed over her. She had half a mind to turn and go back to bed, but she knew the fear would only follow her. She stayed where she was.

"Evelyn?" Mrs. Cook asked, her voice suddenly as weak as Daniel's.

"Aye," Old Dan said.

"Did she know you?" Mrs. Cook asked.

"I didna think so," Old Dan said. "But then this sickness… it makes me very afraid, Evie."

Mrs. Cook let out a noise like an angry sob. "How long will she hound us? Was she not content to destroy us with her lies?"

"It wasn't as though she came after me," the old man said. "We stumbled across each other, quite by accident."

"And John and Mary?" Mrs. Cook said. "Was that an accident? How many more of us will die before she's content to leave us alone?"

Maggie closed her eyes as the shock of what she was hearing sunk in. For a moment she forgot herself and leaned against the door. It swung open and Maggie stumbled into the room. Mrs. Cook jumped half out of her chair, and then sank back into it with a moan. Maggie heard a sigh from the bed. No one spoke.

"I heard you talking," Maggie said. "I don't understand."

"Go back to bed," Mrs. Cook said gently.

Maggie shook her head. "No. John and Mary—you said a woman killed them."

Maggie took a step nearer the rocking chair, almost menacing in her approach. She was trembling. "John and Mary's death was an accident. Wasn't it?"

Mrs. Cook seemed supremely unhappy. She began to answer, bit her lip, and finally nodded. "Yes, Maggie. It was an accident."

"You don't believe that."

"I don't know anything to the contrary."

"But you don't *believe* it. You think this woman killed them. You think they were—" she faltered. "Murdered."

Mrs. Cook reached a weary hand to a strand of grey hair that had worked itself loose from her bun. She brushed it back and regarded the young woman standing before her, eyes pleading.

"Sit down, Maggie," Mrs. Cook said. Maggie obeyed, sinking into the deep green feather blanket on Old Dan's bed.

"No," Mrs. Cook said wearily. "I don't believe the fire was an accident."

Maggie leaned forward. "Then what—?"

Mrs. Cook leaned back in the rocking chair and listened to the pop of the firewood in the hearth. "When we were very young," she said slowly, "we were part of a council. John Davies, and Mary, and Daniel and I. We were studying old legends and phenomena. Things that couldn't be explained naturally."

Daniel spoke up, and his voice seemed stronger than before. "It was glorious," he said.

Mrs. Cook ignored him. "It was dangerous," she said. "There are powers in this world, Maggie—or outside of it, as it may be—that are best left alone."

"Who was the woman?" Maggie couldn't remember the name they had mentioned.

"Evelyn?" Mrs. Cook asked. Her voice suddenly grew more tired. "She was nearly one of us. She would have become one of the council, if we had voted her in. Mary stopped that from happening." Her voice dropped to a whisper. "Thank heavens."

"She were an evil one," Old Dan suddenly added. "Swore she'd kill Mary for opposing her."

Mrs. Cook shot Daniel a scathing look. Maggie felt that Mrs. Cook had planned to leave that part out.

"We didn't think she meant it," Mrs. Cook said. "We didn't think there was any real danger. Not until the fire."

"Do you have any proof?" Maggie asked.

Mrs. Cook shook her head. "Only the warning bells that went off in my own heart, and the memory of her black face all twisted and laughing."

"Laughing," Maggie whispered.

Mrs. Cook looked at the young woman and suddenly burst into tears. "Oh, Maggie," she cried, reaching for the girl who once more looked so orphaned. She rose from her rocking chair and enfolded Maggie in her embrace.

For a long time they remained together, Mrs. Cook holding onto Maggie as though her tight embrace could stop the sorrow from coming. When at long last Maggie lifted a hollow-eyed face, Old Dan was watching them with a rolled up piece of parchment in his hands.

"What is that?" Mrs. Cook asked. She did not sound as though she wanted an answer.

"It was Evelyn's," Old Dan said quite simply. "I took it from her."

Mrs. Cook paled. "When?"

"Not two weeks ago," he said. "When I saw her. She was in Galce, in an inn. I snuck into her room and this was there, and I thought it was important. So I took it."

"Why?" Mrs. Cook asked.

"It's important," Old Dan repeated. "It means something. I've been up to see the laird with it."

A flush of anger rose in Eva Cook's cheeks. "You mean you'd still speak to that—"

Old Dan shrugged. "I don't suppose he's any friend of hers, not after all this time. It was his council she ripped to pieces."

"Why did you come back here?" Mrs. Cook asked.

"The laird wouldn't see me," he said. "So I was takin' the scroll to Pravik. Maybe Jarin Huss can read it." He held up the parchment, and his hand began to shake violently. In a moment his body was racked with the terrible cough, and Maggie saw blood on his hand where he covered his mouth.

"Trouble is," he rasped when he had regained control of his body, "I'm not sure I'll make it to Pravik."

Mrs. Cook walked slowly to Old Dan's side. She laid her hand on his forehead. "You're burning up," she said. "Daniel— what happened to you in Galce?"

"She looked at me," Old Dan said. "I didn't think she recognized me. At least not at the time. But her eyes met mine."

His bony frame sunk back farther into the bed. "All that night I dreamed about her eyes. The coughing fits woke me up. It's been getting worse ever since."

As though to illustrate his words, Old Dan began to cough again. This time, blood ran from his mouth down his chin and onto the sheets and blankets. Mrs. Cook ran from the room for water and rags to clean the blood. Maggie could only stare at the helpless old man, while her own blood ran cold. She knew what they were thinking—somehow, she knew it was true. This was no natural illness, but a living evil that was slowly murdering a frail old man.

When the coughing fit had at last ended, Old Dan gasped for air. Every breath racked his body with pain, and he shivered uncontrollably. Mrs. Cook sat at his side, holding one gnarled hand in her own, whispering words of comfort.

The fire was dying out. Maggie went in search of more coal. In truth, she could think of nothing but escaping from that room.

From the deep recesses of her memory, laughter followed her out.

An hour had passed before Maggie entered again. The room resounded with silence. The fire had nearly gone out. Mrs. Cook was still clutching Old Dan's hand, stroking it. He opened his eyes and Maggie wanted to cry when she saw how much worse he looked. His skin was horribly pale, and there were dark circles under his eyes. He struggled to sit up when he saw her. She hurried to sit down on the bed so that he would not waste his energy.

He slumped back onto the pillows and his fingers reached for the parchment that was laying next to him.

"Evie," he said in a voice that was barely a whisper. "How will it get to Pravik? To Huss . . . it's important."

The energy to speak seemed to drain out of him onto the pillows. Maggie picked up the parchment in one hand and took the fingers of the old man who had once brought her toys at the Orphan House.

"I'll take it," Maggie said. Mrs. Cook's eyes snapped up to look at Maggie's face, her own full of horror.

Maggie only leaned closer to Old Dan, who had closed his eyes again. "Do you hear me?" she whispered. "I'll take it to Pravik."

He nodded, ever so slightly, and a smile tried to struggle free from his face.

He did not move again that night.

As Maggie left the room to trudge back to her bed, she turned to see tears running down Mrs. Cook's face.

* * *

Daniel Seaton died the next morning. If he had other friends in Londren, Mrs. Cook did not know of them. Maggie was sent after the undertaker, and the austere little man arrived before noon. A coffin was available that would do the chore, and the body of Old Dan was taken to an old graveyard and buried before the sun had set on the day of his death.

Maggie and Mrs. Cook watched as the black box was lowered into the ground by men who did not care, while dry autumn leaves blew through the maze of tombstones. A bell was rung in the little stone building that watched over the graveyard, and Maggie held tightly to Mrs. Cook's arm as they leaned on each other.

"Farewell, Daniel Seaton," Eva Cook whispered as the bell pealed its melancholy song.

It was over quickly. The two women climbed into a waiting carriage and began the slow ride back home. The red brick of the Orphan House glared down at them as the horses clopped past, and Maggie turned her face from it. Tucked inside her coat, the parchment scroll burned an awareness of itself into her.

She had decided to leave for Pravik the next day.

2

Run, Boy, Run

"LAST CALL TO BOARD THE *CROSSWIND!*" The deep-voiced call rose up over the noise of the crowds and brought tears to Mrs. Cook's eyes.

"Are you sure you won't reconsider, Maggie?" she asked.

"I need to do this," Maggie said. She smiled as she looked into Mrs. Cook's eyes. "It will be all right," she said. "You'll see. I'll come back soon, and I'll write you the minute I get to Pravik."

"Why did you ever make a promise to that Dan Seaton?" Mrs. Cook asked, shaking her head.

"It's not just the promise," Maggie said. "There are questions in my head that need answering, and somehow I think I'll find the answers in Pravik. I'll be all right, Mrs. Cook, truly. There; now I've made *you* a promise."

She set her ragged little trunk down on the dock and reached for the old woman who had given her so much. They clung tightly to each other, and Maggie felt Mrs. Cook's body stiffen in a gallant effort to keep from sobbing. Maggie pulled away from the embrace and looked up at the sails of the *Crosswind* that would soon catch the sea breeze and head away

from the island she had always called home: away to the
continent—land of history, home of the empire, great dark
place of adventure. She picked up her trunk and squared her
shoulders, willing herself to look her dearest friend in the face
one more time. More than anything she feared the sight of
Mrs. Cook's tears. They were the only thing with the power to
drain her of all resolve and return her to Londren, even now.

Their eyes met, and Maggie's vision of Mrs. Cook's stout
form standing tall and brave misted over, as tears sprang to her
own eyes.

"Good-bye," Maggie croaked. She forced herself to turn
away and walk to the ship that creaked impatiently as it
bobbed on the water of the harbour.

The sailors had begun to haul the gangplank up into the
ship as Maggie ran up, calling out for them to wait. They
frowned at her, and one of the men spit over the side and
muttered something under his breath. Maggie called up her
thanks as they lowered the plank once more.

When she and her battered trunk were safely aboard the
ship, Maggie found a spot at the rail and looked into the crowd
for one more glimpse of Mrs. Cook. All she could see was a
mass of coats and hats and moving bodies, and though she tried
to make sense of the bewildering view, she could not find her
old friend. Perhaps it was best.

It was a clear, sunny day, and the sails filled with wind as
the boat moved swiftly over the water of the Salt Channel,
away from the island of Bryllan. The cries of the gulls in the
harbour changed to the sounds of water and wind, the feel of
salt spray and the warmth of the sun. The chill of the last few
days had given way to warmth, belying the coming winter,

although the spray made Maggie glad of her old brown coat.

After a while Maggie grew tired of standing. She propped her trunk up under the rail and leaned against it, sliding down to the deck. Drowsiness, the effect of far too many conflicting emotions, settled over her. She pulled her cap down to shade her eyes and fell asleep.

* * *

Maggie woke up to the bustle and noise of the crew as the *Crosswind* moved into port in the Galcic town of Calai. The sun had gone into the regression of early evening, and the air had grown colder. Maggie got to her feet unsteadily and reached for her trunk.

Calai was bewildering. The port was full of fishing boats, and the smell of salt and fish mingled in the air, making Maggie's stomach queasy. Fishermen, housemaids, vendors hawking their wares, and children playing tag formed a crushing mass of people. Maggie held tightly to her trunk as she descended the plank.

Suddenly very aware that she wasn't sure what to do next, Maggie allowed herself to be carried by the flow of the crowd. She soon found herself on the outskirts of the harbour, looking into the town. Darkness was settling fast, and street lanterns came on like fireflies as the lamplighters went about their business.

Laughter spilled out from a nearby pub where men from the docks were gathered after a hard day's work. Maggie stopped a big man on his way to the rough-looking place.

"I'm sorry to bother you," she said, trying not to notice

what a grim face he had, "but I—I need to find an inn, and I'm not sure . . ."

She looked up at him for a moment, and the gentleness in his eyes caught her by surprise.

"There's a good one not far from here," the man said. He pointed her down the street and gave her directions which twisted through the town in labyrinthine fashion. Maggie tried hard not to let the string of lefts, rights, and "on the corner of's" blur together.

The man tipped his hat. "Good evening to you," he said, and Maggie set off in the direction he had indicated.

It didn't take long for Maggie to realize that something was wrong, either with the directions or with her recollection of them. She kept going, uneasily, as the town grew darker and less friendly.

She stopped abruptly, and whirled around at the sound of footsteps behind her. She could see nothing in the shadows, but her fingers tightened their grip on her trunk all the same. She knew better than to trust the darkness.

When the street remained still and no more menacing noises found their way to her ears, Maggie turned slowly and began to search out her way once more. A moment later they were there again—footsteps. She picked up her pace.

She had not walked more than a block when she came to a dead end: a high brick wall crumbling with age. She reached out her hand to touch it, willing it to disappear and become the well-lit window of an inn.

Behind her, she heard the sound of a match flaring to life.

"Out a little late, ain't you?" a voice asked. Maggie turned to see two men, the burning light of a small oil lamp illuminating unshaven faces. One of them played with a knife, twirling it in his fingers.

The other man grinned at his fellow, then looked at Maggie again.

"Didn't nobody tell you this ain't a good neighbourhood?" he asked. "It's crawling with rabble."

The man with the knife laughed.

"So, what you got in there?" the speaker asked. He gestured toward the trunk.

"Nothing," Maggie said, finding her voice. "Only some clothes." She thought of what would happen if they got to the money hidden in the bottom of the trunk. She would be stranded here in Galce without a way to get back home, much less reach Pravik.

"Oh, come now," the speaker said again. He moved forward menacingly. "It don't take much to make us happy."

Maggie started to move in front of the trunk, when she gasped in fear. A huge black shadow was moving up behind the men. Glowing eyes announced that the shadow was alive.

A lilting voice, from somewhere behind the shadow, drew the men's attention to the threat behind them.

"Picking fights with women, boys? What would your mothers say?"

The men whirled around, falling back before the black shadow. The first man dropped the lamp as his partner looked for an opening to run. The glass of the lamp cracked in pieces, but a faint light kept burning.

"Don't tell me you give up already?" the voice said. The wiry figure of a young man stepped out from behind the big shadow. "We haven't even come to blows yet."

"We didn't mean nothing," the man with the knife said. "We was just having some fun."

"So am I," the young man said. "Isn't this fun?"

The shadow growled and opened a mouth full of gleaming teeth. The man with the knife dropped to his knees on the pavement. "Let us go," he begged.

The young man sighed, then stepped aside and slapped the shadow on the rump. "All right, Bear," he said. "Move aside."

The shadow moved obligingly, opening the way down the street. The men scrambled to their feet and raced for the safety of the alleys.

Maggie had sunk down to the ground, her back against the crumbling brick wall. The young man watched the ruffians go with his arms crossed over his chest, then turned back to Maggie with a grin. The grin faded fast at the look on her face. He stepped closer to her and offered his hand, pulling her to her feet.

For the first time Maggie got a good look at her rescuer. He was young, as his voice indicated—probably no more than eighteen or nineteen. He was lanky and none too tall. He wore a brown vest over a billowy white shirt, and his trousers were checkered brown, green, and white. His curly black hair seemed a little overdue for a cut, and a bright gold earring glimmered in one ear. His feet were bare.

"I—" Maggie stammered, unsure of what to say. "Thank you."

The young man smiled, a wide grin that showed off straight white teeth and made his eyes dance. "My pleasure," he said, and dropped into a sweeping bow. "Nicolas Fisher, at

30

your service."

He stepped back and placed a hand on the furry black shadow beside him. "And this is Bear."

"Nice to meet you. Both of you." Maggie couldn't help but laugh. "Bear? Doesn't he have a name?"

Nicolas shrugged. "I suppose he does. But he's never told it to me, so I won't insult him by making one up. I call him Bear, and he calls me Boy, and that works quite well since that's what we are."

"Do you do this often?" Maggie asked. "Rescue people, I mean."

"Is that what we did?" Nicolas asked. He seemed amused. "Can't say we've done much of it before, but after this we might have to make a habit of it. More fun than I've had in a while. But I suppose you're not wandering around at night for the lark of it. What did you come here for?"

"I was looking for an inn," Maggie said weakly. "I'm afraid I got lost."

"I'm afraid you did," Nicolas said with a frown. "There's an inn not far from here I can take you to. It's not exactly a high class establishment, but it's a place to sleep—and eat, if you're hungry."

"That sounds good," Maggie said. She reached for her trunk but Nicolas beat her to it. He picked it up and offered Maggie his arm, and she took it with a tentative smile. For all she knew this strange young man could be after the same thing as the alley-dwelling ruffians. Still, she couldn't help liking him—and trusting him.

Nicolas and Bear took Maggie to a dilapidated, two-story establishment with a sign that proclaimed it "The House of

Dreams." Light poured into the street from the wide windows. Inside, the dining room was filled with happy chaos. Bear waited outside while Nicolas led Maggie in.

The brightness of the room hurt her eyes. The walls were painted with brightly coloured murals, showing fantastic, dream-like scenes. Shouting, singing, laughing people packed the room. Galcic men with small pots of ale and Gypsies in brilliantly stitched and coloured clothing sat at round tables, eyeing one another suspiciously while they drank and ate a rich smelling stew. Pipe smoke and noise mingled together and rose to the bright red ceiling.

Lost in observation, Maggie hardly noticed that Nicolas was talking to a gaudy woman wearing huge earrings and a green dress. The din of the room was overwhelming, and it took a moment for her to recognize Nicolas's voice shouting over the cacophony.

"There's a room upstairs for you!" Nicolas said. "Follow me!"

Nicolas and the woman weaved through the crowd. Maggie followed after them, feeling out of place with her drab brown coat and cap and battered trunk, shyly moving through a world filled with colour and laughter and reeking with the pungent smell of ale and cheap wine.

They entered a stairwell on the other side of the room. Inside, the noise instantly died down, as though someone had thrown a blanket over it. The stairs creaked underfoot and their white paint was peeling badly, but Maggie welcomed the quiet.

At the top of the stairs, the woman led Maggie and Nicolas down a long thin hall to the third door on the right.

She pulled out a heavy key ring and unlocked the door, opening a small room with a tiny bed in one corner and a large window without curtains that looked out onto the street.

"It's a nice little room," the woman said. "You will like it. And if there is a problem, you just ask for Madame."

Maggie nodded, and Madame turned to leave. She stopped to pat Nicolas on the cheek and exclaim remorsefully, "And Nicolas! You will not be staying with us? We have missed you."

Nicolas shook his head. "You're too kind," he said with a grin. "But Bear would never forgive me if I left him on the street all night. I promised him we'd be out of Calai before sunrise."

"You're not in trouble?" Madame asked. Nicolas shook his head.

"No, of course no," Madame said. "Just always the wanderer. Someday you come and settle down here. In Calai. It would not be so bad!"

Nicolas only smiled, and Madame heaved a sigh. "Ah well," she said, wiping away a supposed tear. "Someday you will listen."

She turned and swept out of the room, leaving Maggie and Nicolas alone for the moment.

"You're leaving, then?" Maggie asked.

He nodded. "The forest is calling me. Bear's antsy to get away. You'll be all right?"

Maggie nodded. "Thank you. For everything."

Nicolas shrugged, seeming almost embarrassed. Somewhere in the three sentences that had passed between them, he had lost his cocksure attitude.

"Glad I could help," he said, and abruptly left the room. Maggie watched him go with a puzzled frown and wondered why she was so reluctant to let him leave. With a sigh she stretched out on the bed, blew out the oil lamp beside it, and stared out at the chimneys of Calai until her eyes closed of their own accord and she fell asleep.

* * *

Nicolas Fisher could not shut her face out of his mind. He walked along the edge of the gutter and whistled as he tried to conjure up images of the forest he longed for. But each time he tried, another image rose up unbidden: a timid face that didn't know it was soot-streaked, green eyes and auburn hair that was half-hidden under an old cap.

It was a nameless face, and he could kick himself for forgetting to ask her name. Bear grunted as he rambled alongside his master, and Nicolas reached out to bury his hand in Bear's stiff black fur.

"We'll be out soon, old friend," Nicolas said. "Can you smell the trees?" Even as the words left his mouth, the urge to turn back nearly overwhelmed him.

It was not unfamiliar, this feeling, this pull that threatened to carry him all the way back to the House of Dreams. He had felt this way when he first saw Bear, cowering in a cage underneath a circus tent. He hadn't been able to leave then either; not until he had freed the cub and gone dashing off into the night with him. The circus had hunted for them for nearly a week, but had given up at last.

A wind kicked up, swirling the leaves in the street, and

the skin on the back of Nicolas's neck prickled. The wind carried voices with it, faraway voices . . .

The scroll leaves a heavy scent. The hound will have no trouble.

Ugly beast.

Be careful!

He heard sniffing, the deep, dangerous sniffing of a bloodhound catching a scent.

Go!

A long howl filled the air with mournful dread.

It was going for her. For the girl at the House of Dreams. Nicolas was sure of it, as sure as he was that there was not a minute to spare.

He turned and ran for the inn.

* * *

Maggie awoke to the feeling that something was horribly wrong. She tried to sit up and found that dread was pressing her down like a weight. She could hardly move. She thought she would suffocate, and panic began to well up inside of her.

The door to her room banged open and Nicolas rushed in, slamming the door behind him. He turned, grabbed Maggie's trunk, and began frantically shaking her.

"Get up!" he rasped in a hoarse whisper. "Get up! You've got to get out of here, now!"

The pressure broke, and Maggie sat up, light-headed and breathing hard. She slipped down to the floor and began hunting for her shoes.

Nicolas joined her on the floor, snatching one of the shoes

from under the bed. "Hurry!" he said.

"What's going on?" Maggie asked.

"There's something after you." He stopped abruptly as a strange sound welled up from somewhere below, out in the street. It started low and rose till it drowned out the pounding of his heart in his ears.

Howling.

Maggie felt as though her heart had stopped. For a moment both she and Nicolas sat in frozen silence on the floor, and then the panic returned. Maggie pulled her shoes on. Nicolas had moved to the window.

She moved questioningly to his side. He put a finger to his lips in warning. His eyes were fixed on something in the street. She leaned closer to the window, and saw it too. Something huge and black was moving below. It seemed to melt into the night shadows, rendering it nearly invisible. Maggie heard it sniffing, drawing deep breaths and then letting them out again. Tendrils of greenish smoke became visible in the shadows.

It leaped suddenly toward the inn, and Nicolas and Maggie heard a crashing noise underneath their feet. It had broken through the door.

They looked at each other. For a long moment they stood frozen in each other's eyes.

Another howl rose, filling the empty spaces of the inn like water in the swamped hold of a ship. Someone in the inn screamed, even as heavy footfalls tore at the stairs.

It was coming.

Nicolas dropped Maggie's trunk and threw it open, searching through it until he had found the bag of money at the bottom. He thrust it at her and propped the trunk against the door. He moved to the bed and started to push it, but abandoned the effort as the sound of heavy breathing drew near. He ran for the window and yanked it open. Before Maggie realized what he was doing, he had thrown himself out.

She leaned over the sill. Behind her the door shuddered. She threw a desperate glance over her shoulder. Green smoke was curling its way under the door. Her lungs started to constrict again.

She turned back to see Nicolas picking himself up off the street, apparently unharmed.

"Jump!" he called. "I'll catch you!"

Maggie held tightly to the windowsill and lowered herself out as a splintering sound announced the creature's presence in the room. Her fingers clutched the windowsill with a will of their own, frozen by fear.

"Let go!" Nicolas shouted. His voice sounded far away. Maggie's eyes were drawn to the shadow falling slowly across the window. Green smoke twined around her face, playing with her senses. Dimly she knew she should let go, but her fingers wouldn't loosen their grip. The shadow seemed to be moving so slowly it would never arrive. Her eyelids grew heavy, and she smelled flowers. Then wine. Then death.

Far away, she heard Nicolas screaming at her. What was he saying? *Let go . . .*

The creature was at the window. She saw teeth, and claws, and a humped back bristling with black spikes. The beast howled, and in her ears the cry of the hound sounded like a thousand screams.

Her eyes widened in terror as claws swept toward her.

She let go.

Nicolas staggered back with her weight, but he caught her. He lowered her to the ground and she clung to him for an instant, terrified. He pulled away from her, pulled at her.

They ran.

Through the streets, as the city blurred past them, they ran. Behind them came howling, smoke, glowing eyes and the smell of death.

They ran toward the sea, Nicolas in the lead, pulling at Maggie's hand and yelling at her to run faster. She clung to his hand as if it was life itself. To let go meant death. At least if she held on she would not die alone.

Their feet barely touched the cobblestones that glared red with lamplight before them. They seemed to fly like the gulls overhead. The smell of salt filled the damp air as they ran to the nets and docks and black water of the harbour.

Nicolas dashed over the docks. He heard the gulls overhead, crying, calling to him. *It is close. Run. Run, Boy. Run. Seek safety in the sails.*

Nicolas ran to the end of a wooden dock and jumped into the icy water, pulling Maggie after him. She clutched the edge of the dock and watched him with eyes wide with terror, waiting for him. Cold water soaked her skirts and pulled at her. What next?

"Can you swim?" he asked. She nodded and began to pull her skirts up to free her legs. "Then come," he said.

They let go of the dock and struck out for a small ship that floated silently in the ocean a short way out. The water grew colder as it deepened, and Nicolas heard Maggie gasp for air behind him.

He heard howling. And the gulls.

Swim, Boy. Swim.

He reached the anchor rope and began to pull himself up. He stopped and reached back for Maggie. She took his hand and he pulled her up onto the rope. It was slippery in his hands, but he climbed with all of the strength he could muster. The rope shook with the effort.

In minutes the two spilled over the rail onto the deck of the ship. For a moment they simply lay there, letting the wood absorb some of the water from their clothes and hair, panting for breath. Nicolas rolled over on his hands and knees as a low, mournful howl made his hair stand on end. He heard water churning.

It was coming.

There was a skittering noise, a scratching and chirping and squeaking. Mice and rats exploded out of the doors and hatches on the deck and ran down the sides of the ship to the water. A large mouse stopped and stared at Nicolas, whiskers twitching.

In the hold. Burning in the hold. Burn it, Boy. Burn the Hound-thing. Burn the Death-thing.

Nicolas grabbed Maggie's hand and hauled her to her feet. They stumbled toward the door of the hold. It was dark as pitch below, and Nicolas ran his hands over crates and netting, searching desperately. The ship began to rock as something pulled at the anchor rope.

He found a box of matches and muttered a blessing on the mice. He lit one, his hands trembling. It illuminated a hold full of dry wooden crates. The floor was littered with rope and straw. In the match light he could see Maggie's face, drawn and lined with fear. Her eyes burned big and green, and her hair hung in wet strands. Her cap had been lost in the ocean, though the coat still clung to her.

The boat tipped wildly to starboard as something came up the anchor rope.

"Girl," Nicolas whispered hoarsely.

"My name is Maggie," she interrupted.

"Maggie. Go find the lifeboat. Get it into the water and row as fast and as far as you can. If the hound is too close, just jump. Get in the water, understand?"

"What about you?" she asked.

"I'll follow you," he said. "Just do as I say. Go! Now!"

She gave him one last, torn glance and disappeared up the ladder onto the deck. He watched her go, imagery of the hound on deck filling him with dread. Tendrils of green smoke were working their way through the floor into the hold.

Nicolas made a bag with his shirt and stuffed the matchbox into it. Inside an open crate he found six or seven more boxes of matches, all of them full and dry. He added them to the collection and climbed the ladder just as heavy footfalls began to thud across the deck.

He emerged from the door to see the hound staring at him, moving slowly forward. It seemed unsteady on the rolling deck. Nicolas resisted the urge to look back and make sure Maggie was safe. He was sure that if he took his eyes from the beast, it would be on him in a second.

It was less a thing of the shadows here and more solid, more real. Green smoke still played around its face, and the stench of death still desecrated the air around it. Its eyes narrowed as Nicolas stood tall before it. A low growl emerged from the thing, and the deck shuddered underfoot.

Nicolas backed away slowly. The growl rose into the howl of a beast about to finish its hunt. Nicolas turned and ran for the rigging. The beast's crashing footsteps followed.

He threw himself up into the ropes, climbing like a madman. Clawed feet tore at the rigging below him. He swayed wildly in the air, still moving upward. Teeth tore at the rigging on deck, and the ropes Nicolas clung to were severed. He swung through the air, releasing the ropes and flying toward the mast.

He caught hold of the mast and clung to it tightly. Wrapping his legs around the swaying wood, he reached into his shirt and pulled out a box of matches. He struck one furiously, again and again, willing it to ignite. Frustrated, he threw the match away and reached for another. Below, the hound threw its weight against the mast. The whole ship rolled in the waves.

Another two boxes of matches slipped from Nicolas's shirt and spun wildly down toward the beast. He held on desperately with his legs, striking a match again and again.

It lit.

He threw the match back into the box from whence it had come and watched the whole thing blaze to life. The heat in his hand threatened to burn him, and he threw it at the nearby sail.

The white cloth burst into flames.

Still he struck at the matches. The sickening sound of wood splintering filled his ears. In slow motion the mast began to fall, hindered by the rigging all around it.

He threw another blazing missile as the mast gave way.

The matchbox landed on a pile of nets near the hound, and they too flared up. Nicolas reached for a rope as the mast fell, catching it with not a second to spare. He hung by the rope, looking down at the glowing-eyed hound and the blazing nets. The fire was spreading along the deck.

The flames from the sail ate away at the ropes. A heavy piece of cloth suddenly came down, straight at the hound. In an instant the ship underneath the creature's black feet was ablaze, its whole world a sudden flaming hell.

It screamed.

Out on the water, Maggie heard the scream. She clutched the oars of the lifeboat and watched as the blazing ship collapsed on itself. Gulls swirled overhead like vultures around a dying beast. Their calls sounded the word of victory.

The ship exploded.

She buried her face in her sleeve as the waves rocked and tumbled around her. Burning brands landed everywhere around the little boat.

I'll follow you, he had said. *Just go.*

The gulls were calling again, strange cries. Eight or nine of the birds glided in the air over Maggie's head, and she lifted a tear stained face in wonder. What were they . . . ?

"Maggie . . ."

The voice was weak, but definitely there. Maggie jumped to her feet, ignoring the precarious swaying of the boat, and rushed to the side. Nicolas was there, reaching out a shaking hand. His face was streaked with soot and sweat, and a burn glowed on his cheek. Maggie grasped his hand and pulled him toward the boat.

Just before he climbed in, he grinned.

"We did it," he said hoarsely as he slid to the bottom of the boat. Maggie threw her coat around him, and he laid his head back and listened to the gulls.

Won, Boy. You won.

3

When They See Beyond the Sky

TONIGHT I GAZED INTO THE FIRE to shut out the darkness around me. The flames danced in shapes and whispered words. I, the Poet-Prophet, have seen the future. I have seen the signs of his coming again.

No one cares! I wander this world and speak of him softly in their ears, but they do not wish to hear. Not to this generation will he return. Already they forget what it was to have him in the world. Already the people of this earth turn to stone, and forget the heart that once beat in their breasts. Cold-hearted creatures of darkness! Without leadership men squabble and fight. They take refuge in tribes and turn against their neighbours, fighting over bits of land and food like starving animals. And even the animals are not what they once were.

The men of this generation care not what the future holds. Yet I have seen it! I write these words in hope that one day the ice-hearts of men will begin to melt. Then they will read the words of the Prophet, and my words will be to them fuel to begin a raging fire. In those days the fulfillment of this prophecy will come. The Gifted Ones whom I have seen will

walk the earth and awaken it to the King.
Hear, then, what I have heard:

When they see beyond the sky,
When they know beyond the mind,
When they hear the song of the Burning Light;
Take these Gifts of My Outstretched Hand,
Weave them together.
I shall come.

* * *

The fire crackled and warmed Maggie's face and hands. A brisk breeze had nearly dried out her clothes, although her coat still hung over a tree branch next to Nicolas's shirt and vest. Beyond the glow of the fire Maggie could just make out the form of her friend, pacing back and forth on top of an old log, now and then jumping and dancing as though he was caught up in a musical sword fight. He was odd, this Nicolas Fisher; but somehow his presence stole all the menace out of the dark shadows of the woods and took all the danger out of their aloneness in an unknown land. He had led Maggie away from the sea and up into the forests as confidently as if he was taking her through his own house. He seemed to belong to the woods, and Maggie was his guest.

A deep snuffling sound came from somewhere in the trees and made Maggie jump. It was Bear. She could not imagine how the creature had found his way here, but he had, and she relaxed again. His great black form offered protection against the night.

Maggie looked into the fire until the heat and brightness had burned into her eyes. The stillness of the forest worked itself into her. She raised her head to listen when a bird cried somewhere in the dark vastness around. She sighed and stretched out on the ground next to the fire, gazing up through the treetops to the brilliance of the stars. She had been in Cryneth when last she had seen such stars. In Londren, the ever-present chimney haze kept all but the brightest of the distant fires from sending their light to the world below.

Nicolas appeared in the firelight and collapsed into a cross-legged heap. The firelight glinted on the gold in his ear and traced strange shadows on his face.

Maggie rolled over and lifted herself onto her elbows so she could look across the fire at her half-wild friend.

"Why did you come back?" she asked.

"You were in danger," Nicolas said.

"How did you know?" Maggie pressed. "You said you were going to the forest. You should have been halfway across the city by the time the hound reached the inn. What brought you back?"

Nicolas sighed, as though he was going to regret opening his mouth. "I heard someone talking . . . I heard the hound coming after you."

"What do you mean you *heard* it?" Maggie asked.

Nicolas shrugged, a strange little smile tugging at the corners of his mouth. "I heard voices, and I knew you were in danger. So I went back."

"I don't know anything about voices," Maggie said, questioningly. "All I saw was the hound. But you couldn't have . . . I mean, it's not possible to . . ."

"My ears often hear things that no one else can," Nicolas said. "It's a gift."

Curiosity rose up in Maggie. The guardedness had gone out of Nicolas's voice, as though he had let out his secret and didn't care now how much she knew.

"What else do you hear?" Maggie asked. "Besides dangerous voices in the dark."

"I hear the grass grow," Nicolas said slowly, "and I hear the stars singing."

"They sing?" Maggie asked.

Nicolas nodded. "Yes," he said. "I hear other things, too . . . sometimes I can hear what Bear is saying."

Maggie looked up at the hulking form just beyond the glow of the campfire. "Bear talks," she said flatly.

"Well, not exactly *talks*," Nicolas said. "He feels things, and thinks things, and sometimes I hear what he means."

"Does he speak the language of the Empire?" Maggie asked, feeling ridiculous but unable to stop herself from asking.

"No, of course not," Nicolas said. "He just feels things, and sometimes I understand them." Nicolas laughed a little nervously. "That doesn't make much sense to you, does it?"

Maggie ignored the question and asked another of her own. "Have you always been able to understand him?"

"No," he told her. "When I was a child I would listen to rabbits and squirrels and birds, and it was hard to understand them, too. But I kept listening, and trying to understand, and one day I did. I still don't understand everything."

Maggie felt herself drawn to the strange young man across from her. It was fascinating, what he was saying, perhaps absurd. Yet she believed him.

47

"What else can you hear?" she asked, leaning forward with her chin resting in her hand.

Nicolas's eyes met hers. How many people had he ever spoken to like this? Who, in all his life, would ever have believed him? Even the Gypsies thought he was mad when he spoke of hearing, although they were not so quick to dismiss it the way others did. They wondered sometimes, if madness was not a gift.

"When babies cry," Nicolas said, "I know what they want before their own mothers do. Sometimes I can hear a baby talking while it's still in its mother's womb."

"What do they say?" Maggie asked, a smile of wonder beginning to tug at her own face.

"It's hard to understand them," Nicolas said. "But not so hard as with the animals. Mostly they dream about the world out here. And they wonder why so many of the voices they hear are angry and worried. They dream, and they wonder, and then they go back to sleep. And when they wake up they wonder all the same things over again."

Maggie laughed. Nicolas chuckled, but his laugh ended in the creases of a frown. "Sometimes I wish I could tell them to stay in there. If they come out here they'll just join the voices of anger, and worry . . . and fear.

"And once in a while," Nicolas continued, "I hear voices talking, from all over the place. I don't know who they belong to, I can't always tell where they're from. But I can hear them."

His voice trailed off and he looked away. "I haven't told anyone about my hearing for years. Not since I was a child."

Maggie wished he would continue, but she sensed he had already said a great deal more than he'd meant to.

"Where were you going?" he asked, changing the subject abruptly. "Before the hound came, I mean."

"To Pravik," Maggie said. Her expression changed suddenly, and she jumped to her feet. Nicolas was up in an instant, alert as a cat. But only the faint sounds of the night reached his ears as Maggie rushed to the tree where her coat was drying. She reached inside and pulled out a piece of parchment, unrolling it frantically. Nicolas watched curiously. The paper was amazingly strong—the scroll was unharmed, and Maggie breathed a sigh of relief. She realized suddenly that Nicolas was watching her, and that she had cut off their conversation rather rudely. She held up the scroll in explanation.

"I was going to deliver this to someone," she said. "It belonged to an old friend. He would have taken it himself, but he died before he could." Her face clouded over.

Nicolas nodded. He cleared his throat. "I just want to say that I'd be happy to accompany you back to Bryllan . . . as far as the boat, I mean. So you won't have to go alone."

Maggie played with the paper in her hands, and she didn't meet Nicolas's eyes.

"I'm not going back to Bryllan," she said. "Not until I take this where it belongs."

"Maggie," Nicolas began, his voice quiet, "I told you I heard voices before the hound was let loose. Someone sent it after you. They might try again. It can't be safe for you here."

Maggie bowed her head and walked back to the fire. Just as she reached the rim of light, she turned and faced her friend again.

"I have to take this to Pravik," she said. "I'm sorry. I can't explain everything, but I can't turn back now. Especially not now."

She sat down and he joined her. When she looked up at him, her face was apologetic. "Anyway," she said, "suppose I did go back to Londren, and they came after me there. I wouldn't be any safer."

"You know your way around Londren," Nicolas protested, miserably. "You could hide there."

They fell silent. Bear nudged up behind them, hanging his massive head over Nicolas's shoulder.

"Will you help me find the road to Pravik?" Maggie asked after a long silence.

"I'll go with you," Nicolas said.

"Thank you," she said.

"No," he said, looking intensely at her, "I mean I'll go *with* you. To Pravik."

"But—" she protested, "you can't just . . ."

"Do you think I have a life here in Galce to hold me back?" he asked. "Bear's my only family; these forests and the Gypsy caravans are my only home. It's time we see more of the world anyway. We'll come with you."

Her eyes filled with unexpected tears. "I don't know what to say," she started.

He reached out a hand and touched her shoulder lightly. "Go to sleep," he said. "I'll be here in the morning."

* * *

Lord Robert Sinclair, the Laird of Angslie, could not sleep. He had retired to his room on the pretense of a headache. A maid had drawn the bedroom curtains and lit a warm fire, and now he lay stretched out on his bed in his stocking feet. The bed was an unusually long one, to accommodate all six feet, seven inches of the laird's stature. His sixty years had depleted little of his strength of presence. His muscles were still strong, thanks to long days of wandering in the mountains. His mind was as strong as his body: it was quick, and sharp, and it burned with ideas, and old passions, and longings.

Yet, for all of that, the laird was a man on whom life dragged wearingly. The things he longed for were beyond his reach, and he had only memories to keep him alive. Memories, and the strange help of a girl who lived on a mountainside nearby.

It had been nearly a week since he had last seen Virginia Ramsey, and he would go to her soon. He had just spent six days in Cranburgh with people he could hardly tolerate, smiling and simpering until he thought hypocrisy would cause him to explode; vowing every night in his room that he would never go back there, business or no business. He arrived home tense and ready to snap, and then his housekeeper had made her deplorable announcement, looking insufferably proud of herself all the while.

"You wouldn't have liked to see him, sir," she had said with a sniff of disapproval. "He wasn't one of your station. He was bent so you couldn't know his height, and dirty so you couldn't know his age. He was very insistent that he wanted to see you. Said he had something for you. But I put him in his place, I can assure you. I have no use for such peddlers."

"Did he give his name?" Lord Robert had asked.

"Aye, I think he did. Let's see . . . Daniel Seaton, it was."

The terrible words spoken, the laird's anger had drained out of him and he had gone to bed, where he could lay in the old familiarity of his room and let the musty magic of his house calm and console him. He forgot even about going to see Virginia. All he knew was that the longed-for past had come to call, and he had not been home.

In hindsight, it often seemed to him that the only time in his life worth living had been the days of the council. For three short months Angslie had been home to seven self-styled scholars, Daniel Seaton among them, in pursuit of a glorious dream. In the forty years since the abandonment of that dream, those memories had taunted him with what would never be again. Fate was a cruel thing, Lord Robert felt, that it could send Dan Seaton to his very door while he was away enduring the company of men and women who didn't have soul enough to feel the lure of the mysteries that had drawn the council.

Lord Robert abruptly left his bed and began pacing the halls of Angslie. Up stairs and down corridors he stalked, passing long rows of windows that looked out on a brown, mountainous highland wilderness, until at last he had reached the double doors of a long-closed room. It was a room that made the servants whisper when they passed it; a forbidden domain with many a wild story shut behind its doors.

Impulsively, Lord Robert reached out and touched the brass door handle. It turned easily under his hand, and the doors swung open.

The room had not been dusted in forty years. Lord Robert strode to the end of the room and dashed the curtains open. Sunlight poured in as it would pour into an opened tomb, illuminating the clouds of dust that danced in the stale air. He turned from the tall, wide window with its view of the hills to face the room where his dreams had once taken flight over the mountains and far into the past; where the obsession of his life had been birthed.

The sunlight glinted off the gold and red bindings of the books that lined one wall and attempted to sparkle on the brass candlesticks that sat covered with dust and grey wax, arrested in its dripping. The candles sat in the center of the room on a long wooden table that had once served as a meeting place for the Council for Exploration Into Worlds Unseen.

He laid his hand on the table and brought it back covered with the greyness of the years. Had it been so long? The rug on the floor had once been brilliantly red and yellow and green, with its swirling patterns and uniquely woven designs. Now its colours were muted by time and silence. It lay drab and not at all like its memory.

Lord Robert walked slowly to the head of the table, where a wooden chair sat waiting for him as it had so long ago. He drew it out and sat down, his eyes struggling to see through the haze of the years to the ghosts of the past.

He felt as though they were there still there, just beyond the dust. He could hear them talking and laughing, debating and discussing. To his right, his memory could see the small, friendly face of Daniel Seaton, crinkled up in a laugh. Next to Dan sat Eva Brown, plump and pretty, clutching a book of sketches to her bosom as though it was a baby or a precious toy. She was laughing, too, probably at something Daniel had said.

Next to Eva sat John Davies, his craggy, serious young face a great contrast to Daniel. John was quiet, not much of a man for speaking. When he did speak, he usually bore listening to. His grey eyes would pierce through all distractions and make a man sit up and listen. On these days, Lord Robert remembered, John's eyes rarely strayed from the face of the young woman across from him.

Mary Grant was Crynthian, like John. She was beautiful, the laird remembered in a startled way. He had forgotten how beautiful. Dark brown hair fell on small shoulders; wide blue eyes danced with the song that she was always singing. When Mary sang, the very stars above stopped to listen. She sang songs of the ancient days, songs full of glory and valour and prophecy—songs she seemed to hear floating to her from another world.

Lucas Barrington always sat beside Mary. He was handsome and tall, a gentleman of sorts, a young continental with a great deal of wealth and rakish manners. Across the table from Lord Robert sat the other real scholar of the group, talking to Lucas in a strong Eastern accent. Jarin Huss was a thin young man with a neatly trimmed beard and a way of speaking with authority to anyone who would listen.

And then there was Evelyn.

Her seat, when she was allowed into the council meetings, was at Lord Robert's left hand. She, too, was beautiful. Her hair was black like the night, her eyes almost as dark. She moved like a panther, smooth and strong. Mystery hung about her like a mist; a fog that called to the laird to come further into its dangerous embrace. Even now, the memory of her was enough to make his heart ache.

They were all young in those days. In his memory, the laird heard their voices and saw each expression.

In a split second, the memory changed. He saw Mary stand to her feet, saw the chair knocked back behind her as she rose with passion glaring in her eyes. He saw the finger pointed at the woman next to him and heard the hissing hatred in Evelyn's reply. He saw the hardness in the eyes of those who had been his friends. He heard himself responding, shouting, accusing. He saw his arms around the dark, mysterious woman at his side. He saw Jarin shaking his head; he saw the anger in John's grey eyes. He heard Daniel crying. He saw Eva stop crying and grow hard, so hard he thought a hammer would never break her open again.

That day was the end of it all. In less than three days, the council was no more. They had gone away, to Midland, to Cryneth, to Sloczka. Only Lord Robert was left, with Evelyn to stay by his side forever and help him find all the answers he had wanted.

Only, she had gone, too. Less than a year later. And she had not said good-bye.

On that day, Lord Robert had walked into the council room and closed the curtains. He had shut the door and never come back.

Until now.

On the table in front of him was a book bound with red leather. A journal. His fingers brushed away the dust, streaking the dull red cover with brightness. Slowly, he opened it.

It opened to a page that had been dusty even before the end of the council, all those years ago. It was yellow and cracked with age, and on it was written short lines in a sort of rhythm. Poetry.

The words were unreadable, written in a language other

than that of the Empire. Lord Robert sighed as he remembered the first time he had opened the book and looked at the handwriting of some unknown ancient, an author who might have lived before the rule of the Morel dynasty choked out life and freedom in the world.

Jarin Huss had been able to read this language. Huss, Lord Robert reflected, had known many dangerous things. His knowledge of the ancient languages would have been enough to have him arrested. It was a risk that Jarin, as a scholar with an insatiable appetite to *know*, was more than willing to take. The laird remembered the Eastern student's description of the underground university, the clandestine teachings of the professors at the University of Pravik. They had taught ancient languages and legends, and history that did not fit the frame the Empire wished to give it.

The lines of poetry taunted from their resting place on the page. The handwriting swirled and danced across the paper in age-old ink, calling to the laird to understand.

Words tugged at the edge of his memory, and he struggled to recall them as he looked over the poems again and again. The words had been spoken in the Eastern accent of Jarin Huss, as he read the poetry aloud for the first and only time.

> "*When they see beyond the sky,*
> *When they know beyond the mind,*
> *When they hear the song of the Burning Light;*
> *Take these Gifts of My Outstretched Hand,*
> *Weave them together,*
> *I shall come.*"

Lord Robert was surprised at the clarity with which the words came back to him. He picked up the red-bound book and turned it over in his hands. There were more poems, more words written inside. If only he could read them.

"When they see beyond the sky . . ."

He crossed the room to the window and stood between its cobwebbed curtains, hands tucked behind him. His eyes wandered over the hills, along a small path that rounded the side of the mountain and disappeared. The eyes of his memory continued to follow the path, up the steep hillside, to the rocky outcrop where Virginia would be seated even now. He was seized with a sudden desire to visit her, perhaps to recite to her the words of the poem. She had been born on the land of the Sinclair family, had spent most of her life on the side of the mountain, but it had only been three months since the laird had really become aware of her existence. In an accidental way he had heard rumours of the blind girl who could see another side of reality. If her visions were fact and not madness, then the things she saw proved the validity of Lord Robert's lifelong belief in another world alongside his own. She had given him back his old beliefs and reawakened his old longings. He went to see her often, and drank in her words as though they were life-giving water, though she gave it to him only in painfully sparing drops. One day he hoped to break through into the world of Virginia's visions, but for now her words were all he had.

The path called to him. He picked up the red journal and

left the room, shutting the doors tightly behind him.

* * *

Virginia Ramsey's hair was a very dark brown. Most of it was on the verge of turning black, but enough of it was near to turning red to make her overall appearance very striking. Her eyes, which could not see, were green.

She spent most of her time sitting cross-legged on top of an outcrop on the side of the mountain, where she could smell the passing of the seasons and hear the birds fly by. The birds thought her a friend, and they would light on her shoulder and whisper to her. Her right hand usually rested on the head of her shaggy old deerhound, who was as deaf as she was blind.

On the side of the mountain, Virginia Ramsey heard all that she ever wished to hear. She heard wind, grass, and the songs of creation. And sometimes, on the side of the mountain, Virginia could see.

The things she saw were true things, though no one else, it seemed, could see them. She saw beautiful golden creatures and horrible, black shadow-things. She saw people, but not as others saw them. She could see into their souls, into the truth of what they were. She could see the childlike heart of her grandfather, the conniving soul of the village innkeeper, and the burning potential of the innkeeper's son, little Roland MacTavish, that made him look to her like a lion cub: a kitten now, but with all the strength and power of the beast king just waiting to push its way out.

She saw other things, too. Sometimes she saw people in faraway places, and sometimes she saw things that had happened hundreds of years before.

One frequent vision had grown stronger and more urgent with the years: that of a great hunting hound, its muzzle dripping with blood and its eyes with hatred. It was tracking her down. This vision she saw most often at night, and then she would wake up coldly terrified, sure that the universe itself was hunting her.

The people in the village were afraid of her.

They didn't know exactly what it was that Virginia Ramsey could do, but they had the feeling that she knew far more about them than they would like anyone to know. Everyone in the town was polite to her, while most of them would have done anything to keep her sightless green eyes away from them.

The deerhound under her fingertips growled low, sending a rumbling shiver through his lean body.

"Hush," Virginia said. "It's only the laird, I think."

She bowed her head as he approached, tired at the thought of talking to him. He asked such insistent questions, firing them like arrows one after another. What she saw lay deep inside of her soul; to reveal it to another was like tearing open a wound. She did not fault the laird, for he obviously did not understand. He thought that she could explain her sight as easily as he could describe a sunny day. She might have grown angry with him, except that in him was a strength and a spirit she did not possess. He was her protector. Her grandfather knew it, the town knew it, and she hoped that the hunting hound of her visions knew it. Someday she would need him. So she spoke with him when he came.

Besides, underneath all of his selfish questioning, she

sensed a deep need in him. He had wounds of his own, and something in her wished to heal them. At the same time something in him drove her back. His wounds were festering, infected with a blackness that both frightened and drew her.

His voice broke through her thoughts. She heard and felt him sitting near to her, as the deerhound growled low and deep but did not move. And then she felt it: a strange sensation, one she had not known in the laird's presence before. She felt drawn to him . . . no, not to him, but to something with him. Her skin prickled with its nearness.

"I read a poem today," Lord Robert said. "I wondered if you might like to hear it."

The prickling, tingling sensation had grown so strong that she could not quite understand what he had said. Her voice, answering him quickly, was urgent.

"You have something with you?"

There was a pause, as Lord Robert was taken aback by Virginia's intensity.

"Yes," he answered.

She took her hand from the plaid wrapped around her and stretched it out toward him. "May I have it?" she asked.

He made no audible reply, but in a moment she felt the rough, cool leather of an old book in her hand. She took it gently, drawing it close to her and letting it fall open. She ran her fingers over the open page, trying to feel the paths of ink on the rough old paper. Warmth emanated from the handwriting and then began to flow from the page into her hand, traveling up her arms like a shock. She gasped deeply as colours began to flash before her eyes, patterns and pictures whirling before her. The sounds and smells of the Highland hills sank into oblivion before the dizzying force of the vision. In a moment the colours had settled themselves into forms, and scenes began to move through her mind.

She saw a warrior of ancient days, his hair the colour of flax. He rode a spotted horse that moved with the slow, painful steps of exhaustion. Its coat and hooves were flecked with blood. Around and above him was the deep green of a forest; below him, roots tangled in black earth. Others rode all around him, similarly weary, and dressed in the blood-spattered, dirt-ravaged clothing of desperate men. On a white horse at the head of the party rode one whose features Virginia could not describe. Every time she thought she could, his face seemed to change. The only constants were the sense of power that rested on him and an accompanying sense of grief.

The scene dissolved in light. The light formed itself into a pulsing circle. The leader of the men stood before it. Virginia watched as he stepped back, into the circle, and the light enveloped him completely. She watched as the warriors followed him beyond the forest, through the circle. The scene shifted, and she saw the flaxen-haired man sitting alone beside the dying embers of a campfire, holding a red book in his hands. He was writing words that burned their way into the pages.

Suddenly everything changed. She no longer saw the forests. Instead, she saw three black-cloaked figures with eyes like deep pits. The foremost of them held a scroll, newly signed and rolled. One opened his mouth to speak, and from his mouth flowed pestilence.

The scene changed once more, now flashing images at her in rapid succession. She saw faces, and she felt that she was no longer seeing the ancient past, but the present. Through her mind's eye she saw a woman sitting at a harp in a small cottage, singing a beautiful song that wove its way through the visions of others. She saw a boyish face with a thick head of curly black hair, his mouth laughing with delight. She saw a beautiful young woman with long, white-gold hair, tending roses and vines in a quiet garden. She saw two tall figures in black cloaks, stretching out their hands toward a circle of fire. She saw a girl on a mountainside, wrapped in red plaid, and with a shock she realized she had just seen herself.

Once more all the scenes and colours blurred together and then spun out to make a new scene. This time she saw the flaming walls of a city. She saw a tall, hooded man on a horse, lifting up a sword with a mighty shout. Around him the very sky throbbed with golden light: underlying power, passion, mystery. She saw a very old man, with a long beard that reached nearly to his waist, lift his hands up toward heaven while swords clashed all around him. She saw an auburn-haired girl on a castle wall in the city, running along the stones, seemingly oblivious to the danger beneath her.

One last time everything changed, and she saw the raging waves of the sea. Standing in turbulent stillness over the waves was an army, its golden radiance casting a glow on the clouds and black water all around. The sea wind tore through the hair of horses and warriors, armour and steel clashed as thunder and lightning split the sky. Just before blackness overtook the vision, Virginia thought she saw the shape of a man stepping back through a circle of light, speaking words that were just beyond her hearing . . .

And then she took a deep breath of the heathery

mountain air, and she felt Lord Robert's hands gripping her shoulders, and heard the whine of the deerhound.

The laird's voice came through the fading shock. "Are you all right?"

She managed a nod, and his voice dropped to a hesitant whisper. "What happened?"

She moved against his grasp, and he released her. She brought her hands up and covered her face. The deerhound's lean body rubbed against her.

"I have seen," she said, and found that she could not go on.

4

Brightly-Coloured Paths

THE MEN WERE ROUGH AND RUDE, and Roland MacTavish didn't
like them at all. They demanded the best rooms and the finest
food in the inn. The MacTavish, Roland's father and the owner
of the inn, did all but lick the ground where they walked.
Roland took their horses for them and said nothing when they
cursed at him and told him to be careful with the animals, and
called him "Boy" and threw him a shilling for his trouble.

He knew who they were; everyone did. They were
Imperial High Police, imposing figures dressed in black and
green. But that did not give them the right to treat the villagers
like inferiors, Roland thought, here in this land where his
family had lived for hundreds of years, maybe even before
there was any such thing as High Police—even before there
was an Empire. Other boys in the village talked with bright
eyes and high expectations of the day when they might be
recruited by the High Police. They spoke of going to Athrom,
the Great City of the Emperor, to train, and of becoming great
warriors. Roland, the only son of his father, knew that he
might one day be taken into the ranks of Black-and-Greens,
but for him there was no joy in the knowing.

When the men went to bed drunk that night, Roland kept the village children entertained with imitations of their peacock's strut and harsh accents.

He did not learn to be afraid of them until the next day, when they began asking after Virginia Ramsey.

They went to Wee Cameron first, the five-foot-two blacksmith with arms like iron pillars. Roland was in Wee Cam's shop, helping shoe a horse, when the soldiers came in, asking where to find a blind girl who was rumoured to have strange gifts.

Wee Cam chewed on a bit of straw and looked at them with squinty eyes out of a sooty face. "What would you be wanting her for?" he asked.

One soldier answered. "She's wanted in Londren." He grinned.

Wee Cam spit and folded his enormous arms over his chest. "Sorry, but I canna help you."

The soldier stepped forward menacingly. "I'm asking as an officer of the Empire," he said.

Wee Cam drew himself up to his full height and glowered at the soldier from a face that was nearly as ruddy as his hair. His eyes sparkled with heat borrowed from the forge.

"And I'm tellin' you, as a citizen of this village, that I canna help you."

The soldiers backed out of the shop and went in search of more amicable help. A look passed between Roland and Wee Cam, and without a word Roland left the horse to Cam's able care. The men were on their way back to the inn, and Roland followed them with a mounting sense of dread.

He listened as his father told the men how to reach the

side of the mountain. Roland wondered if the men would toss his father a coin for his troubles. No doubt the MacTavish would be properly grateful for it.

Before the MacTavish had finished detailing the way to Virginia's outcrop, Roland was running for Angslie as fast as his feet could fly. He ran first for the little stone house where Grandfather Ramsey would even now be working the land, but he changed direction midway and ran for the great house of Robert Sinclair, Lord of Angslie, instead. This was the laird's land. There had to be something he could do.

* * *

Lord Robert had not been gone half an hour when light began to probe once more at the corners of Virginia's darkness. But there was no shock this time; no swirling, reeling bewilderment of colour and scene. Instead, gentle rays of light found their way through to her eyes. They illuminated no strange scene, but her own hillside. She saw the rock and earth beneath her and the blue sky overhead, speckled with clouds. She saw the colours of her own skirt and the plaid wrapped around her shoulders. She saw the deerhound sleeping by her side, its rib cage rising and falling under a cover of wiry fur.

She turned her head to look at the worn path that stretched away from the outcrop and down the mountainside. Someone was coming up the path toward her.

As he came closer, a breeze rustled through the grass ahead of him. It carried the scent of spring flowers and running water. Virginia felt something stir inside her. His shadow fell over her, but it was not a like a shadow—it was like light coming through raindrops. She looked to his face and found that she could not describe him. He seemed young, but then he seemed old; his skin was neither dark nor white. He wore a homespun robe and his feet were bare.

He came very close, and Virginia stood to meet him. He held out his hand to her and she took it, without hesitation or fear. His touch was strong and warm.

"Do you know who I am?" he asked in a voice as indescribable as his face.

She nodded, slowly. "You are the King."

"Do I look like a king?" he asked, glancing down at his homespun robe and bare, calloused feet.

"Yes," she answered.

He smiled. "You see very clearly, little one. What do you know of me?"

"Only that I will follow you wherever you go, if you will let me come," Virginia said. His presence filled her with a sweetness and peace that she had never known. All that was in her reached out to him. The only fear in this moment was that he might leave, as all visions left.

"You name me king," he said. "Of what kingdom? Can you tell me that?"

"I do not know." Virginia faltered. "But, if my heart can be called a kingdom, then you have a throne in it. Somehow, I think you always have—though I have never seen you before today."

A distant light appeared in his eyes. "Be it known, then," he said, "that I am the king of all the world and all the sky and all the stars, and of all the vast worlds beyond them. There was a time I walked this earth and all hearts knew me. But they have forgotten. They wanted to forget."

The sadness in his voice tore at Virginia's heart, and all she could say was, "I'm so sorry."

"So am I," he said, smiling again. "But you, and a few others, will wake the world to me. Yes, your heart is a kingdom, and I am king in it. Be ready, for I will come soon."

"Can I not go with you now?" Virginia asked, for he had begun to move away from her.

"No," he said. "You will come to me some day, but not for a time. Can you be courageous, little one?"

"Yes," she said.

"My enemies hunt you, and you must face them," he said. "Do not forget who I am. And do not forget who you are, no matter what happens. This day I have called you mine."

Far away, Virginia thought she heard the baying of a hunting hound. For the first time since she had first seen the shadow creature in her visions, she felt no fear at its coming. He looked toward the sound, and his face was solemn.

"Remember me," he said, "and through you I will wake the world."

He let go of her hand and stepped back down the path. Behind him a circle of light flared into being. He faded away into it. In the next instant, Virginia's sight was gone.

The loss of his presence left an echo in her of such deep longing that she fell to her knees on the path and wept.

* * *

Roland fell against the oak door. He pounded on it with all the strength he had left, panting for breath. His knees buckled under him when the door swung open, revealing the housekeeper's stern face.

"What do you want?" she asked.

"Please," the boy gasped. "I need to see the laird. It's about Virginia Ramsey."

"What about her?" said a deep voice from the shadows behind the housekeeper.

Lord Robert stepped up to the door. Roland started to answer, but his words trailed into nothing as the world spun around him. The laird knelt down beside the boy and lifted him up, brushing blond hair back from the child's face.

"Come now, boy. What do you have to tell me?" he asked.

Roland drew a deep breath of air. "They're going to take her away," he said, leaning heavily on Lord Robert's shoulder.

"Who? Who is?" Lord Robert asked.

"The police," Roland gasped out.

"Village police?" The laird's face was a knot of frowns.

"No, no," Roland said. "High Police."

Lord Robert stood and handed Roland over to his housekeeper.

"Get him something to drink," the laird commanded. "I believe he's run the whole six miles from the village."

With Roland safely in the housekeeper's care, Lord Robert dashed out the door in the direction of Virginia's mountainside.

* * *

Virginia heard them coming even before the deerhound began to growl. The breath of a shadow hound echoed in their

69

footsteps. The deerhound tensed and she rubbed his neck soothingly.

"Hush," she said. "Lay still."

The footsteps came closer. The deerhound sprang to his feet, ignoring Virginia's entreaties to lay down. The dog's deep-throated growl rose to a crescendo, and he sprang toward the intruders.

Virginia heard the sound of cursing and the metallic whir of a sword being drawn. The hound's bark ended abruptly in a long whine. Suddenly the men were all around her. The flat edge of a knife pressed underneath Virginia's chin, forcing her face upward as someone wrenched her arms behind her. She felt a man's breath on her face as shackles closed around her wrists.

"Blind as a bat, just like they said," said the man in front of her. His voice became low and taunting.

"We're going to take you away, girl. *They* want to see you, and they don't never let anyone go home again. What do you think of that, eh?"

Virginia said nothing. The knife was pulled away, allowing her head to drop into a bowed position.

"Aw," said one of the men. "She didn't answer. Maybe she's deaf, too."

They laughed. Rough hands grabbed her arms and hauled her to her feet. The heavy iron shackles rubbed painfully against her wrists, and she stumbled as the men propelled her forward. The path, usually so familiar, seemed strange to her feet.

They were still talking, joking with each other, but their voices were only an incoherent noise in Virginia's ears. She thought she heard the deerhound whine nearby, and her thoughts reached out toward him, longing to go and bury her face in his wiry fur. Had they killed him, she wondered—was it only her imagination that heard him whining for help? If he was not dead, he was badly hurt, or he would have been at the men long before. Desperation welled up inside of her, and she moved against the grip of her captors, as though she would tear her hands free from the shackles and run for the cover of the hills. And her old hound, her most faithful and understanding companion, would rise to its feet and run like the wind at her side.

"Look," one of the men said suddenly, "Tears. There's a person in there after all!"

Someone grabbed her hair and yanked her head back, making her clench her teeth against the pain. He stood close enough that she could feel the heat of his body, and shouted into her face, "Are you afraid, girl? Are you afraid?"

She made no reply. He let go of her, shoving her head forward with such strength that she fell to the ground.

"Get her up, and let's get out of here," said the man. "Looks like a storm's brewing."

The hands were back at her arms again, making the iron bite into her wrists. Before she was steadily back on her feet, a familiar voice rang out over the mountainside.

Lord Robert.

He shouted again, a wordless, raging sound. The hands let go of Virginia and she sank down on the path, her heart beating painfully. Her protector had come. She whispered a prayer for his safety—to the one whose words still echoed in her heart. "*Remember me.*"

The sounds of a fight broke out. Metal clashed against metal; bone against bone; and suddenly all was silent.

In a moment the laird touched her shoulder with a hand shaking with adrenaline.

"Are you all right?" the laird asked. His voice was shaking like his hand. Virginia started to nod, and instead found herself being lifted in strong arms.

"I'm going to keep you safe," he said. "But you'll have to come away with me."

In answer she nodded, and then turned her face into his chest and let him carry her away.

* * *

The Galcic forests were deep and golden with the colours of fall. As time passed, Maggie found herself overwhelmed by the abundant presence of tree, rock, stream, and leaf; each one so much like the others, and yet uniquely its own, and all occupying one vast, peaceful world. In this place where insects lived for a brilliant day and trees stood guard for centuries, time ceased to hold much meaning. The solitude of the forest bore down on her, now like a weight, now like a song. At times she wished for nothing more than to see a town, and the next moment she hoped that she might become endlessly lost in the woods, never to see another human settlement with its noise and confusion again.

If it wasn't for Nicolas, she was sure, she would be lost. There were moments when she was quite certain the path led in one direction, but Nicolas and Bear would confidently head in another. When she could see no path at all, they did not slow their steps. Boy and beast seemed equally a part of the forest.

They had been in the forest for three days. Maggie's shoes were beginning to give way under the constant friction of roots and ruts and pebbles. Her whole body ached from walking. Nicolas, his feet bare, did not seem to notice any strain. He walked until he grew tired, and then they would stop and rest in the cool shade of the trees. Nicolas would curl up and sleep soundly, and Maggie soon learned to sleep when he did. If she did not, the chance would be lost. Even at night, they walked.

At first, Maggie was concerned about food. But what Nicolas did not find, Bear did: they ate roots, leaves, nuts, and berries. Nicolas fashioned a spear from a thin branch and caught three fish with it. The scanty fare rarely left Maggie feeling full, but she did not lack for energy.

It was late afternoon, and Nicolas was singing. The song was a nonsensical spinning of melody and words without any meaning. His long branch-spear waved in the air in time to the music, now and then moving quickly enough to whistle in the air and add punctuation to the song.

The path moved steadily downhill. A piece of rock gave way under her foot, and Maggie slipped. She winced at the strain on her sore muscles as she struggled back to her feet.

Nicolas turned at the sound of her fall and ran back to her. He offered his hand, and she gladly took it. She brushed herself off, grimacing as her fingers brushed a tender patch on her leg.

"Oh, that's going to hurt later," she said under her breath, envisioning a purple bruise. She let out a breath of air and started to walk forward again, but Nicolas stopped her.

"You look tired, Maggie," he said. For the first time he seemed to notice the weariness in his companion's step. His face crumpled into such an expression of worry that Maggie almost laughed at the sight. He gestured downhill.

"There's a good resting place, just down there," he said. "Come just a little further. And then you can rest as long and hard as you like."

Maggie couldn't help smiling as he clambered down the hill just ahead of her, now and then telling her how good a resting place they were coming to.

It was a good place, indeed. Maggie almost fainted with relief at the thought of curling up on the patch of moss and leaves and sleeping until she wasn't tired any more. As Bear puttered around nearby, she lowered herself down onto the welcoming carpet and closed her eyes.

She had barely begun to dream when Nicolas's urgent voice penetrated her sleep. She opened her eyes a crack and squinted at him. He was peering down at her with great excitement, rambling on about something. It took Maggie a minute to adjust her senses to the point where she could actually understand what he was saying.

"Come on, Maggie, we've got to go *now* or we'll miss them. You can sleep all you want when we get there."

"That's what you said about *this* nap," Maggie complained, clambering groggily to her feet. "Can't we stay here a little longer?"

Nicolas was pacing back and forth on the path. "It's not far, I promise. You won't regret it."

Maggie's head hurt as she followed Nicolas. She realized that she really needed sleep; needed it very badly.

"Where are we going?" Maggie asked, when she had caught up with Nicolas.

"Didn't you hear me?" he said. "There's a Gypsy camp ahead."

Briefly, Maggie wondered how he knew that, as she had seen no sign of human company in the woods. She bit back her questions. The flight from the inn had given her a sort of faith in Nicolas's instincts—his hearing, or whatever it was he had.

"Tell me," she said as they walked, "Why do we want to catch up with the Gypsies?"

Nicolas looked at her with a twinkle in his eye. "Let me put it this way," he said. "You can ride instead of walking, sleep even when we're moving, and eat meat instead of berries. And they may have feather pillows."

Maggie grinned. "Don't you think we're going too slowly?"

Nicolas laughed. "Well then," he said, "Catch me if you can!"

Without another word he sprinted ahead through the trees, leaping obstacles like a goat. Maggie ran after him, surprised at the strength that rose up in her at his challenge. They ran for a few minutes, until Maggie had to stop for air. She leaned against a tree and gasped in deep breaths, laughing as she did so.

Nicolas came back to stand by her. "There's a clearing just beyond those trees," he said. "Campfires and horse dung all over the place. Looks like they've just moved out. They can't be far."

Maggie nodded. After another minute, they headed down the path again. Their step was slower this time, but they soon came across the abandoned campsite. A much wider path, clearly distinguishable as a road with wheel ruts on either side, led out of the clearing. On another side, a similar road headed out.

"Which one?" Maggie asked, gesturing toward the roads.

Nicolas didn't hesitate, but walked toward the first. "This one," he said. "They're very close. I can hear them."

Maggie shook her head and followed him, Bear at her heels. In a short time she thought she heard voices, and before long, she clearly recognized the sounds of horses, wagons, and shouts. Bear began to grunt as he caught the scent of the camp ahead.

A sudden cracking noise interrupted Maggie's walk, and a small figure fell in a shower of leaves from the overhanging tree branches. Maggie jumped back with a startled cry. The creature had nearly landed on top of her. With her heart still thudding in her chest, she broke into laughter at the sight that met her eyes. A boy, no more than four or five years old, stood in the road, holding a wooden sword. Dark eyes glowered out of a round, dirty face. The boy wore trousers that had once been white, and a green vest without any buttons that exposed a bare chest.

Maggie moved toward him. The child's skinny arm lifted the wooden sword defensively. He snarled like a fox. Suddenly his eyes grew large, and he stepped back. Maggie felt the massive form of Bear just behind her. She reached up a hand to touch the animal's head, and held out another hand toward the boy.

"It's all right," she said. "See? He won't hurt you."

The boy lowered his sword apprehensively, eyeing

Maggie and Bear with evident suspicion. His feet remained rooted to the road.

"Would you like to pet him?" Maggie asked, stepping even closer to Bear to demonstrate the absence of danger.

Curiosity overcame the child's caution. He took three hesitant steps forward. Then, throwing caution to the wind, he let his sword drop limply to his side as he trotted happily forward and reached out to touch Bear's nose.

Bear licked the boy's hand with his long, rough tongue. The child laughed. His laugh was musical and free of fear, and Maggie melted under his charm. She crouched down beside him and laughed with delight as his giggles erupted under the force of Bear's sniffing nose and wet tongue.

Nicolas's voice broke through Maggie's reverie, coming from somewhere oddly far off.

"Don't look now, Maggie," he said, "but you're surrounded."

She jerked her head up, and her mouth dropped open at the sight of the people standing silently all around. They stood on the road and in the midst of the trees, at least twenty of them, dressed in ragged, brilliantly coloured skirts and vests and head scarves. Men and women both wore earrings and necklaces, and the women wore loose bracelets. Their hair was long and dark and curly, and they held weapons of many shapes and sizes in their hands.

Maggie shivered suddenly. Had she been an enemy of the Gypsies, she would not have stood a chance.

Her eyes skirted past the dark, unfamiliar faces to Nicolas. He was standing next to a tall, big-chested man with a black beard and long, curly hair.

The tall man motioned with his hand. Maggie heard a rushing sound as fifteen or so daggers and swords were tucked into homemade sheaths and sashes. She stood awkwardly to her feet as the little boy happily skipped to the side of the tall man next to Nicolas. Bear nudged her arm comfortingly.

Nicolas held out his hand. Maggie left Bear's side, walking past the eyes that silently followed her down the wheel-rutted road. She stepped up to Nicolas and took his hand. He presented her to the tall man with a bow.

"My friend, Maggie," he said.

The tall man cocked his head in question. "Is that all the name she's got?"

Nicolas nodded. "In Bryllan there might be more," he said. "But here she's only Maggie."

The tall man seemed pleased by the answer. He bowed his head politely.

"And I am only the Major," he said. He spread his hands out to encompass the still-silent individuals in the road. "These are my Gypsies. We haven't got much, but we'll share it with you for as long as you like."

Maggie smiled. Her voice expressed gratitude and relief.

"Thank you," she said. Before she could say more, the Major turned and walked down the road, the little boy clinging to his hand and jabbering excitedly. The silence of the crowd broke as the air filled with laughter and talk. Nicolas walked at Maggie's side with a proud little smile.

They soon arrived at a place in the road where horses impatiently stamped and tugged at reins held by children on brightly decorated wagons. The horses were shaggy, small, and strong, with broad backs and light-stepping feet. Their manes were long and unkempt, but their eyes shone brightly, and the wagon wheels rocked as they strained at their bonds.

The Gypsies climbed aboard their wagons. Some reclaimed the reins from their children. At the front of the caravan, the Major stood on the driver's seat of a wagon painted red and yellow. Beside him, a teenage boy smoking a pipe held the reins and waited. Nicolas climbed into the back of the wagon and pulled Maggie in after him.

They moved quickly to the front, where they could see the road and the pipe-smoking boy and the Major standing precariously on the seat.

The Major shouted and Maggie heard a chorus of answering shouts from all around. He raised his bare arm and held it high in the air for a moment, bringing it down with a cry of, "Move out!"

The wagon lurched forward as the pipe-smoker lashed the reins on the horses' backs. They pulled with a jubilant toss of their heads. The jangling sounds of wagons on the move echoed through the trees.

The Major took his seat, his broad back blocking the view of the road. Maggie settled back into the wagon, leaning against a wooden cupboard with a sigh.

Nicolas pushed past a worn green blanket that divided the wagon into two compartments and motioned for Maggie to follow. In the back of the wagon, three bunks were built into the sides: two on the left, one on the right. Nicolas pointed to the single bunk.

"There you go," he said. "Sleep all you like. And look." He snatched up a plump pillow and threw it at Maggie. "Feather pillows. Just like I told you."

"Won't the Major mind?" Maggie asked as she caught the pillow and let her weary body settle onto the bunk.

"Of course not!" Nicolas scoffed. "Anyway, I asked him already. This is your bed for the rest of the trip, so long as you want it."

He turned and positioned himself at the back door, ready to leap out into the dusty road. He turned his curly head back to smile reassuringly. "Good rest, Maggie."

With that, he was gone. Maggie was left with the rocking of the wagon and the lull of the noises outside. She pulled her tattered shoes off her feet for the first time since she had arrived in Calai, swung her feet up on the bed, and laid back slowly, letting herself sink into the softness.

Before she knew her eyes were shut, she was asleep.

* * *

It was dark inside the wagon. Maggie sat up and wondered for a moment where she was. Outside she heard the sound of voices.

She felt around on the floor for her shoes, and soon gave up. The air was still warm despite the night. She groped her way to the door and pushed it open, stumbling into the open air. The ground was hard and cool under her bare feet. The air felt open and sweet after the closeness of the wagon.

Traces of firelight illuminated the shadowed wagon and made its colours dance, aided by the distant moon shining into the clearing. The caravan was arranged in a circle, with the wagons sitting end to end to form a wall of wood and harnesses. Here and there a campfire burned beside individual wagons. In the center of the circle, a large bonfire blazed.

Maggie thought she could see Nicolas's slim form in the silhouettes around the fire. She moved toward him. Before she had quite joined those seated around the fire, Nicolas jumped to his feet. He stood with his back to the flames, voice rising. Maggie slipped into the circle, sitting cross-legged in listening silence. The little boy from the road, now wearing a long cotton shirt, spotted her and plopped himself onto her lap. His fingers twined in her sleeve as he listened, wide-eyed, to Nicolas's story.

"The creature was so close I could feel its breath through the floorboards," Nicolas said. "I took all the matches I could find and climbed up on deck. There it was, staring at me, with its horrible green breath and glowing eyes. It took one look at me and roared like a lion. It shook the whole ship."

The little boy huddled closer to Maggie. She put her arms around him as she watched Nicolas.

"I turned and ran for the ropes," Nicolas said.

"Were you scared?" interrupted a boy of about eleven.

Nicolas drew himself up to his full height and did his best to look offended. "I am never scared," he said haughtily. "I used my head—and I knew that I would be at better advantage in the rigging than on deck with the monster."

The boy nodded apologetically. Nicolas continued.

"I hung high above the raging sea. The wind tore at my clothes and the monster paced on the deck below."

Maggie hid a smile in the little boy's hair. Her own memory recalled a calm sea. She had, after all, been out on it.

"My eyes fell on a dry pile of rope right next to the beast," Nicolas went on. "I reached for my matches—struck one. But the match would not burn! I threw it from me and lit another . . . and another . . . and another!" His voice dropped nearly to a whisper. Maggie leaned forward with the rest of the crowd to hear him. "Still, they would not light. And then at last, one match caught! But even as I prepared to throw it, the mast on which I perched swayed and cracked. The monster had attacked from below! I lost my footing. I fell!"

Maggie was holding her breath. The little boy's fingers dug into her wrists.

"Down, down I plunged, until I reached out and grabbed a rope! Saved! I swung out like a bird over the ocean, flying in the wind, and then back over the ship once more."

The eleven-year-old once again failed to contain himself. "What happened to the match?" he asked.

The question derailed Nicolas for half a second. He made a comical picture, posed dramatically with the fire raging behind him, quite unsure of what to say.

"What match?" he asked.

"The one you lit before you fell," the boy prompted.

"Oh, the match. The match had fallen from my fingers when the mast gave way beneath me. It flew down through the tangle of rigging and landed in the midst of the ropes. As I swung back over the ship, I was greeted by the terrifying sight of flames licking up the wood."

"But you weren't afraid?" came the voice again.

"Of course not!" Nicolas frowned at the boy. "Where was I?"

"Swinging over the terrifying flames," Maggie spoke up. Nicolas turned to her, noticing her for the first time. Maggie smiled.

"We assume you mean that the flames were terrifying to the beast . . . since you, as you said, were not afraid," she said. To her surprise, a brilliant smile lit Nicolas's face. He laughed.

"Come up here, Maggie," he said. "Come on!"

Voices rose in general accord. Maggie removed the little one from her lap, stood, and joined Nicolas in front of the fire where she waited self-consciously as Nicolas picked up the narrative. In less than a minute her attention had gone from the audience back to Nicolas, as the heat of the fire brought back the memories. For a moment her mind left the Gypsy camp altogether and returned to the little wooden boat out on the sea. She felt the hot wind of the explosion on her face, heard the deafening silence that overwhelmed all noise for a split second afterwards; and then she heard the cries of the seagulls and the voice calling to her from the water.

Pieces of Nicolas's retelling pulled her back to the present, but now she had no fear of the audience.

"The black waters washed over my head," he said. "As I fought my way to the surface I heard a sound."

Maggie cut him off, and he fell silent before her. "The ship exploded like a dying star," she said. "In the moments that followed, all that could be heard was silence. The waves still moved, and the sea gulls still cried, but I could hear nothing."

"I swam through the waters," Nicolas said, quietly.

". . . and I thought of how my friend must have perished. I bowed my head and cried, and the gulls sang a mourning song over my head. And then a new sound broke through my silence. I heard my name being called."

"She reached for me and dragged me into the boat," Nicolas finished.

"We let the waves carry us as we watched the last burning remnants of the ship," Maggie said.

"And that," Nicolas said with a flourish, "is how I—we—defeated the shadow creature."

Maggie was delighted when the audience clapped in appreciation. The Major jumped to his feet and put his arm around Nicolas's shoulders.

"Well," he said. "Who knew we had such heroes among us? And such good storytellers. They are welcome by our fire any day!" Maggie saw the respect in his eyes as he looked at her.

Nicolas and Maggie returned to their places in the circle. Someone slapped Nicolas on the back, and the little boy climbed back into Maggie's lap.

"And now we shall have another story!" the Major said. "Peter! Will you tell us the story of the apple barrels?"

The pipe-smoking boy shook his head in amusement. "No, sir, Major," he said. "I will let that story rest until it becomes new again . . . or until a new story comes my way!"

The Major chuckled. "All right, then. Marja! Tell us a tale of the old days."

This request was met with a chorus of encouragement.

"Yes, Marja!"

"Tell us of the birds, Marja."

The Major sat down. A tall, willowy girl rose from the audience to take her place before the bonfire. She wore a long, crimson skirt that ended just above her bare feet. A red scarf adorned her head, tying at the nape of her neck and trailing down her back along with her black hair, which curled and fell nearly to her waist. Maggie didn't think she could be more than seventeen years old, but the smile that played on her face spoke of confidence and beauty and a half-hidden strangeness that intrigued all who looked on it.

She moved with the bewitching grace of a dancer as she spoke. Maggie cast a glance at Nicolas and saw that he was watching with rapt attention.

"Long ago," Marja began, "when every man in the world was a wanderer, and all peoples of the earth were free, there was one who called himself Rinco. He was the father of my own people, who are called the People of the Sky because of their friendship with the birds. This friendship began with Rinco, and this was the way of it.

"It came about that as Rinco wandered in the green forests of the earth, he saw a great flock flying overhead, toward the southern reaches of the world. It was not his way to let any pass by without sharing with him what news they had, so he determined to speak with the birds. He climbed up into the highest tree and called to them by name:

"'Ho eagle! Ho dove! Ho nightingale and wild goose! Won't you wait and speak with me? I wish to know where you fly, and what is the news that carries you so far from your homes?'

"But the birds paid him no heed: all except the raven, who was angered that Rinco would try to stop him in flight. He screamed at Rinco and flew in his face, and scratched him from his eyebrow to his jaw, so that Rinco was blinded in one eye. For this reason the People of the Sky have no friendship with the raven, though they respect him. He is one of the lords of the sky although he is cruel.

"At last it came to Rinco to try and call to the birds in

their own language, and so he listened closely for their cries and tried to imitate them. But the best he could do was to whistle, long and low, and he clung to the top of the tree and whistled, while the flock of birds darkened the sky with their numbers.

"Near the end of this great flock flew the sparrows, innocent children among the lords of the sky. The sparrows heard the whistle and took pity on Rinco, for they saw that the raven had marked him. And so three of them stopped their flying, and lighted in the tree where Rinco waited to talk with them.

"'Where do you fly in such great numbers?' Rinco asked.

"'We fly to the southernmost part of the world,' the smallest sparrow answered.

"'And what news carries you so far from your homes?' Rinco asked.

"'News of the King,' said the next to oldest sparrow.

"'Tell me of this king,' Rinco said, 'for I have never heard his name spoken before. Is he of the lords of the sky—a bird, as you are?'

"'Nay, son of men,' said the oldest sparrow. 'He is surely a lord of the sky, as he is the lord of all the earth, and all the stars above it. But he is not like us. He is the Heart of the World. There is none like him, in earth or in heaven.'

"'He is the sun-king, and the moon-king, and all-the-stars-king, and he shines like them all together,' said the next to oldest sparrow.

"'Has he sent for you?' Rinco asked.

"The youngest sparrow shook its head sadly. 'No one has spoken to the King in many years,' it said. 'But we have heard a rumour that he has come to the deepest south, and so we go there to meet him.'

"'And must I stay here while such a man is waiting to be met?' cried Rinco in dismay. 'Take me with you, dear friends, and I will do whatever you ask.'

"The oldest sparrow thought for a long moment. Then he said, 'We sparrows are not the wisest of the birds. Yet you spoke with us, and not with Master Owl. Nor are we the grandest, but you were not ashamed to be seen with us while Master Eagle flew by. And we are not the most valiant, not bold or strong like Master Raven, and yet you ask us for favour. And so we will grant it, because you have honoured us. We ask only that you promise us your friendship forever, and the friendship of your children to ours.'

"'I grant your request with all of my heart,' Rinco answered.

"'Then we will take you with us,' said the sparrows. 'In a few moments you will see us again. When you do, whistle for us as you did before.'

"Then the sparrows lifted up into the air and were lost in the great flock overhead. Rinco saw them soon returning, a great number of strong birds with them. So he whistled, as they had said, and the birds flew down and took hold of him and lifted him up. They flew over the green forests of the earth, and over the southern sea, into the deepest south. There at last their flight was ended. They came to rest on an ice island at the edge of the earth, where the sun shone only dimly.

"There they waited for the King to come, but alas, the rumours were false. Long they waited. Rinco was kept warm by the feathers of the geese and fed by the skill of the fisher hawks, until at last the birds determined to make their journey home. So they lifted Rinco up once more and flew back over the southern sea, over the green forests of the earth, and they set him down in the top of the tree where first they had met him.

"Rinco climbed down and began once more to wander, as his people always had done and would do forever after. The time came when he took a wife who bore him children, and he taught them to greet the birds whenever they met. Some say it is the People of the Sky who have kept the Gypsies free, for whenever they witness the flight of the birds, they cannot bear the thought of bondage under the Empire. So they keep all the Gypsies longing to wander.

"Every year the birds fly south, for they remember that once the King was to meet them there, and they hope that one day he will come. All of Rinco's life he would climb to the top of the tallest tree in the season of the great flight. He would watch the birds fly past, and he would greet them and dream of the deepest south and the time he spent there.

"And when he came down from the tree, his children would sometimes hear him say, 'He is the sun-king, and the moon-king, and all-the-stars king, and he shines like them all together.'"

The little boy had fallen asleep in Maggie's lap. She carried him to his caravan thoughtfully and retired to her own bed full of thoughts of birds, and of Gypsies, and of a king who shone like the stars.

5

A Decision is Made

ONCE AGAIN I HAVE BEEN THINKING *of the day of his return. I will not be here to see it, I know that well. I must pass through the borders of the world and join my exiled Master. When I do, light shall be my companion again, for the Blackness has no place outside this universe. When I have passed beyond the sky I will not spare much thought for this earth, where now I sit by the dying embers of last night's fire and write.*

Yet it troubles me to think that I will be forgotten to this world, for I have loved it, though it bears no love for me. I leave this journal, then, for those children of men who will one day be; and I hope that they will remember me.

My name is Aneryn. I am a Poet, and I am a Prophet. I fought beside the King in the Great War. The Brethren of the Earth—spirits of wind and tree and beast, of water and of fire—fought alongside me. There were men on our side as well. Few they were, and weak, as I am, but nobility and courage were in their hearts. This skeletal world without a heart and without flesh does not know what it means to feel courage, or to feel love. They, my sword brothers, knew. And I know. I alone know.

In the end the heart of the world was broken. The King took himself away. He took the faithful children of men with him, beyond the sky, to the kingdoms of light. The Earth Brethren were left alone. They continued to battle the Blackness, but they were overcome quickly by the strength of the enemy. They would have gone with the King if it had been permitted them, but they are bound to the Seventh World and cannot leave it. I know not where they are now. They live still, I believe, but as captives. They wait for the day of his return.

I alone remain of all the hosts of the King. I watched as my sword brothers and my Lord passed through the sky circle into the kingdoms of light, but their path was denied me. I was left here, for it is not good that the earth forget completely. Someone must remain who remembers. I am that one.

I write these things, so that the world can never really forget. Those who care to look will find the truth. When I am finished and my pen is at last run dry, then I will lie down and let my wounds drain me of life.

And I, too, will journey beyond the sky.

* * *

The Major's Gypsies were on the move once more. Nicolas sat on the driver's seat of the Major's wagon. Peter the Pipe-Smoker rode a shaggy little mare at the back of the caravan, and the Major, having declared an itching for a good walk, kept up a powerful stride next to a wagon further back.

Maggie sat on her bunk and rode with the back door open so that she could see out. She watched as the Major stretched out his arms so that Tiny Paul, Maggie's four-year-old friend, could climb up on his shoulders. Together they strode along: the Major, with a heavy sword swinging at his side, and Paul, waving his wooden one furiously.

The wagon bumped and jolted over the ruts in the road, and Maggie sighed with contentment as she leaned against the wall. A flock of birds burst suddenly from the trees and flew, cackling, over the heads of the Gypsy band. Maggie heard a long, high whistle rise from one of the wagons. It was the second time she had heard such a sound that morning. The first time, Nicolas had explained that Marja was hailing the birds.

Maggie stood unsteadily, taking a moment to get her balance in the rocking wagon, and then pushed aside the green blanket. She stumbled past the cupboards and climbed onto the driver's seat beside Nicolas. They sat in happy silence, rumbling down the road at the head of the Gypsy band.

The voices of the Major and Tiny Paul mingled with the sounds of horses and wagons as they sang a raucous song at the top of their lungs. Maggie grinned at the sound, then turned to Nicolas.

"Why do they call him the Major?" she asked.

"He was in the High Police," Nicolas said with an ironic grin. "Not a very respectable position for a Gypsy. Members of the Wandering Race are not usually drafted into the Emperor's service."

"Was he really a major then?" Maggie asked.

Nicolas shook his head. "No," he said. "I can't be sure—Gypsy stories get a little tangled with time—but I don't believe he belonged to the police more than a week. Just long enough to make him the butt of many a fireside joke."

"They seem to respect him," Maggie said.

"Oh yes," Nicolas said. "Yes, they respect him. He's like a father to them. It's been a while since anyone made fun of him. He laughs at the police just as hard as the rest."

"Have you known him a long time?" Maggie asked.

Nicolas was silent for a moment, and then he said, "Yes."

Maggie knew that she was prying, but another question came almost without her bidding it. "Are you a Gypsy?"

He sighed quietly and did not look at her. "Half," he said at last. "Actually, if it weren't for my gift of hearing, I'd have grown up in a respectable Midland home like you did."

Maggie didn't bother to correct him, as memories of the Orphan House with its high iron gates filled her mind. She didn't prompt him again, but Nicolas had decided to talk.

"My father was a Gypsy," he said, "but a Galcic family adopted him when he was a boy. My mother was Midlandish." Something in his face softened. "She was a good lady," he said, "but she died when I was six. Scarlet fever. My father . . . well, he left before I was two. I don't remember him."

"I'm sorry," Maggie said softly. Nicolas didn't seem to hear her.

"My mother's family was going to take me back to Bryllan, but some of them had an idea that I was crazy. See, when I was little I thought everyone could hear things like I could. Animals, and babies, you know. So I would tell people, and they all decided I was a little off in the head. One night I heard my mother's sister—she was a mean old lady—talking about putting me in an Orphan House in Londren."

He shivered, too preoccupied with his own thoughts to see the look on Maggie's face. "You have no idea what that meant to me," he said. "I had seen Orphan Houses in Galce, and there is no nightmare that could have been worse. You don't know what it was like."

Maggie said nothing.

"So I ran off, through the streets in the city where I was—I don't even know where. I got lost in the city, and an old Gypsy woman found me. She took me on the road with her. I lived with the Gypsies until I was thirteen, and then I started wandering on my own. I found Bear, and I learned to like living by myself."

"But you seem so happy here," Maggie said.

Nicolas nodded and smiled wryly. "Thing is, even the Gypsies think I'm a bit crazy. I don't really fit in here, Maggie. But you're right—when I'm here, I'm happy. At least for the first while."

They were silent for a long time, and then Maggie asked, "What happened to the old woman who took you with her?"

"She's dead," Nicolas said. "She was the Major's mother."

Before anything more could be said, Nicolas pulled up on the reins and signaled to the caravan to halt. The Major strode forward to see what the hold-up was, handing Tiny Paul to Maggie as he joined Nicolas.

A dead deer lay in the road, and a flock of ravens picked at the remains. The largest, an enormous black bird, opened its mouth and cawed. Its malevolent stare was fixed on the caravan, and Maggie shivered.

Nicolas jumped down from the driver's seat, and he and the Major approached the carcass, throwing a few stones to get rid of the birds. The large raven flew onto a branch overhead and sat watching.

Peter rode up to the front of the caravan, his pipe hanging

from his mouth, his brown head wreathed in smoke.

"Any meat worth saving?" he asked, taking his pipe in one hand.

"No," the Major said. "Doesn't look to be safe eating. We'll have to get it out of the road."

Peter called for rope, and Marja appeared at the front of the caravan with a long coil. As the men tied the deer to the saddle of Peter's shaggy mare, Maggie saw Marja's face go pale. She followed the Gypsy girl's gaze to the raven on the overhanging branch.

Slowly, Marja let out a long, eerie whistle. The raven ruffled its feathers and did not move. Maggie thought she saw Marja's face turn even whiter.

As Peter's horse hauled the deer carcass out of the road, the Major came back to his wagon and reached for Tiny Paul. Maggie handed the child over. She heard Marja say in a low voice,

"The raven's a bad omen. He ought to move on with the dead. Yet he stays and watches us."

The Major looked over his shoulder uneasily at the huge black bird. It had not moved from its perch. With little conviction, he said, "It's just a bird, Marja."

"It's a sign," Marja insisted. "And not a good one. It's an omen of death. The scavenger waits for carrion when he sees danger approaching."

Maggie found her eyes drawn to the raven. Once again she shivered. Marja's worries were nothing but superstition, yet the bird frightened her somehow. There was something familiar about it, as though she had seen it in a nightmare.

Peter and Nicolas returned from disposing of the deer.

Peter re-lit his pipe and headed for the back of the caravan, Marja disappeared into a wagon, and the Major again walked with Tiny Paul on his shoulders. But something had changed; Maggie could feel it. The Major did not pick up his song, and Nicolas did not continue his stories.

An ominous cloud had fallen over the Gypsy band, and the raven left its branch and followed the wagons.

* * *

Eva Cook wanted very much to be happy. She had cause to be: Pat was coming home. She would be back in Londren within two days. It had been months since the young woman had left for Cryneth to work as a seamstress for an acting troupe—an unusual occupation, but one that suited Pat well.

But Mrs. Cook was worried. There had been no letter from Maggie yet. She had received the mail every day with a thrilling heart, but there was nothing. She had chided herself time and again for worrying. Pat habitually went for weeks without writing, and Mrs. Cook had not worried then.

Maggie had not been gone long. She was busy; she had probably forgotten all about writing.

So Mrs. Cook told herself, but she continued to worry, and brood, and frown. An idea was beginning to shape itself in her mind: that when Pat arrived, the two of them would go to Pravik and find Maggie. Everything would be fine, of course. But Maggie would be glad to see them anyhow.

The fact was, deep inside, Mrs. Cook was sure that everything was *not* fine.

Mrs. Cook stared through the steam rising from her

teacup to the little pile of letters on the table in front of her. She mentally went through the pile again. A bill, from the coal seller. A letter addressed to her husband, Charles Cook, dead of a heart attack fifteen years earlier. The letter came from a Londren club that Charles had sometimes patronized; she had sent letters back to them before with the word "Deceased" written on them in big black letters, but evidently someone at the club didn't consider death an obstacle when it came to soliciting money. And there was a stiff little packet addressed to the yellow house at the end of the street.

Mrs. Cook sipped her tea slowly and looked out the kitchen window at the cold drizzle. It would be a miserable walk to the yellow house to deliver the misdirected letter, but it was better than sitting around doing nothing. She finished her tea, stood up, and took the packet from the bottom of the pile.

She pulled on her dull blue cloak and boots and opened the front door. The hinge squealed loudly as the door opened on a grey, puddled street. Mrs. Cook made a face at the weather as she stepped ponderously down the three front steps. She reached the bottom and looked up the street. Her heart caught for a moment and refused to beat.

A very tall man was walking through the rain toward her, carrying a girl in his arms. His step was purposeful and strong, and Mrs. Cook knew that she had seen him walking just that way before. She knew his stride, his form, his way of holding his head up.

But it was impossible.

He stopped three feet away from her. His blue eyes, set in a face older and more lined than she remembered, spoke a thousand words. He bowed his head slightly, every inch a gentleman. He had always been a gentleman. His sideburns were grey, though the hair that curled under his ears was still dark blond.

She tore her eyes away from his face and looked at the girl. She was pale, her eyes closed. Mrs. Cook might have thought her dead except that she could see her breathing. The girl's dress was black with a tartan skirt of red, white, and black —she came from the Northern Highlands. Her arms were twisted behind her.

Lord Robert's voice, low and urgent, broke through the rainy stillness. "We need your help, Eva. I'm not welcome here, I know. But look at this girl and tell me you can turn us away."

She wanted to tell him to get away, to turn back down the street and disappear in the rain and never come back. But in spite of herself, her eyes went back to the girl's face. There was something there that pleaded silently for help, and something else . . . something that shook Mrs. Cook with the force of old longing suddenly revived. She realized with a start that the girl's hands were chained.

Mrs. Cook took a step back, and then turned from the pair in the street and climbed the steps to her house. She pushed the door open, and stood frozen for a moment in the doorway. Leaning on the door frame wearily, she turned her face back to the laird.

"Come in," she said.

Lord Robert stooped as he awkwardly maneuvered through the door. He moved straight to the couch by the fire and laid the girl down gently. Mrs. Cook stood in the kitchen doorway and watched as the laird sank down onto his knees beside the couch and leaned wearily against it. He closed his eyes for a moment before looking up at his hostess.

"Thank you," he said.

She nodded and then gestured toward the girl.

"Who . . . ?"

"Her name is Virginia Ramsey," he said. "She is the granddaughter of a tenant farmer on my land." He sighed deeply, and his eyes went back to the figure on the couch. "She fainted some miles back," he said. "Of weariness, I suppose. We've been three days on the road, walking and riding and walking again." His voice trailed off. "I won't lie to you, Evie . . . it's Mrs. Cook now, isn't it? That's what the postmaster told me." He saw her slight nod of acknowledgment and asked, "Is Mr. Cook at home?"

"He's passed on," Mrs. Cook said. "Some fifteen years ago."

Lord Robert nodded. "I'm sorry to hear it. He was a good man?"

"Very," Mrs. Cook said. There was a note of rebuke in her voice. He heard it and understood. It had been a long time since she had thought of Lord Robert Sinclair as a good man.

"You were beginning to tell me something," she prompted.

"There are High Police after us," he said. "Your hospitality to us is kind, but not advantageous to you. We'll move on again if you wish. Only let us stay until Virginia has some strength back."

"Those irons?" Mrs. Cook asked, gesturing at the chains.

Lord Robert's face flushed with anger. "The gentility of

the High Police," he said. "How anyone could think it necessary to chain a blind girl . . . I tried to get them off, but they're fine pieces of iron. I could do nothing without attracting attention. There were High Police all over the roads. I couldn't risk taking her to a locksmith."

"There's a locksmith five blocks from here," Mrs. Cook said. "He's a good man. He won't be into the shop till noon today, but you can fetch him then."

Lord Robert said, "It may not be wise for me to show my face. I already fear what asking for you at the post might have done."

"Of course," Mrs. Cook said, flustered. "I'll go after him myself, then."

Her face paled slightly as Lord Robert's words sank in. Was her past involvement with the laird to be her undoing now? It had already taken Maggie away from her.

"Why did you come here?" she asked, suddenly angry.

"I didn't know where else to turn," he said. "I found myself in Londren and realized I couldn't run forever. My society 'friends' would have turned me in to the police."

His weary blue eyes looked straight into hers, catching her off guard. "I was despairing, and your name came to me like an arrow. I went to the postmaster and asked after you, and the man knew you personally. Well enough to know that you were the Eva Brown I asked for. I know you do not think kindly of me, but in heaven's name, Eva, I didn't know where else to go."

"That seems to happen a lot lately," Mrs. Cook muttered bitterly. "Dan Seaton slept in this very house just over a week ago."

99

Excitement suddenly animated the laird's face. "He came here?" he asked. "Where is he now?"

"He's dead," Mrs. Cook said. "Died in that room behind you."

The unexpected news checked Lord Robert's enthusiasm, if only for a moment. "Did he bring anything with him?"

Mrs. Cook sat down in the high-backed chair near the fire. "He did. A scroll, all written up in some ancient tongue."

The laird rose to his feet. "Do you have it?" he asked.

Mrs. Cook pulled herself up on her own feet, her height dwarfed by the laird. "No," she said sharply. "I don't deal in mysteries anymore, Lord Robert. I haven't done so for forty years. The thing is far from here now, where its curse can't touch me."

Lord Robert sank back down to the floor, but he was quiet only for a moment. Then he said abruptly, "Can you truly have turned your back on everything we lived for? Did the scroll do nothing to you when you saw it? My housekeeper said it was very old. Think what it might have contained!"

"I don't care to know," Mrs. Cook said.

"Daniel came to me with the scroll," Lord Robert said, "and the fool of a woman who keeps my house turned him away. Do you know what I did when I heard of it? I went back to our old council room. Do you remember the journal Huss began to translate in the last days? It's still there! Don't you remember, Eva, how the lore of old days just seemed to come to us, as though it wanted us to find it? And now it is coming to us again, calling us again!"

"Let it call," Mrs. Cook said. "It shall have no answer from me."

Lord Robert did not seem to hear her, but went on. "And it's not only the scroll. Do you see this girl, Eva? Do you sense the way the air changes when she comes near? She is Gifted."

"As Evelyn was Gifted?" Mrs. Cook said. Her eyes flashed with anger. "Evelyn, who destroyed us all?"

"Our own foolishness destroyed us," Lord Robert said. "Not Evelyn."

"No?" Mrs. Cook said. "Do you still defend her? After everything that happened, can you still be so blind? We tried to reach into another world, and that world would have taken our very souls if we'd let it. As Evelyn let it."

With those words she turned and stalked into the kitchen, leaving the laird alone with Virginia..

An hour later, when Mrs. Cook could bring herself to leave the laird of Angslie unsupervised in her house, she went after the locksmith. He was a man of average height, with copper hair, a hooked nose, and a very discreet tongue. His name was Benjamin Warne.

He took in the scene without a word and set to work at Virginia's shackles. They were off in the space of thirty minutes, and he held the iron chains up with disdain.

"If I were you," he said to Lord Robert, "I should take these out and bury them somewhere away from here. If I'm not mistaken, there are High Police inquiring for you all over the city."

A quick glance passed between Lord Robert and Mrs. Cook. It did not go unnoticed by Benjamin Warne. Lord Robert reached into his waistcoat pocket and pulled out sufficient funds to pay for the locksmith's service, and extra to keep his tongue.

Warne waved the money away. "No," he said. "I'll not
accept money for a job compassion would have bound me to
do. Take care of the girl; her skin is badly torn. And don't fear
for my silence . . . that cannot be bought, but my words will
not bring chains on her again, or on you."

They thanked him profusely. When he was gone, they
heard a sound in the sitting room. Virginia was awake.

Lord Robert rushed to her as Mrs. Cook fetched water to
bathe Virginia's wrists. When she returned, she knelt down
and gently began to clean the wounds. As the locksmith had
said, the skin had torn deeply and painfully, and the iron soot
had worked its way into the raw flesh. Virginia winced with
pain as Mrs. Cook worked, but said nothing.

When dry blood had turned the water to rust, Mrs. Cook
sent Lord Robert upstairs in search of a balm. Before he
returned, Virginia spoke.

"I don't know who you are," she said, "but your hands are
very gentle. Thank you."

Something about the simplicity of the thanks and the way
that Virginia's eyes stared into nothing when she spoke
brought Mrs. Cook to tears.

"No, dear," she said. "No, no, there's nothing to thank me
for."

Virginia's hands reached hesitantly for Mrs. Cook, and
the elderly woman allowed the young one's fingers to trace the
lines and wrinkles of her face. The fingers met with tears, and
Virginia smiled tenderly.

"Is it for me you are crying?" she asked. "Or for something
else?"

Mrs. Cook nodded and took the searching hands in her

own. "For you, dear," she said.

They heard the laird's feet pounding down the stairs, and Lord Robert appeared with a small bottle. Mrs. Cook took it and started to apply the ointment to the wounds. Virginia bit her lip and worked to hold back tears of her own. In moments, the stinging cream began to work its healing magic and the pain ceased. Mrs. Cook wrapped Virginia's wrists in bandages and then touched the young woman's cheek kindly.

"Finished," she announced.

Mrs. Cook had never had children of her own, but her motherly instincts had not suffered for lack of use. She ordered Lord Robert to escort Virginia to the kitchen, where she soon laid out a hearty meal of bread, cheese and sausage from the cold room, and plenty of hot tea. While they ate, she bustled around the house: the lower room, where Old Dan had stayed, was prepared for Virginia, and Maggie's room upstairs was reluctantly made ready for Lord Robert.

When the rooms were ready, Mrs. Cook brought Virginia a clean dress of Maggie's so that she could wash her travel-stained clothing. To Lord Robert's chagrin, she insisted on washing his clothes as well. "I don't care what you look like," she said, handing him a nightshirt and a blanket to wear until his clothes were dry, "but I won't have you smelling like last week's rubbish while you're in my house."

Late that night, Lord Robert left the house in slightly damp trousers and shirt, with a shovel and the blood-rusted shackles. He carried them down the street and over the fence to the yard of the yellow house, where he dug a hole under the shadow of a young oak tree.

The rain had ceased earlier that evening. There was no

sound in the night except for that of the shovel penetrating earth. Lord Robert gritted his teeth as he worked. Even this was too loud. What if someone in the house looked out? But the yellow house seemed very much asleep. The windows were dark, and no light or sound stirred in its bulk.

A sufficient hole dug, Lord Robert dropped the shackles in and grimaced at the clanking sound they made in the darkness. He thought he heard something stir in the alley beyond the fence, and stood stock still while his heart beat out the minutes. There was nothing.

He shoveled the dirt back quickly and spread damp oak leaves over the spot to disguise the newly turned earth. With that he stood tall, wiped the nervous sweat from his forehead, and climbed back over the fence.

Shovel in hand, he had just started up the steps to Eva Cook's home when he heard the sound of running footsteps behind him. He started to turn, his body unable to move with the speed he wished for. A searing pain flashed through him as something heavy hit below the base of his skull. He fell to the steps with a cry. A foot landed squarely in his back and pushed him off the steps onto the street. His eyes, fighting black spots as he struggled against the pain, could just make out a slim form standing over him, hands raised in the air with something clutched between them.

The object rushed down toward him, and he heard Mrs. Cook's door swing open. The elderly woman's voice cried out, "Pat! Stop! He's a friend!"

And then he could not see, or hear, anything. The laird's body lay still on the cobblestones as he slipped into unconsciousness.

He awoke to the unpleasantness of smelling salts under his nose and a throbbing pain in the back of his head. Mrs. Cook was peering down at him with obvious concern while the hand of an unfamiliar young woman held the salts unmercifully. She was thin and dressed like a boy. As she stood, Lord Robert could see that she was as tall as Mrs. Cook. Her straight, dark hair was cropped short. In the shadows of the street, she could easily have been mistaken for a young man.

Lord Robert struggled to sit up. The young woman had wandered over to the window and was peering out through the curtains at the street.

"You're all right then," Mrs. Cook said. "I was afraid she'd killed you."

"Who is she?" Lord Robert asked, putting his hand behind his head to feel the growing lump there. "And does she have a good reason for attacking me?"

The young woman answered his questions on her own, walking back to the couch with her arms folded in front of her. Her face was serious and her glare met the laird's eyes dead-on.

"My name is Patricia Black," she said. "I live here. And I had a very good reason for popping you. I thought you were the High Police."

The blood drained from Mrs. Cook's face as Lord Robert quietly said, "Do you often have High Police sneaking around in the middle of the night?"

"They're on their way," Pat said. "On my way here I overheard a racket at the postmaster's. They're looking for someone. You, I suppose, though they said you had a girl with you. The postmaster let it slip that you'd come here, but he

105

gave them a good run around on directions. Must have felt guilty for ratting you out."

"We've got to get out of here," Lord Robert said. He stood up, ignoring a wave of nausea that hit him at his sudden rise, and pulled his coat from the tall rack that stood by the door. Three long strides took him to Virginia's door. He knocked loudly.

"It's time to go," he said. His voice broke in mid-sentence. When he turned to Mrs. Cook, his face was weary.

"You don't know who we were," he said. "We seemed to need help, was all. We left hours ago, saying something about going to the country. Cryneth. Understood?"

Mrs. Cook did not even nod as she pushed into Virginia's room to help the young woman get ready to leave.

"Pat," she called over her shoulder, "get them some food from the pantry. As much as they can carry."

Pat disappeared into the kitchen, leaving Lord Robert to pace in the living room, now and then going to the window to look out nervously. Pat reappeared just as Virginia emerged from the bedroom, guided by Mrs. Cook's hand on her elbow. Pat looked the newcomer over quickly. Her eyes betrayed nothing of what she thought.

The laird pulled himself up straight and looked at Pat. He'd been thinking.

"Do you make a habit of attacking police when you see them? Wouldn't it have been more effective for you to make up a story about your innocence? You might have had the every soldier in Midland down on you."

Pat looked away from him suddenly. Mrs. Cook sought to hold the young woman's eyes and could not. Pat had turned her gaze to the curtains.

"I meant to tell you," she said in a muffled voice, "that I'll be going away again. Now."

"Now?" Mrs. Cook said. Her voice was beginning to shake. "You've only just come back!"

Pat reached for the old woman and gathered her in a sudden and unexpected embrace. "I'll be back soon," she said. "But I can't stay. I ran into a bit of trouble in Cryneth. It's best if I lay low a few months."

"Oh, Pat," Mrs. Cook said in a whisper.

"Where's Maggie?" Pat asked.

"Who knows?" Mrs. Cook, said, dropping bitterly into her high-backed chair. "She's gone off to Pravik, and I haven't heard from her."

Lord Robert jumped on her words immediately.

"With the scroll?" he asked. The question made no sense to Pat or to Virginia, who was listening to the proceedings while she leaned against the wall. Lord Robert dropped down to his knees beside Mrs. Cook, who looked at him resentfully.

"Did she take the scroll to Pravik?" he asked. "To Huss?"

Mrs. Cook nodded. Her eyes were full of tears, and she turned them away from Lord Robert.

Pat stepped defensively toward Mrs. Cook. "What's going on?"

"We'll go," Lord Robert said, ignoring Pat. "Why not? We'll go to Pravik. There's nowhere else to go."

Mrs. Cook stood up abruptly and pulled her cloak around her shoulders.

"What are you doing?" Lord Robert asked.

"You're right," Mrs. Cook said, shoving one foot into a

boot. "There's nowhere else to go. I can't stand another minute not knowing where Maggie is. Come on, Pat, we're going to Pravik."

"You mean to say you're coming with us?" Lord Robert asked, the beginnings of a smile on his face.

"That's what I said," Mrs. Cook snapped. "Someone's got to look after that girl of yours. Heaven knows you're not qualified to do it."

Virginia smiled to herself, and Pat approached her.

"Well, we may as well get ready," she snorted. "Seeing as no one cares to ask what we think of all this."

"I'm glad for your company," Virginia said.

"Yes, well, I can't say I'm sorry myself," Pat answered.

They pulled on outdoor clothes while Mrs. Cook muttered under her breath about temporary insanity and not knowing what she was thinking. Lord Robert gloated to himself. Virginia stood still against the wall, relieved that she would not be alone with the laird on the coming journey.

In minutes they were out in the rainy street, leaving an empty house for the police to puzzle over.

6

The Blackness Has Wings

MAGGIE AWOKE TO THE DEEP SENSATION OF FEAR. It seemed to her that she had been having a nightmare, but the memories of it had already receded into the far reaches of her mind. For a moment she lay awake, staring into the pitch darkness of the wagon. In the bunks beside her, she could hear the Major snoring lightly, and she could just make out the shape of Nicolas's hand hanging down from the top. The inside of the wagon was familiar to her, but its familiarity refused to slow down the beating of her heart or bring even an ounce of comfort to stop the creeping of fear over her skin. She shivered.

And then she saw it.

The raven was perched on the foot of her bed, and it was staring at her with green eyes. Eyes like the death-hound.

Maggie felt its eyes peering into her own, penetrating her courage, draining strength from her. She fought against the bird's malevolent grip, even as the air seemed to close in around her. She could barely breathe. At last she tore her eyes away from its hypnotic stare, to catch sight of something in the bird's claws.

She gasped, air coming to her in a rush. It was the scroll.

Her coat was hanging on a hook near the front of the wagon. Somehow the bird had taken the parchment from her pocket. Its black claws gripped the ancient paper with utmost care. Breathing hard now, with sweat gathering on her brow, Maggie watched as the bird's wings stretched up and its body tensed for flight.

She knew she had to grab the scroll, but she was unable to move. Her fingers strained against imaginary bonds as she willed herself to move, to reach for the scroll before it was too late.

Suddenly, a form sprang across the wagon. Nicolas landed on the bed with his hands grasping the raven's wings.

"Quick, Maggie," he yelled. "Get the scroll!"

Maggie lurched forward, her immobility broken. The bird fought against Nicolas with all its strength, and the force of its struggle knocked him down to the floor of the wagon. Maggie grabbed at the scroll, crying out with pain as the bird's beak speared at the skin on the back of her hand, the force of its blow deflected just enough to tear her skin without impaling her. She wrenched at the scroll and it came free from the creature's grasp.

Maggie scrambled to her feet and pushed her way to the front of the wagon as Nicolas rolled on the floor, desperate to hang on to the creature. The Major, awakened by Nicolas's initial yell, let out a war-like cry just as the raven tore its wings from Nicolas's grasp and flew out the back door of the wagon.

Nicolas leaped out after the bird while the Major pulled on his tall boots. He ran for the front of the wagon as Maggie cried out, her voice mingling with the horrible caw of the raven.

The Major emerged from the wagon to see Maggie wielding a stick, doing her best to beat the raven off. Nicolas, on the ground below her, threw a rock at the bird, only managing to clip its wing, and dropped to his knees in search of another missile. The Major gave a ferocious cry and grabbed his sword from its resting place just inside the front of the wagon. He swung out at the bird as Maggie ducked out of the way. The raven darted up to dodge the blow and came right back at Maggie again. Once more the sword cut the air, with all of the Major's impressive strength behind it, enough force to split the bird in two. Again, the raven flew back just out of range. It cawed as one of Nicolas's stones hit its neck.

Throughout the caravan, the Gypsies awakened to the strange battle. Lights bobbed in the camp as stocking feet stumbled out of the wagons with many a sleepy exclamation in tow. Pipe-smoking Peter leapt onto his mare's bare back, and the ragged pair came up beside the wagon as the Major's sword lashed out again. The bird moved out of range, but this time it darted forward again almost instantly, headed straight for Maggie and the scroll she had tucked inside her shirt. She pressed against the wagon, and the Major threw himself in the way. The bird's claws tore down his face, leaving bloody tracks across his forehead, nose, and cheek. It just missed the big man's eyes.

"Here, Maggie!" Peter called. Maggie launched herself off the wagon onto the horse's back. Peter drew a thin sword and called out Nicolas's name. Nicolas turned and caught the weapon as Peter tossed it to him. He was on the wagon beside the Major in an instant, slashing at the darting foe.

From all over the caravan, the Major's Gypsies came to witness the battle. They surrounded Peter and Maggie with rocks and sticks and swords in their hands, every one ready to take his or her own shot at the hellish creature in their midst.

But the raven seemed determined to deny them the pleasure. All of a sudden, it pulled away from the fight and flew off like a ghost into the blackness of the woods.

Deafening silence filled the clearing as the Major stood on the wagon, breathing hard, his sword still drawn. Nicolas crouched with his weapon at the ready, listening. The entire camp seemed to hold its breath.

From somewhere far away, they heard a rushing sound.

"What . . ." Maggie heard Peter say under his breath.

The ravens exploded from the trees in a burst of wings and claws and green, glowing eyes, cawing and screaming. There were thirty of them at least, though there seemed to be hundreds, and they descended on the Gypsies like vengeful spirits.

Peter wheeled his mare around and drove his heels into the animal's side. The Gypsies melted away from their path as the mare fled from the scene. Behind them, Maggie could hear the beating of wings. She turned her head to see five ravens after them, low to the ground. She buried her head in Peter's back, while behind her, the Gypsies attacked the birds with rocks and sticks and swords. She heard the birds' unearthly screams as the Gypsies cut them out of the sky.

On the wagon, Nicolas and the Major ducked and spun and slashed as the ravens flung themselves toward them. The wounds on the Major's face ran with blood as wings beat on his head and shoulders. Black feathers attacked his eyes like fits of blindness. The cries of men and birds filled the air, mingled with the slashing of swords and axes and the dull thud of clubs and stones. Somewhere in the melee, a child's wailing rose above the sounds of battle.

Peter's mare kept a frenetic rhythm as her hooves beat down the rutted road away from the caravan. Maggie clung to Peter's waist as she tried to slow the pounding of her heart. His clothes smelled like pipe smoke. The forest flew past in a blur of shadows and tangled shapes. One shape took form before them, and Peter tensed. He pulled up on the reins. They stopped, the mare prancing with the suddenness of it.

A raven was perched on a low-hanging branch over the road, glaring menacingly at the riders. Peter's mare fought against his control, stamping impatiently, as Peter stared at the bird.

The mare was breathing hard, her sides heaving under the riders' legs, as Maggie's eyes caught those of the raven. Without warning she felt the same fear that had paralyzed her in the wagon. A strangled cry died in her throat. The bird stretched up its wings and floated up off the branch, hovering in the air just before them, just before the attack they knew would come. Maggie wondered why Peter did not move, and then realized that the paralyzing eyes had taken hold of him as well.

But the mare had not looked into the raven's eyes.

With a frantic neigh, the mare tore the reins from Peter's hands with a jerk of her neck and galloped back down the road to the caravan. With their backs turned on the black bird, both Peter and Maggie came to their senses. Peter drove his heels into the mare while Maggie leaned forward, willing herself to be lighter, to be wings to the mare. The scroll inside her coat felt like a weight holding them back.

The Gypsies, scratched, beaten, and bleeding, had dragged fifteen of the ravens to their deaths on the ground. The remaining birds circled overhead like vultures. Below, the Gypsies stood waiting, their bodies tense for the battle that was surely not over.

The sound of wings suddenly beat in Maggie's ears, and she cried out in pain as claws ripped into her back. Peter twisted himself around, but he could not move to help. The raven cawed wildly, its wings beating all about Maggie's head and shoulders. The mare reared onto her hind legs in terror. Maggie, arms thrown up to protect her eyes, slipped from the horse's back.

The bird flew up just before Maggie hit the ground and dove toward her again. She rolled out of the way just as it plummeted; it pulled back into the sky rather than crashing into the ground. Maggie's heart pounded in her ears, blocking out all other sounds. From the corners of her eyes she could see the brightly painted wagons and blurred motion as the Gypsies battled the ravens who had once more descended on them. But she could not tear her eyes from the raven, the nightmare that hovered just above her, screaming victory.

Then a low whistle pierced through Maggie's isolation, and the bird's wings were suddenly tangled in the strong cords of a net.

Maggie scrambled backwards and to her feet, eyes riveted as Marja struggled with the raven. It cawed and snapped its beak, fighting to free itself from the net. Its strength wrenched at Marja's arms and threw her from side to side, but the Gypsy girl did not let go.

Maggie turned her head to see Nicolas standing beside her. He was watching Marja with fascination, and Maggie realized that all of the Gypsies had turned their attention to Marja's battle. The still-living ravens had withdrawn once again.

Maggie looked up to the birds that circled high above. An icy fear struck her as she realized that something was happening to them. Nicolas saw the look of horror on her face and looked up with her, his face paling beneath bright red scratches.

The ravens seemed to be losing their shape. Feathers gave way to ragged edges; claws and beaks disappeared as the birds lost their bird-shape and became turbulent, black scraps of energy.

Then Maggie saw it. Slowly, pieces of the bird-things were being torn away, drawn into a larger power . . . and the raven in the net was growing.

Larger and larger it grew, until its wings began to snap the cords of the net. Green smoke played around its beak and eyes. With an ear-shattering cry the bird broke free of the net, and still it grew. It was as big now, thought Maggie, as the hell-hound.

The raven dove, knocking Marja to the ground. She threw up her hands to protect her face as the enormous thing descended on her. The Gypsies threw off their fascination and hurled themselves into action. They rushed forward with a battle cry. Maggie grabbed a club that lay abandoned on the ground and joined the attack.

The raven beat its wings furiously, rising above the onslaught of steel and club. Maggie gasped at the sight. Marja clung to one of the creature's feet as it swept her into the air above the battle scene. People shouted. "Let go! We'll catch you!" Marja seemed not to hear. Peter fought his way through to the front of the crowd. Maggie heard him scream Marja's name.

Marja looked down at the sound of Peter's voice. Their eyes met, and he heaved his sword into the air with all of his strength. Marja held to the creature's leg with one hand, and slid down far enough to catch the sword. With a triumphant cry, she drove the blade up into the underside of the raven. The bird screamed and clawed at her, ripping into her side. The waiting crowd heard her cry out in pain as she fell into their arms. The raven circled overhead, cawing, and then dove once again into the battle. This time, the Major was waiting for it.

As the Gypsies scattered from the bird's attack, the Major leapt from the top of a wagon to the raven's back. His sword hacked into the joint of the bird's wing, penetrating the feathers to the bone. The raven screamed and threw itself straight up, sending the Major hurtling to the ground.

But it was clear that the creature had been dealt a blow. Its crippled wing dragged it down as it struggled to rise, and the Major bellowed a warning to the waiting band below. They gave a triumphant roar as the bird crashed to the ground.

A man ran forward, sword at the ready, but a blow from the raven's wing sent him crashing back into his fellows. On the ground, with its beak like the tip of a giant spear and its massive wings threatening, the bird looked as dangerous as it had in the air. Its green eyes glared with hatred at the Gypsy band that surrounded it.

A cry of "Rope!" rose over the crowd. A long coil quickly made its way into the Major's hands, one end tied around a rock. He whirled it in the air above his head and threw the end over the bird's neck to Peter, who waited on the other side. Peter grabbed it, only to be pulled off his feet as the raven jerked its head up. He was dragged four feet on his stomach as the raven strained against the rope. With another jerk, the rope came loose from the Major's hand, and Peter scrambled to his feet.

But now ropes were everywhere. They flew through the air to waiting hands, over the raven's head, neck, tail, and wings. Older children ran through the crowd with wooden stakes, sticks, and rocks, pounding them into the ground to secure the web. At last, the raven lay trapped beneath a net far stronger than the one Marja had wielded.

The Major climbed onto the raven's neck and lifted his sword high. He held it for a moment, steadying himself as the creature's body strained beneath him. The crowd broke into a shout of victory as he brought the sword down into the raven's head. The strength of his thrust shattered the bird's skull. The Major threw himself clear as the raven shuddered. It let out one last scream and lay still.

Marja's whistle rose over the silence, sending a note of mourning into the night breeze. As the Major's Gypsies watched, the breeze turned into a wind and stirred the feathers of the creature. Slowly, the carcass began to dissolve, becoming no more feathers and bone and sinew, but ragged bits of energy that caught on the wind and disappeared, until all that was left of the great bird was a maze of ropes and stakes.

* * *

The Gypsies returned to their wagons. A few tried painfully to sleep; others sat and whispered away the last few hours before dawn. In the camp of the caravan, before the embers of the great bonfire, the Major and a few of his band stood with Nicolas and Maggie.

"I'm sorry to do this," the Major said, his torn face dark with drying blood. "But I have my people to consider. We have enough battles of our own to fight."

"I understand," Nicolas said.

Maggie stood next to him with her head bowed. She was unable to look the Major in the eye. She had brought this upon them; she and the scroll. Brought it, too, upon Nicolas. Because of her he would have to leave these people with whom he was so much at home. She felt as though she had made him an outcast again. The burden of it weighed on her.

Nicolas began to turn away, but the Major stopped him with a hand on his shoulder. "We part now," the Major said in a voice deep with concern, "but we part friends."

Nicolas turned back and placed his own hand on the massive shoulder of the Major.

"You have done more than I can thank you for," Nicolas said.

Maggie looked up then. Her eyes wandered to the others who stood by the bonfire. Marja, her face white and her clothing stained crimson with blood where the raven's claws had ripped into her, leaned heavily on Peter. She was silent and her face was racked with pain. But she had come to say good-bye—or at least, to make sure that the danger left with them.

The Major stepped back from Nicolas and looked at Maggie. His face broke into an unexpected smile. "I hope you will come back to us someday," the Major said. "Tiny Paul will miss you. And we will all miss your storytelling."

A lump rose in Maggie's throat, and she blinked back tears. "I—" she began, and faltered. She thought she saw encouragement in the faces of Peter and Marja, so she continued. "I'm a long way from home," she said. "But for a little while, you made me forget the distance. Thank you."

The Major nodded. Nicolas and Maggie turned and began to leave the small company, but pipe-smoking Peter's voice stopped them.

"You can't go on foot," he said. "You'll never get where you're going that way . . . anyhow, we have two horses for you."

He walked past them and led them to the dark area where the caravan's horses were kept. Maggie shook her head when Peter handed her the reins of his own little mare.

"I can't," she said. "Your own horse . . . No, Peter, I can't take her."

"She's strong," Peter said, puffing smoke and talking out of the side of his mouth. "She might not look like much, but Nancy'll get you where you need to go."

"I know she will, but . . ." Maggie's voice trailed off. Nicolas shook his head at her. She took a deep breath and looked Peter in the eyes.

"Thank you," she said. "I'll take good care of her . . . and bring her back to you."

Peter nodded. "No rush," he said. "She's not hardly a loss." But he could not resist patting the mare's neck one last time, and Maggie thought she saw tears glinting in his eyes.

She stroked Nancy's shaggy head and smiled at the warmth in the little creature's eyes. Away in the darkness she heard Nicolas holding counsel with Bear.

"I know you don't want to stay, but it's for your own good," she heard him say. "You wait for me outside Pravik, you understand? I'll come back to you soon. And stay with these Gypsies a while. Protect them."

Bear made a sound that was a little like crying, and then Nicolas swung onto the bare back of a gelding, and they rode away.

* * *

It was noon when four passengers disembarked from a cab at the white-cliffed harbour of Daren. The harbour was busy as it was sunny, and a brisk wind threatened to take Lord Robert's hat off of his head. He held it tightly as he went to inquire after fare to Galce, leaving the women behind to wander as inconspicuously as they could through the crowds.

Pat was the first to see the green and black police uniform through the morass of fishermen, sailors, and housewives. Hands in her pockets, she stepped in front of Virginia and Mrs. Cook and whispered, "Trouble."

The three women moved in the opposite direction of the uniform, each holding one of Virginia's arms a bit too tightly. As they went, Mrs. Cook and Pat saw another soldier, standing so close that a turn of his head would reveal them. He was talking animatedly to a fisherman, who was looking at the soldier as though he suspected he might not be quite right in the head.

Virginia's sharp ears caught the words, "Dangerous fugitive . . . murderers . . ." and ". . . blind."

"They're looking for us," she whispered. Mrs. Cook moved to block Virginia from the soldier's line of vision, and Pat hustled them through the crowd toward the water.

Behind them, they heard the laird's voice begging pardon as he made his way through the crowds. He greeted them with an agitated whisper, his hat in his hand and the wind blowing his dark blond hair. It made him look wild and almost young.

"There are soldiers everywhere," he said. "We don't have a chance at boarding a ship. They've set every sailor in the harbour on the watch for us. Even if one would let us board, his mate would be sure to betray us. They're offering a reward."

"How could they know we're here?" Pat asked. "Are they watching every harbour in Midland?"

"They have the men for it," Lord Robert answered. His eyes fell on Virginia, who held her head high as she drank in her surroundings through every sense available to her. Her wrists were still bandaged and painfully raw. Mrs. Cook stood at her side, holding her arm. Overheard instructions came back to him: *Stop them however you can . . . but we need the girl alive.* Lord Robert set his jaw and turned back to Pat.

"We've got no choice. She's not safe in the Isles."

"Nor are you," Pat said. "If I'm not mistaken, you're on the hit list as well as she is."

"Aye," Lord Robert said, "but she's the one they want."

His voice dropped too low for anyone to hear. "I'd give anything to know why."

Lord Robert's eyes scanned the harbour, looking over the heads of the crowd to the boats moored on the docks. A little fishing boat humbly bobbed on the water, barely noticeable in the midst of larger ships. It was tiny and, from all appearances, ancient, but it looked seaworthy.

"Come," Lord Robert said, and led the way to the tiny boat. Pat and Mrs. Cook looked it over dubiously, but the nearness of the High Police choked their protests.

Lord Robert climbed aboard and held out his hand for Virginia. She took it and made the guided leap from the dock to the boat, her heart only in her throat a little. Lord Robert helped her sit near the back of the tiny craft. Next, Mrs. Cook jumped for the boat, gasping through clenched teeth as it rocked underneath her. Pat knelt on the dock and untied the thick knot that held the boat to the shore. In a moment she stood and jumped in, the rope in her hands.

Lord Robert grabbed the oars and began to steer the drifting boat away from the harbour. Waves lapped gently against its sides, and Mrs. Cook held on tightly. Pat dug around beneath the front seat and came up with a small spyglass, some maps, and a waterproof wooden box full of hard tack and tobacco. A fishing net, wet and tangled, lay at Virginia's feet.

Pat put the glass to her eye and stood up, surefooted even on the waves, looking back at the harbour.

"Black-and-Greens everywhere," she commented. "It doesn't look like they're onto us."

She turned, looked out to sea, and whistled. "Black clouds rolling in. Methinks we're in for a rough ride."

"You don't need the spyglass to see that," Lord Robert said.

Pat put the glass down and saw that clouds were quickly blocking out the sun that had felt so warm in the harbour. The wind was picking up, and the water was white with choppy waves. Mrs. Cook's face was pale. Virginia sat beside her, facing the wind with implacable courage. For a moment Pat wondered if Virginia was unaware of what was happening, but the changing temperature and motion of the water had told the blind girl all she needed to know.

No one suggested that they turn back.

The storm held off for hours, until Daren was nothing but a fading vision of white cliffs behind them. Then lightning streaked a path down to the sea, and deafening thunder tumbled after it. Rain lashed the craft and its inhabitants furiously. The waves stirred as though a giant beneath them had awakened.

The oars were useless against the crushing force of the water, and Lord Robert struggled to pull them into the boat. A cracking, splintering sound met his efforts, and the remains of the oars came suddenly up out of the water, jagged ends outlined in a flash of lightning.

A huge wave rushed violently down over their heads, and filled the little boat with water. Pat grabbed the wooden box and dumped the contents overboard, struggling to keep her balance as the boat bucked and tossed beneath her. The water was up to their ankles and cold enough to steal their breath away, and Pat bailed furiously. Mrs. Cook joined in, bailing with her cupped hands.

Again and again the wind and waves and rain battered

the tiny boat, while its inhabitants bailed stubbornly and furiously. Only Virginia was calm. She sat in the back of the boat and looked up, unmoved, while her face met the onslaught of the rain without fear. She neither helped nor hindered the efforts of the others, and to them she seemed not to belong to them—to be a creature of the air.

As the numbing cold and painful lashing of the water drained the strength from those who tried to fight it, a great stillness overtook Virginia. No hint of expression passed over her face, and even the sea around her calmed. Pat wiped her hair out of her eyes and stared at the strange young woman, whose very calmness seemed to take the fury out of the storm.

"Look!" Virginia commanded suddenly, and the three ceased working against the water and raised their eyes to the sky.

They were surrounded by an army of beautiful giants.

In the blackness of the clouds warriors and horses waited, wearing golden armour and cloaks of deep scarlet and forest green. They stood facing the wind, and their horses stamped impatiently. The air was filled with the sounds of swords swinging, harnesses jangling, and hooves stamping. The wind made the white manes of the horses and the long hair of the warriors stream out behind them. For a moment only, even the earthy smells of the creatures reached the sailors in the tiny boat.

And then it was gone.

Lord Robert looked away from the sky and at Virginia with wild eyes. He had seen it. It was real. She had opened the Otherworld to him at last.

The rain continued to fall, but it did not chill them as it

had before. The wind died down and the waves that had beaten the boat now caressed it, and carried the little craft through the water to Galce.

The sun was setting fiery orange over the water when the fishing boat scraped against the sands of the continent. Lord Robert and Pat jumped into the surf and pulled the boat to shore, where they helped Mrs. Cook and Virginia out. The setting sun brought the changing colours of the forest to blazing, brilliant life. Somewhere deep in the trees, a bird was singing.

Virginia shivered with the cold, fully human again, as water dripped from her skirts onto the sand. Mrs. Cook moved close and put her arms around her. Virginia leaned her head on Mrs. Cook's shoulder, and they stood in silence. Lord Robert let the fading warmth of the sun play on his neck and bare head, and he sighed low. He gazed a moment at Virginia, but she did not seem aware of his presence.

"Where do we go from here?" Mrs. Cook asked finally

The question brought Lord Robert back to himself. He looked around at the sandy shore. His eyes fell on a tall white stone that rose from the water out in the channel, the sun causing it to shine like a strange moon rising from the depths.

"I know this place," the laird announced. He pointed out at the stone. "That's the Giant's Tooth. I came here often as a child. We're not ten miles from Calai."

"Which way?" Pat asked.

Lord Robert started off briskly. "This way, I'm nearly certain of it! We haven't got time to waste, now come on."

They started to walk, but Virginia suddenly stumbled and nearly fell to the sand. Mrs. Cook held her up, and cast a wrathful glance at the two who led the way.

"She can't walk all that way now, and though I don't like to complain, neither can I," she said. "You two can march on if you like, but we're resting here."

Lord Robert bowed his head, and Pat threw herself down on the sand next to Mrs. Cook, stretching out with a long sigh.

"I'm sorry," Lord Robert said. "Of course a rest is needed."

Virginia lay down on the sand, and Lord Robert came and sat by her head. He reached out to touch her, but she flinched and moved away. He drew his hand back as though it had been bitten.

No one else had seen, but Lord Robert felt the rejection keenly. Not for the first time, he wondered darkly what it was that had sent the High Police after Virginia Ramsey.

7

A World in Turmoil

TONIGHT THE MOON BURNS RED. *I have seen it thus before: in the days of the Great War, the anger of the heavens burned in her face. Such a world she looks down on must kindle great wrath! Evil walks among men, though the Blackness itself is kept away behind the Veil.*

It is a great mystery, the Veil. I will tell the tale of it, for it is a thing of mourning and of wonder.

There once walked among us a race of beings called the Shearim, the Fairest of Creation. In them was great wisdom, great beauty, and great strength. They took what shapes they wished and moved about clothed with the forms of men and women and children. Men sometimes called them the Virtues, for they took names to themselves after those qualities which men most honoured and revered: Justice and Wisdom, Harmony, Innocence, Hope, and Beauty. The child-hearts among the Shearim were called Merriment, Laughter, and Melody.

Some kept to themselves, but many were dear to men, for they would often come among them, easing burdens with their touch and filling hearts with their laughter and strength. It was sometimes said that those who had been with the Shearim would afterwards glow as if they had touched the sun.

When the Blackness began to grow in the Seventh World, the Shearim first sought to hold it off by exerting their influence for the good, but it was to no avail. At last the Shearim, in their own way, became warriors, and they battled the creatures of shadow before even the Great War. Those were days of grief and hardship for the Fairest of Creation, for the Blackness was cruel and ruthless, and loved to torment its enemies.

In the end, men became allied with the Blackness and went to war against the King and his army. In those days the Great War began, as men and shadow fought against the Earth Brethren and the few remaining faithful of men. But this was a clash in which the Shearim did not take part, for they were bound by their own law, and could not take up weapons against men. They watched, and moved among the wounded and dying, and ministered to them as best they could. It is said that the Eldest Seven stayed by the King and served him. But in the end even their ministrations were to no avail, for the King's heart was broken and he went into exile.

It was then that the love of the Shearim for all creation became fully manifested. With the King gone and the Blackness growing, the Fairest of Creation, weeping for all that had come to pass, saw that there was one last thing they could do to save the rebellious ones. They joined themselves together and called upon the power of their law to undo them. While the raging Blackness watched, the life-force of the Shearim was woven together into a new thing: an impenetrable Veil, a living division between the Blackness and men.

And so the Blackness was for a time thwarted, and the children of men were left free to build their own world, and someday, perhaps, to reach out for the King again. For this slender chance of redemption the Shearim gave themselves.

But now they are gone from creation forever and always, for the Veil must one day be destroyed, and the makers of it can never be re-made themselves. They sacrificed themselves to defeat the Blackness and to save men, and the world will ever weep for them.

O Children of Men, will you only be dry-eyed in the face of this thing? You for whom it was done, you for whom all was sacrificed—will you not weep?

* * *

Virginia lay on the beach sands, listening to the gentle thunder of waves on the shore blend with the soft sound of snoring. Her clothes had dried to an uncomfortable damp. The wet sand felt warm under her body. The air around her was cold, and she knew that the sun had gone down. In the forest, insects were chirping.

A breeze blew through her hair and died away. A sudden unease gripped her, and she raised herself up on her hands and sat with her head cocked, listening.

Once again the air stirred around her, and this time she felt as though fingers were reaching for her through the wind. She flinched at the touch of the breeze, and suddenly a blinding flash of colour—purple and red and living, pulsing blackness—shot through her eyes. For an instant she could see two eyes in a shadowed face, staring at her. She looked back, unable to tear her eyes away, and then it was gone. There was nothing but the gentle rhythm of the sea against the sands.

Something had found her. She could not hide much longer.

* * *

The walk into Calai should have been miserable, as the little company staggered along on storm-battered muscles. But something about the day lightened both their steps and their moods. Sun diamonds sparkled and flashed on the water, and the seabirds shouted glad tidings to the white clouds. Mrs. Cook and Pat fell to talking, catching up on each other's lives since they had parted a few months before.

Lord Robert walked with his hands in his pockets, his mind filled with the memory of the vision in the storm, and with wonderings and thoughts of the future that waited in Pravik. Only Virginia, walking by the laird's side, seemed unaffected by the cheerfulness of the day. She was silent and shadowed, every step taken with grim determination.

There was no sign of the High Police in Calai. Lord Robert hailed a cab, and before the heat of mid-afternoon had begun to beat down, the foursome were resting comfortably on an iron train bound for Pravik. They rode in a private compartment, with red velvet seats and windows, faintly etched with dragons and serpents, that looked out on the country as it passed.

That night, Lord Robert sat with his chin in his hand, gazing at the curved moon that stood watch high above the black trees. Moonlight caused the swirling patterns etched in the glass windows to sparkle, snake scales shining in crystal. Pat slept beside him, her head resting against the wall. She had pulled her legs up on the seat, and lay curled up like a cat.

In the seat across from them, Mrs. Cook was snoring softly. Virginia was wide awake.

Lord Robert listened to the rhythmic clacking of the train wheels as the car rocked gently back and forth, rushing through the forest. He imagined himself in a study in Pravik, pouring over the contents of the mysterious scroll with Jarin Huss, just as in the days of the council. For so long he had sought the Otherworld, only to find every door closed to him. Now windows such as he would never have imagined were flinging themselves open at every turn, and the Otherworld was seeking *him* again. Seeking him through Virginia. Her nearness to him made his pulse quicken with the awareness of the other side of reality, and he felt a determination to make her open up to him. He knew that he did not have her confidence—her trust—but he meant to win it. She held the key to the worlds unseen, and she must open them to him someday.

His thoughts were interrupted by the sound of Virginia's voice. "Laird?" she asked.

He turned away from the moon to face her. "What is it?" he asked.

"You saw, didn't you?" she asked. "All of you—you saw the riders."

"Yes," the laird said, sitting forward. "We saw them. I have waited all my life to see such a sight."

"And I have seen such things for as long as I can

remember," Virginia said. "But I have never desired to. The visions come without my wish or command, and they fill me with joy or horror as they will."

"As a young man I would have given anything to see as you do," Lord Robert said. "The powers of the Otherworld did not grant me such a gift. Only, here and there, they would seek me out. They would give me a hint in one place and a whisper in another, always tantalizing, always calling me to come farther. But I had no stepping stones to reach them."

"You speak as though the Otherworld had a human spirit," Virginia said.

"Perhaps it does, or more than one," Lord Robert said, carefully. He was baiting her; waiting for her to tell him the things she had always kept hidden.

"You should be careful," was all Virginia said, "whose call you answer."

"Are you worried about me?" he asked, and said, without waiting for an answer, "You don't need to be. I can take care of myself."

"So says every man, before he is lost," said Virginia. "I do fear for you. I have seen you, sometimes, and there is a great black cloud around you that whispers and calls to you. And a woman."

"I don't know what you're talking about," Lord Robert said, suddenly irritated. "I suppose everyone has a 'cloud' at times, of emotion of one sort or another. And what do you mean, a woman?"

"A woman who occupies your thoughts and your longings," Virginia said. "I have seen her in your memories."

Lord Robert laughed a short, humorless laugh and said,

"It's just this sort of thing that makes the villagers hate you."

"I know," Virginia answered, and said nothing more. Lord Robert silently chided himself. He had let something slip through his fingers, he was sure of it. After a while he turned to apologize, feeling sincerely guilty for his words—but Virginia was asleep.

The laird did not sleep well that night.

* * *

Dusk had fallen when Nicolas and Maggie rode into the city of Pravik and wound their way through the narrow streets. The black waters of the Vltava River cut through a ravine in the center of the city, dividing level streets from those that rose up the sides of a high plateau, crowned by the dark aspect of Pravik Castle. Fifteen bridges spanned the river, their lamps glinting off the water far below. The dark shapes of mountains and foothills stood sentinel beyond the city.

The streets were still and empty, and the step of the horses beat hollowly on the cobblestones. The air was uneasy; it whispered in Nicolas's ears and twitched in the horses' tails. Maggie leaned over and stroked Nancy's neck just before they stepped onto the Guardian Bridge, a silent archway lined with white marble statues.

Nicolas pointed up the steep hill on the other side of the bridge, to the place high on the plateau where torchlight glistened and the milling silhouettes of a body of people could just be made out.

"That's Pravik Castle," he said. "Looks like something's happening up there."

Maggie squinted into the darkness at the shadowy bulk of the castle. Nancy stamped nervously, and Nicolas said, "Let's go see. Come on!"

Maggie followed Nicolas onto the bridge, where the strange white figures held out their hands in silent pleas. The lamplight on the bridge flickered off the statues' empty eyes and lit the sides of the ravine, carved deep and narrow by centuries of water. Halfway across the bridge, the sounds of unrest from the crowd around the castle began to mingle with the rushing spray of the river. Nicolas spurred his horse on faster.

They rode up the streets until they reached the edge of the crowd. There were hundreds of men gathered around the gates of the castle: merchants and university students, chimney sweeps and lamplighters. They carried weapons, such as they had. On the other side of the gates, half-hidden by the shadows, stood row after row of High Police, the ends of their spears shining in the torchlight. Their swords, long and sharp, rested in black scabbards. The soldiers were as silent and unmoving as the statues on the bridge, but their eyes glistened with threats.

A young man, tall and darkly handsome, had mounted a wagon, where he shouted in a strong voice. The crowd around him had quieted, and only their muttered agreements betrayed how strongly his words struck their hearts.

"The Overlord has no right to deny us a voice!" the young man said. "The Governing Council speaks for *us*, the people . . . how can they if they will not hear us? Let the Overlord know that we will not leave these gates until they are opened to us, and we are given the right to speak!"

An old man in the crowd shouted something back at the
young man, who answered with an imploring look at those
around him. "We cannot allow the Overlord to take more from
us. Already he bleeds us dry! In our schools, our universities,
he denies us the right to know what is true. I know! I am a
student, and every day I must sit and listen only to those things
which the Overlord—indeed, even the Emperor himself—
deems necessary for me to know! And you, the workers and
merchants who are the lifeblood of this city! The taxes taken
from you snatch the very food from your children's mouths.
Now they will take those same children from you. The Man
Tax is an evil that ought to have been strangled the day it was
born. Instead it has taken your sons from your hearths and sent
them to become wolves."

He gestured to the silent rows of soldiers who watched
and listened from the other side of the gate. "The High Police!
What are they but slaves, taken from our numbers before they
knew enough to know what was worth fighting for? My
brother was taken from my parents when he was thirteen years
old—as you have all lost brothers, and sons, to their ranks. And
now they will lower the age of the tax, and we will lose our
children when they have scarcely learned to walk and talk!
Seven years old! That is what the Emperor has decreed. That is
what our Overlord bows to without protest. We shall not allow
it! We are here to protest, and our cries will rise above Pravik
until they reach the throne of Athrom itself! All we ask is a
voice in the council tonight. Stand strong, and be heard!"

The young man jumped down from the wagon, and
Maggie found that she could still see his head above the crowd.
He strode up to the gates and shook them until the iron rattled

deafeningly.

"Tell me!" he demanded of the soldiers. "What does the Overlord say? Will he listen now? When will the gates open to us?"

In answer there was only silence, only the glaring malice of the High Police.

Nicolas leaned over and whispered, "Some of those soldiers could be looking their own fathers in the face now, and it wouldn't make a difference to them. The Empire has trained away every shred of family loyalty and love that ever existed under those uniforms. That's why the Man Tax is so hated."

Maggie looked back at the glinting spears behind the gates and shivered. "It is the same in Bryllan," she said. "Only our boys are taken much older, when they are nearly men. Why so young here?"

"Because the Eastern Lands have always been breeding grounds for revolutionaries," Nicolas told her. "Gypsies wander here, and they taunt all men with a vision of freedom—even if it is a tattered, starving, outcast freedom. And there are others who work to keep revolution alive. In the universities. The Eastern Lands are a threat to the Empire and they always have been."

The young man leaped back onto his wagon and continued to speak, but Maggie was engrossed in the faces of the crowd, and his words were lost on her ears. The men in the crowd showed faces filled with fear and anger; some lined with age and some smooth with youth; fathers who longed for their sons and boys who wished for their brothers. Many in the crowd were young, clean-shaven men who bore the good clothes and uncalloused hands of university students, and they, who had perhaps suffered least, seemed most determined to bring change. Maggie noticed a few men who wore homespun clothing and carried pitchforks and homemade spears— farmers, these, with rough hands and weathered faces. They seemed out of place, awkward though not fearful, and they kept silence and watched the others.

The crowd fell quickly silent as a man approached from the inside of the gates and ceremoniously unlocked them. He stepped out into the street and surveyed the crowd with a look of high disdain.

"The Overlord of the Eastern Lands, his lordship Antonin Zarras, wishes me to inform you that you will not tonight, nor ever, be admitted inside of these gates." His announcement was greeted with an angry murmur from the crowd.

"And if we refuse to leave," the young leader answered, jumping down from the wagon again so that he stood looking down into the eyes of the official, "then his lordship the Overlord will not be admitted *outside* of these gates." There was a cheer of encouragement, and the young man wrestled his way in between the slightly open gates. "We have a right to be heard!" he shouted, even as he allowed the man to shove him back outside and clang the gates tightly shut.

"Give us our voice!" a big man shouted at the retreating back of the official, and his call was taken up by the crowd. "Give us our voice! Give us our voice!" The chant became a deafening chorus.

Once again the gates were opened. This time an old man and a young woman were escorted through. High Police stood silently beside and behind them, and the old man held up his hands for silence. Amazingly, the crowd began to calm.

"Professor Huss," one of the university students called. "Tell us what is happening in the council!"

Maggie snapped her attention to the old man at the sound of his name. Jarin Huss. He was old and tall and rail-thin, and he wore long red and brown robes. A thin grey beard twisted its way nearly to his waist. The respect he commanded was obvious; his quavering voice quieted the mob. The woman who stood beside him was young, but there was a deep gravity in her face that made her look much older. She wore a long, regal blue dress with gold trim, and her long, light brown hair fell past her waist in graceful curls. She bowed her head respectfully to the crowd, and Maggie saw heads bowing in response as recognition lit in many eyes.

"My friends," Professor Huss said, "the Overlord will not admit you to the council. You know this. We have done all we can, but the council will not be moved on your behalf tonight."

"Is there nothing you can do?" an old man cried, and Nicolas flinched at the sound of the heartbreak in his voice.

"Not tonight," Professor Huss answered. "I am sorry."

"We will not leave." It was the deep voice of the big man, who stood with his brawny arms crossed over his chest. "We have a right to speak."

"Speak, then!" Huss said in frustration. "I cannot force the council to listen. My friends, go home. Sleep in your own beds tonight. We will do all we can for you and your children; yes, even tonight, we will continue to fight the battle of words for you. But I implore you, do not stay here. I do not know what will happen if you do."

"You are only one man," said a young man, a university

student with a nervous face. "Professor, you have already tried to sway the council. I do not mean to offend, but . . . well, have you not failed?"

There was a long quiet as Professor Huss bowed his head, and the woman put out her hand and touched his arm comfortingly. It was she who answered, her voice tense.

"We have not failed until we are dead," she said. "Do not give the Overlord an excuse to move against you. Spill blood tonight, and that is failure. Go home, my people. There is nothing else to be done."

Maggie found herself searching out the young man who had so galvanized the crowd with his words. She found him easily. He was standing near the gate, listening with his head half-bowed. As she watched, the young man lifted his head and met the eyes of Huss. She thought she saw a smile's shadow on the professor's face, though it was a sad one, and he spoke quietly. She thought she could make out the words from the shape of his mouth: "You tried."

The guard who had previously appeared at the gate stepped out of the shadows and bowed slightly.

"Professor, my lady," he said, "You are wanted inside. By order of the Overlord."

The soldiers around them crowded in, and the two turned unwillingly and disappeared into the darkness of the courtyard.

Outside the gates there was a forbidding calm. The air felt suddenly hot and heavy, like the air before a storm.

In that moment the big man who had challenged Professor Huss cried out and drew back his arm to let a huge stone fly. Before the stone could be loosed, a tall man in a dark cloak stepped out of the crowd and shoved the man back.

"No!" he said. "Did you not hear the lady? Tonight is not the time to spill blood!"

The big man shoved back. "And who are you to decide what will be?" he spat. "You hide your face in your hood like a coward. Show yourself, or do not pretend to be lord over me!"

The crowd was tensed and watching. Even the High Police, still standing unmoving behind the gates, seemed to stiffen in anticipation. The young man who had led the crowd stepped forward as though to intervene.

The man in the cloak spoke quietly. "I am no one," he said. "No one but a farmer who does not want to die tonight."

The big man shoved him again, and the hooded man did not fight back. The young man was at his side in a moment, his body tense, forcibly restrained.

"Cowards," the big man said. Before anyone had time to react, he whipped his hand back and let the stone fly. It flew straight through the gate and struck a soldier in the head. The soldier stood still a moment, then lurched to the ground.

The crowd poured itself on the gates. Young men scaled the bars; shouts echoed all through the yard. Axes and swords and torches were thrust through the iron bars while voices called, challenging, calling for the High Police to come and fight. The young leader and his hooded friend were lost in the press of bodies.

Nicolas took Maggie's arm and whispered urgently in her ear, "We've got to get out of here before . . ."

His last words were drowned out by the sound of a trumpet blast. The High Police surged forward as one. The gates were forced open from the inside, pushing the rioters back. The nervous young student, high on the gates, cried out as he fell into the hands of the crowd and then down to the ground. A black-handled spear quivered deep in his chest.

The gates were opened and the High Police flooded into the crowd. There were dozens of them, marching from the bowels of the castle out through the courtyard. They were armed and trained, and they were without mercy. The cries and screams of dying men filled the air as Maggie and Nicolas tried to force their way to the back of the crowd. They had reached the street when one man's anguished cry rose above the crowd. It was the big man who had started the riot.

"You will not have my son!" he cried. His voice was cut off unnaturally. Maggie bowed her head in sudden grief. She felt Nicolas pulling on her arm.

"Let's go, Maggie!" he was saying.

But Maggie could not bring herself to leave yet. Impulsively, she climbed up a lamppost, where she could see into the torch-lit mob.

The handsome young leader fought near the gates. He was skilled and seemed to be holding his own. His nervous young companion lay bleeding his life out on the cobblestones beside him. Maggie saw the tall hooded man fighting like a whirlwind with a spear he had wrenched from a soldier. He flew to the rescue of an old man and arrived only seconds too late.

A trumpet blast issued from somewhere inside the courtyard. The sound of horse hooves could be heard even above the riot. Row after row of mounted soldiers issued forth from the courtyard, riding through and over the crowd without remorse and without pity.

Maggie watched the people fall. Then all she could see

was the deep crimson of blood.

* * *

"Maggie!" It was an intense whisper, spoken from a parched throat. "Maggie, wake up!"

Maggie groaned and opened her eyes. She was looking into Nicolas's concerned face, and he was holding her head up. The rest of her was stretched out on the ground.

"Is it over?" she asked.

"Can't you hear it?" Nicolas asked.

Maggie closed her eyes and let the sounds of the fight reach her ears again. "Yes," she breathed, stomach sinking lower than it had been. "Where are we?" she asked after a moment, and struggled to sit up.

"Hiding," Nicolas said. "You fainted."

Maggie put one hand to her aching head and looked around her. They were in the shadow of an old house. A wrought iron fence surrounded the small courtyard where they sat, and Nicolas leaned against the wall of a stable. The street outside the yard was still and dark, lit only by the dim light of a street lamp. On cobblestones far down the street, the shadows quivered with the lights of the riot.

"What's happening down there?" Maggie asked.

"Just what you saw," Nicolas said. "Those farmers don't have a chance. They should have listened."

"They ran out of hope," Maggie said. "People with no hope do strange things." The old burn scars on her hands ached a little, and she rubbed them.

"You sound like you know," Nicolas said. He was looking

down to the quivering shadows and was not expecting an answer, so Maggie didn't give one. The big man's dying cry was still echoing in her ears.

"*You will not have my son!*"

Maggie sobbed once, and turned so that Nicolas wouldn't see how close she was to losing control.

What sort of world had she come to? As a child in the Orphan House life had been a terrible dream, but she had awakened from it when Mrs. Cook took her in. Snatches of the nightmare had returned—especially when John and Mary died. But now to discover that it was life with Mrs. Cook that was the real dream, and the nightmare was reality . . . dread welled up inside of her, and she struggled to force it back. Hounds and ravens and bloody injustice could not be the stuff of reality. Surely they could not.

Nicolas began to move back farther into the shadows, and his voice was terse. "Someone's coming."

The wrought iron gates of the courtyard swung open, and the dark forms of men rushed through. Some were limping. Two carried a third, who groaned pitifully. One man, who stood head and shoulders above the others, was recognizable as the hooded man. Maggie and Nicolas watched, fascinated, as he dropped to his knees in the courtyard and began to strike the ground with his fist. After a moment, he stood back. A piece of the ground slowly rose in the air.

A trapdoor.

The tall man descended into the ground, and the others followed him. The trapdoor remained open for a few minutes after the last head had disappeared, then slowly closed.

Maggie and Nicolas looked at each other, speechless.

143

Maggie wanted to speak, but there was nothing to say; the darkness of the night—so much more than physical darkness— kept her quiet.

The courtyard was cold. Maggie and Nicolas sat with their backs against each other to keep warm. Maggie was tired, and after a while her head began to nod.

"Wake up," Nicolas said sharply into her sleep. "There's someone else."

The gates opened slowly this time. The newcomer was in no hurry. He stepped into the courtyard wearily, pulling the gates shut as though they were too heavy for him.

He shuffled slowly into the courtyard, leaning on a walking staff, red and brown robes dragging after him. His shoulders were stooped and his head bowed, and Maggie knew him immediately.

Jarin Huss.

He approached the place in the ground where the trapdoor was, and lifted his staff. He struck the ground with it three times, and the trapdoor lifted. Huss slowly disappeared into the earth. The door closed after him.

"That's the man we're looking for, right?" Nicolas said after a few minutes. "It'd be a shame to lose him now." He stood, stretching his cramped legs, and approached the hidden trapdoor.

Maggie stood warily and followed him. Nicolas scrutinized the ground, his eyes searching for something that was not to be found. He went on his knees and felt around, looking for the way to open the door.

Maggie watched and even tried looking herself. Nothing presented itself to her tired eyes but a small knot-shaped pattern in one stone.

She pointed. "Maybe that's . . ." she began to say, and then she noticed that Nicolas's eyes were closed.

He was listening.

She watched in fascination as his hand moved slowly over the ground, coming to rest on a completely ordinary bit of stone. He made a fist and raised his hand over the ground, bringing it sharply down three times. There was a faint groaning sound, and the ground began to open.

Nicolas grinned. Maggie smiled and caught his eyes. He blushed suddenly and looked away.

"Let's go," he said, and descended into darkness.

Maggie followed after him. In a moment the small light of a candle flickered in his hands.

"Where did . . . ?" Maggie started to ask. Nicolas put a finger to his lips to silence her. He pointed up to a small ledge near the top of the stairway, where a number of burned-out matches lay beside two candles.

The stairs led deep into the cold earth, until they reached a narrow corridor with a smooth stone floor. The air was damp, and small streams of water trickled down the walls, collecting in small gutters on either side. Every drop of water echoed in the corridor. Wind howled down it and fell silent again. It was eerie and unwelcoming, and Maggie was glad for the sound of her own footsteps.

The passage went on for a long time, and ended in a heavy wooden door with light shining through the cracks into the corridor. Nicolas walked softly to the door and put his ear against it. He motioned for Maggie to come too. She walked tentatively forward.

Before she reached the door, a scream issued from beyond it. Nicolas started back, surprised. Maggie was horrified. There was another scream, as tortured as the first, and it trailed off into a whining moan.

Nicolas pushed against the door. It swung open on well-oiled hinges. For a moment he and Maggie stood in the doorway with the scene before them etched in their eyes like a painting.

A long table sat in the middle of the room, and a young man who was little more than a boy lay on it. He wore no shirt, and his bare skin was spattered with blood. His arms were linked with those of the handsome young university student, the eloquent leader from outside the castle, who stood behind him. The regal lady in blue sat on one side of the table, holding the boy's hand tightly. Huss stood on the other side, with the dripping head of a spear in his hand. It had just been pulled from the boy's side.

The walls were lined with men—farmers. In the farthest corner of the room stood the tall man, still hooded, his face in shadow. He held the black-shafted spear Maggie had seen him fighting with, but he had broken off the spear end and was leaning on the staff. His clothes were homespun and simple, but a large ruby glinted on one of his fingers.

The boy's face was the colour of bone. His dark eyes stood out in his head, full of pain and fear. He had heard the door open, and Maggie and Nicolas watched as his eyes slowly moved to them and opened wider at the sight.

They were surrounded before they could move. Nicolas raised his hands in surrender. Maggie followed his example. Professor Huss turned to regard them, slowly, as unhurried as he had been in the courtyard. He drew himself up and searched both of their faces. Neither met his eyes.

"As no one has spoken for you, I assume that you are friend to no one in this room," Huss said at last. "So you have come here either by accident, or by curiosity, or to seek out someone whom you have not found. Which is it?"

It was Maggie who answered, to Nicolas's surprise. "Not any of those," she said, half faltering. "We *are* friends to one in this room—to you."

Huss's eyebrows popped up. Maggie thought she saw a smile playing at his thin mouth. "Is that so?" he asked. "Well, then, friends . . ." He looked around as though he had forgotten where he was. "We will have to talk later." His eyes came back to them. "At the moment my attention is otherwise occupied."

He motioned to the men who stood all around Nicolas and Maggie. "Let them go," he said. "But do not let them leave."

The men stood back. Nicolas and Maggie pressed themselves against a wall. Attention diverted from them as thoroughly as if they had sunk into the stone itself. No one seemed to care who they were.

Huss produced a needle and thread from his robe and leaned over the boy. His back prevented Maggie from seeing the operation in detail, and she was glad for it. The woman who sat beside the boy still clung to his hand, but her face was pale and her mouth tight.

At last it was over, and Huss stood. His hands were bloody and he looked at them reflectively. "I don't suppose anyone thought to bring a washbasin," he said, then shook his head. "Of course not."

He looked up and addressed the room. "He is too ill to go back to the country with you."

"He must go back, tonight." It was the hooded man who spoke. He moved out of the corner as he did so. "This city is not safe for him."

"He will die on the road if you take him," said Huss.

The hooded man spread out his hands to indicate his surroundings. "He can't stay here. The cold and damp will kill him."

"He will stay with me," the woman said. She rose to her feet. Her eyes met those of the hooded man, and Nicolas saw something pass between them. The look sounded thunderous in his ears.

The university student said, "He can stay in the school, my lady. The risk is great if he is found in your house."

"No greater than it is for us if he is found sheltered in the university," Jarin Huss said, sharply. "What you have done— and not done—tonight may be enough to destroy us. It will not do to have a member of a rebel militia discovered. That is . . ." He looked up at the hooded man. "If there is a rebel militia."

"I saw enough tonight," the hooded man said. "The Overlord will not listen. I was right to train my people in the use of force. Yes, Professor. There is a militia."

"Professor Huss is right," the woman said. Her dress was spattered with blood and her hair was pulled back from a face that was weary but determined. She looked back to the hooded man. "He cannot stay in the school. He will come with me. When he is well I will send him to you." Another look passed between them, a look with something gold and fiery in it. "You must not come here again until the echoes of tonight have stopped sounding."

The words sounded strange in Nicolas's ears. As he looked at the hooded man, his head filled with voices. Every sound in the room grew faint, as though he was moving far away, and other sounds took their place.

"It is the peace of death we break . . ."

"Rise up! Blackness no longer!"

He heard the sound of fire roaring and swords clashing; the sound of horses as though there was thunder in their hooves—horses as of giants. He heard the battle cries of men, rising from a thousand throats all at once.

The sounds faded. Nicolas was back in the stone room once more. Maggie seemed to have noticed that something was wrong. Her hand rested on Nicolas's shoulder. He turned to look at her but quickly shied away from the question in her eyes.

The decision was made. There was nothing more to be said. The hooded man stood for a long minute at the table, looking down at the pale face of the boy. He touched the boy's forehead and smiled sadly; looked up at the woman and drew a deep breath.

Then he turned and was gone. Everyone went with him except the professor, his student, the woman, and the boy. And Nicolas and Maggie.

"Jerome, take the boy to his refuge," Huss commanded. Jerome, the student leader, looked at him questioningly. He motioned to the wall against which Nicolas and Maggie were huddled. Huss chuckled.

"I am not afraid to be left alone with them," the professor said. "And you will be back soon to avenge me if I am wrong to be unafraid."

Jerome nodded unhappily, but said nothing. He bent down and picked the boy up gently, cradling him in his arms. The woman put her hand on Huss's shoulder.

"Thank you for everything," she said, and she and Jerome left the room.

Huss turned to Nicolas and Maggie.

"Now we are alone," he said, looking at them both in turn. "And you have something to say. Speak."

8

Revelations

MAGGIE REACHED INTO HER COAT and brought out the scroll. She
held it out, mutely. Jarin Huss took it with a puzzled
expression on his face.

He unrolled the scroll and stood for a long time, perusing
its contents. Maggie saw a shadow pass over his face, followed
by a strange elation. One thing was certain: the scroll was not
an indecipherable puzzle to him. He knew what it meant.

After a long while, Huss looked up from the parchment
and fixed his eyes on Maggie.

"And who are you, young woman?" he asked.

"My name is Maggie Sheffield," Maggie said. "That is,
I . . ." She closed her eyes. "I represent the Council for
Exploration Into Worlds Unseen."

"Oh?" Jarin Huss said, his expression conveying more
surprise than he meant it to. "Well, this is a noteworthy
meeting, isn't it?" His forehead wrinkled in thought. "This is
hardly the place for a noteworthy meeting. Do come with me,
Maggie Sheffield. And . . . ?"

"Nicolas Fisher." Nicolas shifted his feet uncomfortably
under Jarin Huss's steady gaze.

Huss nodded as though the name meant something to him. "I see. You are also welcome to come with me, Nicolas Fisher. Now, let us go."

Huss removed a torch from the wall and led the way back down the damp corridor. The room behind them fell into darkness as they left.

Jarin Huss said nothing as they walked, and neither Maggie nor Nicolas felt leave to begin a conversation. They followed until they had emerged from the ground into the strong light of the moon. Huss took them through the courtyard to the high front door of the old house. He pulled a key from his robes and fit it into the lock, turning it loudly.

They stepped into a room which might once have been a grand entrance, but which was now grey and drab and falling to pieces. Wide doors led into other rooms, probably sitting rooms, but in the darkness Maggie could not see them well. Across from the door, a tall staircase led to the upper floor.

Huss did not bother to light any lamps, but held onto his torch. They climbed up the long staircase to a wide loft that overlooked the entrance. At the top of the stairs they were greeted by the grey-eyed stare of a cat perched on the banister. When they had all passed by, the cat silently dropped from its place and padded after them.

At the end of the hallway, Huss pushed open a door into a small room. He extinguished the torch and lit lamps all around the room, filling it with warm light. He finished by touching a match to an oil lamp that squatted on an oak desk covered with open books and papers. The room, Maggie thought, resembled the professor himself in its aged and scholarly warmth.

Bookshelves lined three walls, lending the rich colours of

book bindings to the glow of the oil lamps. Against one wall, the cat had made itself comfortable on a small bed with high posts. At the foot of the bed a window looked down on the street, and the lights of the castle could be seen. Huss stared out the window for a moment and then drew heavy gold curtains across it. Maggie was glad that the castle and the disturbing scenes connected with it were shut out of the room.

Between the bed and the desk, an old table with charmingly curved legs sat, surrounded by four chairs. Huss pulled out one of them.

"Here, sit and be comfortable," he said, taking his own advice. Maggie and Nicolas awkwardly obeyed. Maggie was trying very hard to think of what she was going to say. Nicolas seemed overawed by the room. Books and papers were foreign and intimidating to him. He found himself longing suddenly for Bear and the outdoors.

Huss took the scroll from his robes and laid it out on the table. Maggie looked down at the strange letters and shivered. There was something about the open scroll that felt wrong. It seemed an obscenity that ought to be kept hidden in the presence of decency. She felt stupid for thinking so, as the professor didn't seem bothered. She raised her eyes to him as he spoke and tried to forget that the scroll was there.

"I was not aware that the Council for Exploration Into Worlds Unseen was an operative body again," he said. "I am very surprised to hear it."

Maggie looked away from his steady eyes and said, "It isn't, sir. That is, there is no council in operation, but I do come from it . . . them."

Huss smiled faintly. "Suppose you just tell me who sent

you? That might be easier than trying to explain the existence or lack thereof of a council which has not been together in forty years."

"I was sent by Daniel Seaton," Maggie said. "In the interests of John and Mary Davies. And although Eva Cook didn't want me to come, in a way I represent her more than the others."

"I see," Huss said, now clearly amused. "So you are the whole council unto yourself, are you?" He chuckled and tapped the scroll with a long finger. "And where did you get this?"

"From Old Dan—Daniel Seaton," Maggie said. "He brought it to Mrs. Cook and me before he died. He said he had taken it from a woman called Evelyn."

The effect of Maggie's words on the professor was profound. He shot halfway to his feet, then sank back down, muttering something to himself. After a moment he returned to his surroundings and said, "Daniel is dead, then?"

"Yes," Maggie said, sorry that she had not broken the news gently. "He said he had been to the Highlands of Bryllan to try and take the scroll to Lord Robert Sinclair, but he had not been able to get in to see him. On his way back to Midland, he fell sick. When he came to us he was dying."

"And he sent you to me?" Huss said.

"He said you would want to see the scroll. He thought it was very important."

Huss nodded. "What have you to do with Eva Cook?" he asked. "Who, I assume, is the Eva Brown I once knew."

"I live with her," Maggie said. "I am her foster child, one of two. She and her husband, who is now gone, took me from an orphanage when I was ten."

Nicolas was looking at Maggie strangely, but she did not notice.

"And John and Mary?" Huss asked. "You are here in their interests as well?"

"They are also dead, sir," Maggie said. She spoke the words carefully this time, aware that Huss did not expect to hear them. She saw the strain and sorrow on his face as she spoke, and was sorry for it. "They fostered me for three years, until I was thirteen, when they died in a fire. It was a tragic accident."

"Was it?" Huss asked, his voice terse.

Maggie sought to meet Huss's eyes, no longer awkward, reaching out to meet him in the pain he shared with her. For a moment they looked at each other with an understanding of mutual loss.

"I had hoped you could tell me," Maggie said at last.

Instead of answering, Huss stood and walked to the window, his hands clasped behind his back. He stood and stared at the drawn curtains for a long time. Nicolas tried to catch Maggie's eye, but she was watching the professor intently and did not spare a glance for him.

Jarin Huss turned and smiled wanly at Maggie. "I am quite sure they were murdered," he said. "Just as I am quite sure Daniel was murdered. Just as I am quite sure that Mrs. Cook is not safe, and that I am not safe, and that you are most certainly not safe."

"If she wanted safety she would've stayed at home," Nicolas said, "instead of risking her life to get you that piece of paper. Now are you going to help her, or aren't you?"

Huss raised an eyebrow, but there was no irony in the

gesture—only comprehension. "They have come after you already, then," he said.

"Who has?" Maggie asked. Huss did not answer, and Maggie stood in frustration. "Who has?" she asked again, leaning over the table toward him with her palms on the wood, fingertips nearly touching the scroll.

Huss bowed his head and looked suddenly very weary. "Them," he said. "The Order. The scourge of mankind." He sat back down at the table. His legs seemed to have lost the strength to hold him up. "You will be safe here for a few days at least. Goodness knows we can't give it back to them."

The door to the study opened with a bang. Maggie jumped up in alarm. She found herself facing Jerome.

"Oh," she breathed, and sat back down, her heart racing.

"I frightened you," Jerome said. "I'm sorry."

"You should be," Nicolas muttered. No one seemed to notice.

"This is Jerome," Huss said, "my apprentice—the future leader of the Underground University of Pravik, which is of course a very deep secret—one you shall both be careful to keep. Jerome, this is Maggie Sheffield and Nicolas Fisher."

Jerome nodded courteously to them and said to his master, "The boy is sleeping safely in Libuse's home."

"Thank you," said Huss. He sounded exhausted.

"Is something wrong?" Jerome asked.

Huss smiled thinly. "Everything is wrong, Jerome, and everything is right. Our gain is our snare, as it always is."

His words made no sense to Maggie or Nicolas, and they glanced at each other, a bemused smile on each face. It was the first time Maggie had looked at Nicolas since entering the room. He knew it acutely, though she hadn't noticed.

Jerome noticed the scroll, and he came to stand by Maggie. "I assume *this* has something to do with it," he said.

"You should never make assumptions," Huss said. "But as it is, this time you are right." He shook his head and muttered, "I fear it will draw them like a magnet."

"Let them come, whoever they are," Jerome said. "We will hold them at bay."

Huss smiled and patted Jerome on the cheek as though he was a little boy. "You're very brave," Huss said. "As brave as you are ignorant. But perhaps bravery is better than cowardice, even if it is brought on by stupidity."

"Will someone kindly tell *us* what is going on?" Nicolas asked. "Maggie brought that thing to you, and we both put our necks on the line to do it. We ought to know what's happening."

"Of course," Huss said. "In the morning."

"What?" Nicolas sputtered.

"In the morning," Huss repeated. "I suppose we have one more night in which we may sleep safely. I will explain all that I can in the morning. I confess I wasn't prepared for you. I want some time to think."

Maggie thanked him, but Nicolas did not seem to have heard. He was staring at Jerome with his ears full of voices, and his face was dismayed.

They were ushered to two small rooms down the hall. Both rooms were dusty and cobwebbed, but the linens were clean and the beds, while old and a bit springy, were comfortable enough. Maggie fell asleep quickly. Nicolas lay in bed and thought about the woods, and about Bear, and the

Gypsies, and things that he could hear and no one else could.

* * *

As she slept, Virginia saw the black-cloaked shadow that
moved from car to car, peering into the compartments. She saw
it, and she knew why it had come.

She opened her eyes and found that she could see,
although a mist over her eyes made every form uncertain and
blurred the mute colours of the train. The crystal dragons
etched in the window glass stood out with strange clarity,
glinting through the mist. She saw Mrs. Cook beside her,
slumbering deeply. Across the compartment, Lord Robert and
Pat were also sleeping.

It was best, she thought.

She stood and left the compartment. Her fingers lingered
long on the door. Those inside would never willingly let her
go, she knew that. Just as she knew that she had to leave, that
she could not endanger these who had given so much for her.
She felt a pang of guilt nonetheless, and sorrow at leaving
them.

She bowed her head and walked away slowly. It would
not do to meet her adversary here on the train. If she did,
others would be placed in danger. For one fleeting moment she
felt an urge to run back and beg the laird to protect her. But
the words of the King were to her both a prophecy and a
command: "*My enemies hunt you, and you must face them.*"

Face them she would, then. The courage of the King
returned to her and she steeled herself for the battle ahead.

"*Do not forget who I am. Do not forget who you are.*

Remember me . . ."

Virginia walked from car to car until she had reached the end of the train. She pushed open the door and found herself standing on a small platform, protected by an iron rail, while the cold night wind whipped at her clothes and hair and stung her eyes.

Through the mist she could see the forest rising all around, choking out the track that wound endlessly back the way they had come. She hesitated only for a moment. She could feel danger approaching. Once again a vision flashed before her eyes, of a dark hand reaching out to open the very door behind her.

With a deep breath Virginia flung herself over the railing. Even as she did, the mist faded away and she was blind again.

* * *

Maggie walked in dreamland that night. She saw herself in the Gypsy camp, surrounded by bright caravan wheels and the stillness of the forest at night. A full moon was glowing brightly. A low fog hung about the wagons. They were moving although it was night, and she was driving a wagon of her own.

She felt the closeness of someone beside her, and she turned to ask a question of Nicolas. But it was not Nicolas with her—it was Jerome. She was startled, even in her dream, but somehow it was good to have him near.

He reached over and gently took the reins from her hands, pulling the wagon to a stop. "We will miss our chance if we keep going," he explained in his deep voice. He stood on the seat of the wagon and pulled her up beside him. Together they looked up at the moon. Across its pale face they saw a great flock of shining white seabirds winging silently toward them.

The birds were slender, yet each was bigger than the wagon. Jerome seated himself on the neck of one of the birds, and she felt a nudge as another lowered its head for her to climb on. She did, and the birds lifted into the air with a motion smooth and white as cream.

The birds flew high above the earth until they seemed surrounded by stars. When Maggie looked down the earth was a dusky colour, streaked with the glowing silver of rivers, lakes, and the seas themselves.

The birds flew over the glistening sea, farther and farther south, until Maggie could see a ridge of snow-covered mountains ahead. The birds' wings beat in great, sweeping motions. They rose up over the tops of the mountains. As the ridge dropped away beneath them, a light burst over it with such brilliance that Maggie covered her eyes with her hands. She looked to the side, and then she saw that the bird carrying Jerome was continuing up over the mountains, and the one carrying her was dropping away, back toward the sea and the north.

Maggie cried out something that she could not understand and reached for Jerome. His eyes met hers and she saw silver tears in them, but he smiled, and turned his face back toward the brilliant light—and the dream was over.

She sat up in bed and clutched the sheets under her chin, wondering why the dream—beautiful as it had been—troubled her so much. She played the scenes in her mind until she could not bear the silence of the room anymore. She got up and walked on bare feet to the bedroom door. When she opened it she was looking into Jerome's face.

He was standing across the hall from her door, leaning on the rail, fully dressed. His head was bowed and his eyes were closed, his breathing deep and regular. He had a sword strapped to his side, and one of his hands rested close to the hilt. She looked at him curiously, and a smile played on her face.

His eyes opened quite suddenly. He looked up at her, and said, his voice only a little sleepy, "Why are you smiling?"

"Why are you standing there?" Maggie asked.

"Because I think you need protection," he said.

She rubbed her arms. "Why do you think so?"

"Master Huss said that evil was coming," Jerome said. "He does not think it will arrive tonight, but I do not like to take chances."

Maggie thought suddenly that she had never seen anyone who looked as strong or as gentle as Jerome did at that moment. The thought disconcerted her. She tried to regain the smile that had been on her face a moment ago.

"But you were sleeping," she said, teasingly.

He did not smile, but nodded seriously, and frowned. "I am sorry," he said. "I did not mean to—but I have been dreaming, and the dream was not eager to let me go before it had run its course."

"What did you dream?" Maggie asked in a whisper.

"That is not a question to ask, Little One," Jerome said. "Every man's dreams are his own."

"Professor Huss said that you will take over for him when he is gone," Maggie said. She was curious to know more about

161

him.

He nodded. "I will."

"Do you look forward to that?" Maggie asked.

"No," he told her. "For me to be master means that my own master must be dead, and he is like a father to me."

He was quiet for a moment. "Even so, perhaps I could look forward to it if I believed that the future would be as the past."

"What do you mean?"

"The Underground University of Pravik has existed for hundreds of years, teaching and keeping hope alive. And whether the masters of the University have known it or not, their work has all been for one final goal—that the Eastern Lands might wrench themselves free from the grasp of the Empire. We're very close to reaching that goal now. Very close. We work toward the day when we will change the world." Jerome seemed lost in his own reflections for a moment. "We have been free in the past," he said. "We can be so again. The Eastern Lands are headed for war, and the university will be at the forefront of it."

"I should think you would be glad," Maggie said. "I was at the castle tonight—I heard what you said. You will make a great leader."

Jerome smiled sadly and said, "Ah, but you see, Little One, I do not want it to come in my time. I urge it on, I speak words to inspire and give courage because that is my part in this story, and all the while I am a coward in my own heart. Peace is a dreadful thing to break, Maggie."

"Must it be broken, then?" Maggie asked. "Why not continue to live as we have, under the Empire?"

"We cannot," Jerome said. "A man I know says that the peace of the Empire is the peace of death. He is right—and even he does not realize the truth of it all. We seek to bring not only revolution, but resurrection."

They stopped talking, but the silence was not awkward. They looked into each other's eyes, searched there, and both found that they were at home.

"I also dreamed tonight," Maggie said after a long while.

Jerome was very close to her now, but neither knew when the other had moved. He smiled gently.

"What did you see?" he whispered.

Maggie started to speak, but her voice caught in her throat. "I don't think I can tell you," was all she could say.

* * *

Nicolas did not dream, but neither did he sleep well. At last his restlessness awoke him altogether. He lay in the darkness and replayed thoughts of the day. He felt closed in behind the city walls—like a spirit wishing to leave an ailing body. He had been curious about the scroll, and for Maggie's sake he had wanted Huss to explain himself, but all of his curiosity was gone now. He only wanted to get outside. To get away.

She needs me, he thought.

Not anymore, his own mind answered back.

He closed his eyes tightly and tried to shut out the feelings, but for a moment he thought the breeze was blowing, and it smelled like falling leaves and a new dawn.

It was still early. If he left soon enough he could be out of the city in time to truly smell the dawn. Out, to welcome the sun. He could already feel the roughness of a forest path under his feet.

Slowly, quietly, Nicolas climbed out of bed. His mattress creaked slightly in protest, but he paid it no mind. He pushed open his bedroom door, and it made no sound; nor did his feet as he stepped into the hallway.

Jerome was laying outside of Maggie's door, breathing deeply, a sword by his side. He was stretched out so that no one could get through the door without waking him.

Nicolas stepped deftly over the young man. He, who could hear all, could easily keep from being heard. He was grateful for it.

* * *

Maggie awoke with the gentle feeling of sunlight on her face. It was bravely filtering its way through the grime on the windowpane, illuminating a tiny room with a layer of dust on everything and cobwebs in the corners.

The house was silent. Maggie was struck by the feeling that everyone was gone, and she was the only one left in the house—or in the world, for that matter. She sat up and swung her legs out of bed, tucking her unruly auburn hair behind her ears.

The door creaked loudly when she opened it. The sound only deepened her sense of aloneness. There was no one in the hallway, and the doors to both Nicolas's room and Huss's study were closed.

Maggie slowly padded down the hallway, rubbing her

arms for comfort. She looked to her left, where she could see over the banister to the ghostly house downstairs. She jumped as grey eyes met hers, and then the cat dropped down and stalked past her. She almost laughed at her own nerves. She neared the door to Huss's study and heard low voices talking on the other side. Breathing an embarrassed sigh of relief, she raised her hand to knock, but before her knuckles fell on the door, words made their way through it to her ears. Her hand stayed raised in mid-air as she listened.

"The boy died early this morning," a familiar woman's voice said. "There was nothing I could do."

"I am sorry, Libuse," said Huss.

"He deserves to be buried with princes, Master Huss," said the woman. "And I cannot even risk taking him to an undertaker for fear that his dying in my house will shed suspicion on me."

"Send him back to the country," Huss said, softly, "as you promised you would. His comrades will give him a burial fit for princes, if not among them."

"Yes," Libuse said. "My carriage can carry a dead body as well as a live one."

There was a long pause, and Libuse said, "If only last night . . ."

"If onlys do us no good, my lady," Huss said. "You know that as well as I do. Better, perhaps."

Maggie felt suddenly guilty for eavesdropping. She knocked sharply on the door.

"Come in," called Huss.

Maggie opened the door. The woman from the night before was sitting at the table with Huss. Neither Nicolas nor

Jerome were in the room.

Libuse's hair was plaited and hung nearly to her waist. She wore a blue dress made of expensive cloth and tailored beautifully. She held her head high. Her back was straight, and her face was solemn and lined with a grief that belied her relative youth. She was beautiful and regal, and Maggie felt embarrassed in her presence.

The woman stood when Maggie entered the room. She took Huss's hand and squeezed it warmly.

"Thank you, Professor," she said. "You are a great strength to me."

Huss smiled. "Perhaps I am," he said. "Or perhaps I am a snare to you."

The woman smiled without mirth. "Be that as it may," she said. "I am glad to be caught in your trap."

She turned to Maggie and motioned for her to sit down. "Come," she said. "Master Huss tells me you have much to talk about. I will not stay to prevent you." She smiled, and her smile was kind. She made sure that Maggie was seated comfortably before she left the room.

"Eat," Huss said, handing Maggie a sticky roll. "Breakfast is a rare occasion in this house, and I do not mean to eat it alone."

Maggie obeyed awkwardly. The table held a plate of pastries, a pot of some dark liquid that was not tea but smelled good, and a bowl of fresh fruit.

"This looks good," Maggie said, venturing to look Huss in the face. His expression was open and kind.

"Yes it does," he said. "Libuse is good not to call on me empty-handed. She knows that an old professor like me does not earn the wages of a king. Also, when my head is buried in my books I often forget to eat."

"Who is she?" Maggie asked. Her fingers were sticky from the roll, and she resisted the urge to lick them.

"She is a princess," Huss said, enjoying the look of surprise on Maggie's face. "Yes," he repeated, "A princess of the ancient days. Her ancestors ruled this land from Pravik Castle before the days of the Empire. In deference to her heritage, Libuse is allowed to serve on the Governing Council of the Eastern Lands. As do I. The council answers to the Emperor, of course."

As an afterthought, Huss added, "She was also a student of mine once."

Maggie said, "Old Dan said you were a student at the university, but he didn't know you'd gone on to be a teacher. I planned to look for you through the school when we came here, but I didn't dream I'd find you so quickly."

"I am a scholar," Huss said. "I would chafe at anything else. Teaching is the only way of earning a living that suits me, although I prefer studying to trying to teach the thick-headed subjects of the Empire anything. Of course," he said, his eyes gleaming, "I do find a gem hidden in the mire once in a while. When I do, my teaching becomes unorthodox."

Huss reached for the pot and poured Maggie a cup of the thick liquid. "Drink," he said. "It's far more palatable than it looks."

Maggie reached for the cup and took a sip. The taste was bittersweet and not unpleasant. She took another sip, and became conscious that Huss was watching her very closely.

She put the cup down and rubbed her arm. "Where's

Nicolas?" she asked.

"Gone," Huss said.

"Gone?" she repeated, alarmed at first. She calmed herself down and asked, "When will he be back?"

"When it suits him, I suppose," Huss said, his eyes still on Maggie's face. He poured himself a cup of the dark liquid. "He left us sometime last night. When I looked in on him this morning he had already departed."

Maggie sat in silence, too shocked to speak. "Why would he leave?" she asked at last, quietly. Huss didn't answer, and she kept talking, mostly to herself. "It's not like he said he would stay . . . all he promised to do was bring me here, and he did that."

Huss spoke now. "Your friend is an unusual young man," he said. "And a Gypsy, at that. Perhaps the wanderlust took him, and he found our city closing in on him too much."

Maggie nodded. She tried not to show the tears in her eyes. "I'm sure that was it," she said.

"Perhaps," Huss said. He was silent a moment, then said abruptly, "Perhaps not. But you came to me with questions of your own, and today I mean to answer them as best I can. So we will have to stop mourning the flight of our wild bird, and get to work."

He stood. Maggie started to stand with him, but he motioned for her to sit back down. "Finish your breakfast," he said.

Maggie nodded and ate a few more bites, but the news of Nicolas's disappearance had stolen her appetite. Huss took a book from his shelves and leafed through it a few minutes, then sat with his long fingers entwined, watching her until he was satisfied that she had eaten as much as she could be expected to.

"Now," he said, "you didn't bring me the scroll out of idle curiosity, and you did not bring it because you felt duty-bound to Daniel Seaton. By your own admission you went against Mrs. Cook's wishes to come here, and you did it because there is something *you* are looking for—something you want to know. What is it?"

Maggie was quiet for a long time, her brow creased. It was true enough; she had come because she was looking for something. Without realizing it herself, she had believed that this aged professor would hold all the answers, but now, faced with the reality of Jarin Huss's questioning face, Maggie did not know what to ask him or why she had thought he would know.

"I'm not sure what I want you to tell me," Maggie said. "I'm not really sure what I'm looking for."

Jarin Huss leaned back and nodded. 'Then tell me about yourself," he said. "Together perhaps we can unearth the questions you want to ask."

Maggie looked the professor in the eyes, and she slowly let her walls down. She could trust him, she felt. She had to trust him.

"When I was ten," she said slowly, "Mrs. Cook and her husband bought me from the Orphan House in Londren. I stayed with them a short time, and then I was sent to Cryneth, to live with John and Mary Davies."

She faltered, but continued, her voice full of emotion. "When I went to the Davies', I was like a bird that had been caged all its life and didn't even know there was such a thing as

169

a sky. And they set me free. I can't even explain how . . . they loved me. And Mary would sing to me, and play the harp, and my heart would fly.

"One day, when I was thirteen, I was out with the sheep when I saw smoke over the hill. I dropped my staff and ran, and when I got over the hill I saw that the house had burned to the ground. I knew that Mary was dead, and John too. I'm not sure how I knew, but . . ." Her voice trailed away and she took a deep breath. She was looking down at the wooden table.

"I thought I heard laughter. I thought it was an evil spirit laughing. To tell the truth, I don't know what I heard. Maybe nothing. I don't remember anything after that. They tell me I ran to the house and started digging through the ashes, calling for John and Mary."

She held up her hands, the burn scars visible reminders of that day. "They say the villagers tried to help me, and I ran away. I ran all the way to Londren. I do remember being alone, and in pain, and cold. I remember sleeping on the streets and sneaking rides on wagons, and I think I remember falling down on Mrs. Cook's doorstep.

"And then one day I woke up, and Mrs. Cook was there, and Pat . . . another girl they took from the Orphan House, before me. And my hands were burned."

She looked up suddenly, meeting Huss's eyes with terrible urgency. "I lost everything the day John and Mary died," she said. "I lost my heart. Paradise was stolen from me. But I recovered . . . I survived, because people loved me and I knew how to love them back, because of what Mary had taught me." Tears stung her eyes and she blinked them away, leaning forward.

"This may sound strange, Professor Huss, but I have always felt that there was something more that I was supposed to learn from Mary. And from John. I feel as though I was on a path when I lived with them, and when I went back to Londren, the path was lost and I never found it again. I know that doesn't make sense. But maybe I'm here trying to find the path again?"

Huss was listening with an odd glow on his face, but Maggie hardly noticed it.

"And then Old Dan came, and he and Mrs. Cook said that John and Mary's death wasn't an accident. They said it was murder; that Evelyn killed them. I want to know why, Professor. I want to know who Evelyn is, and what the Council for Worlds Unseen was, and why the people I loved most had to die."

A sudden picture came into Maggie's head, a parable that Mary had once shown her. The mental image was strong, unblurred by the tears in her eyes. "Have you ever seen the underside of a cross-stitch, Professor?"

"I haven't," Jarin Huss answered, obviously surprised.

"It looks like a mess," Maggie told him. "A lot of threads and unconnected bits of this and that, strewn around. But if you turn it over, you can see that all of that mess has made a beautiful picture on the other side. My life so far has been a lot of threads and unconnected bits. I want to see the picture."

"To bring cosmos out of chaos," Huss said with a smile. "I understand completely. Though I don't know how much help I can be to you, I will try to bring at least a little order into the unconnected bits of your life. Unfortunately, you will have to sit and listen to me talk for a good while, and I am sure you will need plenty of patience."

Maggie smiled. "Mrs. Cook used to say I had more
patience than was good for me."

"Very well, then," Huss said, but his eyes grew solemn.
He stood and paced as he talked. "I am not surprised to know
that John and Mary are dead, although I am exceedingly sorry
to hear it. Evelyn had threatened Mary . . . perhaps Mrs. Cook
told you?"

Maggie nodded. "She told me a little."

"I have long pondered the mystery of Evelyn," said Huss,
"and I believe that I know now who she is. She is an important
piece of a puzzle I have been studying for forty years. You see,
I have been trying to bring my own cosmos out of chaos. In my
life I have run down many a false trail, but I do think I have
found the truth of the thing at last. I met Evelyn first through
the Council for Exploration Into Worlds Unseen, forty years
ago.

"I was in the Isle of Bryllan, in Cranburgh of the
Highlands, for a conference of scholars. The conference was
dry and dull, even for a such a dull young man as I was—all
brains, and books. Nothing else mattered to me. Still, I was
young—even I hungered for entertainment at times. There was
a festival in Cranburgh at the time, and one day I skipped out
of the conference and wandered in the streets.

"In the midst of the acrobats and jugglers and freakish
human beings, a young Highland gentleman was holding a
group of listeners spellbound with some very strange tales—
tales he took quite seriously. His name was Lord Robert
Sinclair, and he claimed to be the founder of a new branch of
study: a study of what he called the 'other side of reality,' the

Worlds Unseen.

"His theories were a delightful patchwork of history and folk tales and imagination, but they gripped me somehow. I talked with him for hours. In the end he invited me to come to his estate, Angslie, and help him carry on his new science. I went with him, though I have never been sure why. And others did, as well, most of them visitors to Cranburgh just as I was. There were six of us: myself, Lord Robert, Eva Brown, your guardian, Mary Grant and John Davies, who fell in love in those days, Daniel Seaton, and a dashing young fellow called Lucas Barrington.

"We all lived together in Angslie and studied, if you could call it that. We read stories and spun tapestries out of their many threads. Lord Robert had an impressive collection of ancient documents, the kind you can be arrested for owning, and I was able to read them—you see, Maggie, much as the Empire wishes the ancient languages extinct, they are not. There are some who can still read them and understand, and I am such a one. We hunted down other documents; we tracked down stories; and we drowned ourselves in wonder and fear. We pieced together a history of the world much different than what we are taught under the Emperor's rule . . . and you understand, my dear, if the history of something is not what we think it is, the future of that thing is also not what we think."

He stopped a moment, and began again.

"It seems to me as though those days were spent in another time and another world. Sometimes Mary would sing and play her harp. Stories and legends with words like fire, that caught all of our hearts aflame. Her songs were alive, and somehow ancient, and she never claimed to write them—she told me once that she sang what she heard. I can't quite describe the way they sounded."

"I know," Maggie interjected quietly. "She sang to me, too. Sometimes I think her songs are in me, somewhere—if only I could hear them."

Huss looked at Maggie strangely for a moment before continuing. "And then one day, Evelyn came. She was a young, beautiful woman. The laird had met her while he was in Cranburgh on business. He was fascinated with her, all the more because she seemed to have knowledge of the other world. She spoke sometimes of visions and strange powers, and claimed that miracles had been done at her hands." He grimaced as he said the word "miracles"; Maggie could see the distaste he felt for it. "It was the laird's dream come true—that we might find some way to bring the Otherworld into our own.

"Lord Robert wanted her to join the council, but there was something in her that the rest of us could not trust. Mary, especially, was opposed to Evelyn. At first she was quiet about it. She managed to discover where Evelyn came from, and then she left us for a few days. When she came back, she stood up in the council and denounced Evelyn as a witch. Mary claimed that she had gone to Evelyn's hometown, and found that the people of the village were deathly afraid of her. Rumour said— and Mary believed every word of it—that Evelyn had grown angry with two young men in the village and publicly cursed them. Later that same day, both young men came down with strange and horrible diseases. They were dead in less than three days."

A vision of Old Dan dying in Mrs. Cook's guest room assailed Maggie, and she shivered.

"That meeting was the undoing of the council," Huss continued. "Lord Robert took Evelyn's part—blind fool that he was. The rest of us were divided. Accusations began to fly between us all, until at last it was hopeless to think of working together anymore. In less than three days the council was no more. Evelyn, in that meeting, swore to kill Mary someday. Even then, Lord Robert could not see what she was.

"And that is all there is to tell of the Council for Worlds Unseen. I came back to Pravik, nearly crippled by the shattering of a dream that had become more to me than I knew. But just as you recovered after the death of your foster parents, so I recovered after the death of my vision. I became a teacher, carrying on the work here in Pravik, keeping true history alive and out of the clutches of the Empire. I teach ancient languages, and legends, and dreams, but I teach only those who are worthy to learn."

He drew himself up as he spoke till he looked taller and somehow older than before.

"I keep the memory of freedom alive in men's hearts," he said. "It is an extremely important work, and I am the only one left to do it. The old masters are dead, and I alone have taken up their mantle. To most of the world I am an eccentric old teacher of history, but to a few, like Jerome and Libuse, I am the single Professor of the Underground University of Pravik."

For a moment he stood, carried off by his own thoughts, and then he seemed to snap. His shoulders stooped back into their normal posture, and he smiled a little.

"Listen to me," he said. "So caught up in my own

175

importance I've forgotten what I meant to say."

Very little order had appeared to Maggie in what Jarin Huss had said, and the pieces of her questions remained unconnected. But she said, "Tell me about the scroll. What does it have to do with everything?"

"Yes, the scroll," Huss muttered. He sat back down at the table abruptly. "The scroll is the sort of artifact that our council would have been very glad to get our hands on in the old days in Angslie. It dates back to the first year of the Empire, and contains the signature, written, I think, in blood, of Lucius Morel himself."

Maggie sat back in her chair. She caught her breath to think that she had carried something so old. She shook her head in disbelief as she remembered all the scroll had come through, amazed that the thing hadn't crumbled to dust in her hands.

"You can read it," Maggie said. "What does it say?"

Huss's face became clouded, and his voice low. "It is a covenant," he said. "A promise of power to the Morel family in return for an empire."

Maggie did not understand. "A covenant with who?" she asked, her own voice unconsciously lowering.

"With a creature whose name will not be familiar to you," Huss answered. "According to the scroll, his power must be passed to the Morels through a mediator—or rather, through a body of mediators. Mediators who have found what Lord Robert always sought—a way to bring the Otherworld into connection with our own."

He stood to his feet again, pacing. "I have known of this body for some time but did not completely understand their relationship to the Morels until you brought me the scroll. You have shed light on a most unpleasant secret, Maggie Sheffield. Even so, it is better to see it in the light than to fear it in the darkness. They are known as the Order of the Spider. I believe Evelyn is one of them."

Maggie felt a creeping sensation on the back of her neck. Huss had stopped pacing, but he did not seem about to say anything more. There was a long and uncomfortable silence.

Maggie mustered up enough courage to say, "I don't think I understand."

Huss looked at her as though he had forgotten she was there.

"Do you believe in legends?" he asked, and smiled at Maggie's puzzled expression. He sat down and leaned forward so that their heads were close together.

"Once upon a time," he said, "there was a king who ruled over all the world, a good king, and a just one. Under his reign the earth flourished, and its people were at peace and happy.

"But among the King's advisers was one who grew dissatisfied with his position in life. He envied his master, and he began to whisper in the ears of human beings, who were never inclined to be very strong, or very faithful. They listened, along with other beings who were not human— beings much like the discontented adviser himself.

"There was a war. The adviser and his followers, human and otherwise, attempted to overthrow the King, and in the end, they succeeded. He went into exile, taking many of his followers with him.

"The adviser, whose name was Morning Star, prepared to take the lordship of the Seventh World upon his own shoulders. But before he could, a Veil fell over the world—dividing that which was human and earthly from that which was not. Morning Star and his fellow creatures were cut off from humanity, and man was left to rebuild his world on his own—free from good and evil lords alike.

"Thus began the Tribal Age, the beginning of history as we know it. Men divided into a thousand little factions and fought each other and starved, until Lucius Morel gathered an army and conquered them all. So now we have an Empire."

"The last part of your legend is history," Maggie said, remembering her few lessons at the Orphan House, and their mention of the Tribal Age and the way that Lucius Morel had heroically united the world.

"It is *all* history," Professor Huss said, "though many would disagree with me, even call me a fool. It is history gathered from the ancient folk tales of the people of this world, stories long forgotten to most, but long remembered in the Underground University. But you are right: for centuries the teachers of our secret school treated the King as a legend only. His tale is nothing but a dream."

"But you don't believe that," Maggie said.

"No," Huss said, the smallest of smiles on his lips. "I do not. I believe that there was a king once, and I believe in the rebellion of Morning Star, and of the falling of the Veil. It was Lord Robert who first showed me that our university legends could be true."

Maggie cocked her head in question.

"Lord Robert believed in another side of reality—the other side of the Veil, Maggie, though he did not know the old stories. Beyond the Veil there are things too wonderful to imagine, but there is also a great Blackness."

"Morning Star," Maggie said.

"Yes," Huss answered. He drew the scroll out from his robes and laid it on the table, pushing remnants of breakfast aside to make room for it.

Huss's long fingers tapped the parchment. "It is Morning Star's name that is signed here along with Lucius Morel's. Somehow the Order of the Spider is able to draw power from beyond the Veil, from Morning Star himself. That power has kept the Seventh World under the thumb of the Morel family for five hundred years."

Maggie's throat had gone dry, and she licked her lips. "But you said that the power was in exchange for an Empire," she said.

"Yes." Huss nodded. The smile had vanished from his face. "Morning Star intends to come back and claim the world he won in battle long ago."

"He can't come through the Veil," Maggie said.

"The Veil is wearing thin," Huss said. "Creatures have come through it. And there are other signs that the end is near."

Maggie shut her eyes as thoughts of the unearthly hound and the ravens washed over her. She wanted to deny that what Huss said was true; she wanted to make it only a legend and forget it. But she could not, for she had seen evidence of his words with her own eyes, roaming the forests and cities of the continent.

"What can we do?" she asked at last.

"Absolutely nothing," Huss answered. Then a smile began to appear on his wizened old face once more, and he said, "But *he* can."

Maggie felt that Huss meant something very significant, but it was quite beyond her reach. He continued.

"Lord Robert had one ancient piece of writing that held particular fascination for me," he said. "It was a very old journal, and the language was nearly beyond even my abilities to decipher. The laird acquired it only a few short weeks before the council split up, in our third month together, so I had little time to translate from it. I did manage to render one poem into our modern language. I can still remember the words of it, though the journal is still in Angslie."

Jarin Huss closed his eyes and intoned,

> *"When they see beyond the sky,*
> *When they know beyond the mind,*
> *When they hear the song of the Burning Light;*
> *Take these gifts of My Outstretched Hand,*
> > *Weave them together,*
> > *I shall come."*

Maggie shook her head, frustrated at her own inability to understand, but Huss went on.

"It is a prophecy," he said. "There are other such hints in the folklore and legends of the world . . . *'I shall come.'* The words of the King, unless I am greatly mistaken."

Strange words came to Maggie's mind, and she spoke them without thinking. "He is the sun-king, and the moon-king, and all-the-stars king, and he shines like them all together." In her mind she saw Marja in the vivid firelight, and the smoke from Peter the Pipe-Smoker's pipe rising early in the frigid morning. She blushed at the realization that Huss was looking at her with a very odd expression on his face, and she hastened to explain, "I heard a Gypsy girl say it. She told a story about a man who went with the birds to meet the King, only . . . he didn't come."

"The Gypsies remember a great deal that the rest of the world has forgotten," Huss said. "In a way they are the last remnant of the Tribal Age. Yet, it is doubtful that your friend the Gypsy thinks of her story as anything more than a fairy tale."

"I suppose not," Maggie said, and was glad to say no more. Huss began once again to talk.

"The prophecy I quoted you was written before even the scroll," he said. "I believe it foretells the coming of the King to this land. But it also gives a sign of his coming . . . the advent of the Gifted."

"The what?" Maggie asked.

"The Gifted," Huss repeated. "'When they see beyond the sky; When they know beyond the mind; When they hear the song of the burning light . . .' People with gifts of sight, of hearing, of healing, of knowing . . . of song." He smiled tenderly. "Mary was Gifted, Maggie."

She looked at his piercing eyes, and could almost hear the songs that poured from Mary's harp and soul . . . the songs that seemed to be within her still, just out of reach. Gifted. Yes.

"In the council we were aware of Gifting," Huss said, "although we did not know what it was, or how it was connected to the King. Lord Robert thought Evelyn was Gifted, and she may well have been. It only shows what blind fools we were that we never saw the Gift in Mary. John did, I think.

181

And I know now, too late."

"The King is coming back," Maggie said, just to feel the words on her tongue. It seemed as though they had to be spoken aloud; as though her voice had to say them. She shook her head suddenly. "How is that possible?" she asked. "He must have died centuries ago."

"You would be right, if he were human," Huss said. "But he is no more human than Morning Star is . . . than a star is, or a sunrise, or the wind." He reached down and touched the scroll. "Let us hope he returns before Morning Star does."

They fell silent for a while. Huss said, "What I have told you is not common knowledge even among my students. Jerome knows. He is my apprentice; he will be the leader of the university when I am gone, so it is necessary that he know. But I do not know if he *believes*. And Libuse knows a little, but her mind is very occupied with matters of the here and now."

"What are you going to do with the scroll?" Maggie asked. "I don't know why the Order wants it back so badly, but they must . . . someone must, because I've been hunted by—by otherworldly creatures."

Huss held the scroll up in his hands. "I am not sure what to do with it, but I know that we cannot give it back to them. This, Maggie, is a weapon in our hands. It is the greatest weapon we could have been given. It is mightier than any sword could ever be."

"A piece of paper?" Maggie asked incredulously. "A tool of the enemy?"

"The *truth*!" Huss said. "The truth that peels away five hundred years of deception. There is nothing the enemy fears more than that! That is why they destroyed the council at

Angslie. Because we were treading on the borders of Truth, and that is a land they cannot risk our getting into. If we did we might shake free of them."

They were silent for a moment, but inside Maggie questions were shouting. Before she had a chance to ask them, the door burst open and Jerome stumbled in. His face was dark with anger.

"Master Huss," he said. "Forgive my interruption. The High Police have arrested Libuse."

9

Salvation

THIS DAY I STAND MOST ALONE OF ALL LIVING THINGS. This day I have seen Blackness, and there is no power of good beside me to fight it; this day I have seen treachery, and I have not the strength to speak out. My pen must do what my arm cannot; it must say what my tongue cannot. These words on paper must inspire men to return to the high things and turn away from the evil that drags and sucks and covers with filth.

I, Aneryn the Prophet, have seen a great Spider in the Blackness beyond the Veil. I have seen a great treachery. In this moment I wish for the tongue of the Shearim, that I might sing out against evil; I wish for the strength of the Brethren of the Earth, that I might battle it; I wish for the companionship of men, that together we might form a fortress of hearts which the Blackness cannot penetrate. But none of these things is given me; I am alone; I am forsaken; and in darkness and sorrow I see . . .

The Spider weaves a web and its strands pierce through the Veil, joined to the souls of men. Men themselves have called it to them. They have reached for the Blackness, and the Spider has answered them.

On the strands of the web, power flows to the children of men. Even now they form an alliance one with another; Blackness calls to blackness in their souls. This night I have seen them light a fire, and it burns blue before my eyes. A brotherhood, they call themselves, to subject the world in darkness. This is their covenant with Morning Star.

The tapestries of time flow before my eyes and I see the days to come. I know what this Order will do to the Seventh World. I see the bondage the Spider weaves.

But I remember the King. I remember other visions. He will return, for he has spoken it in my soul, and I, the Poet, I, the Prophet, have heard. The Gifted Ones will challenge the Order of the Spider and they will conquer.

I have seen it.

* * *

Virginia crawled forward on her hands and knees, feeling her way through the forest underbrush. The earth was cool and tangled with roots and leaves and moss. Insects ran over her hands as she moved. She felt it behind her: the power of darkness at her heels. Her wrists ached from the wounds inflicted by the shackles, her body from the jump from the train, and every pain grew sharper as the pursuer drew near.

The ground sloped down. The sound of running water filled Virginia's ears. She moved until her fingers found the cool brook, and she paused to bring the water up in her hands and drink.

She stood and waded through the brook; then stayed still for a moment and strained her ears for the sound of footsteps through the rushing of the water.

The darkness swirled around her for a split second and she saw a black-robed figure moving through the woods as silently as death.

And then she smelled flowers, and heather-covered hills, and the coming of spring, though in reality the world was drawing close to winter. It was the smell of the King. His strength and love filled her with a fierce, quiet joy. She whispered, "I remember."

Somewhere in the distance a wolf's long, lonely howl rose and hovered above the trees.

Virginia turned to face the one she knew was standing just behind her. The air stirred slightly, and once again she caught the scent of spring, borne on the wind from some far country. But as she turned, the smell was overwhelmed by the fearful stench emanating from the one on the other side of the brook.

"Who are you?" Virginia asked.

The voice that answered was low and rich. A woman's voice.

"I am one like you," the voice said. "I have come to help you, Virginia Ramsey."

"I want no help from you," Virginia said.

The voice sounded wounded. "I have come to offer you friendship," she said. "Do not turn me away. You have already experienced the friendship this world has to offer."

"My friends have risked their lives for me," Virginia replied.

"Do you think that will last?" the woman hissed. "They are afraid of you! Afraid like all the others, and as your power grows they will turn against you. They will cry for the High Police to come and take you away! You feel their fear already. And do you think the Lord of Angslie is your friend? To him you are a prize possession—though evidently not worth protecting, as you are now alone."

"How do you know me?" Virginia asked.

"We of the Gifted take care of our own," the woman said. "We have known of you for some time. We have been watching to see when you would need our help. You need us now, child. I know . . . I, too, have been alone."

For an instant Virginia's resolve faltered. Her heart reached out to this being who knew what it meant to be different. But then she gasped as the world swirled around her and she saw, with the eyes that only she possessed, that the creature standing across from her had the scales, the eyes, and the tongue of a serpent. She saw a cloud of pestilence hanging around the woman's cloak, tiny vermin screaming hatred and violence.

The vision passed as quickly as it had come. Virginia raised her head high.

"Do you know me?" she asked. "Then know that I also know you! I have seen the death that clings to you, and I have seen the tongue of a serpent that you possess. Say what you will: I know you for a liar. I am not one of you."

The woman screamed with rage. The sound lashed across Virginia's face like a whip. She cried out in pain, and she heard the woman spit out words that cut like knives and bound Virginia so that she could not move. She fell to the ground as otherworldly bands tightened around her till she could hardly breathe.

Under the palm of her hand, Virginia felt the ground
growing hot until the heat was burning her skin, and she
pulled her hand away with all of the strength she could muster.
The smell of smoke filled her senses, and suddenly the ground
all around her was in flames, a fire that grew with the urging of
the cloaked woman's voice. Virginia lay in a prison of fire. The
bands around her snapped; she could move again. She curled
herself up as tightly as she could while the fire roared in her
ears. Only the sound of laughter rose above the noise.

Then she felt the woman's presence with her, inside the
circle of flames. A hand reached out and grabbed her hair,
pulling her up to her knees.

"A serpent's tongue, have I?" the woman asked. "A
dragon's power! And you? Do you have the power to fight me?
You have nothing! You have scorned me, scorned my help, and
here you are—more helpless than a child. Blind! You are a
freak of nature; blind and yet able to see. Without my help you
are nothing. But you will learn. We will teach you to fear the
power of the Covenant Flame!"

Virginia made no answer. Then, slowly, a smile appeared
on her face. The woman jerked away as though she had seen
something repulsive in Virginia's face.

"I have seen the end of you and your power," Virginia
said quietly. "I have seen the King."

Slowly and deliberately, Virginia rose to her feet. As she
did, colour and shape began to take form before her eyes. She
saw the circle of flames all around her. The fire was dying
down, the earth beneath it scorched black. The woman,
cloaked in black, was standing in the very center of it, her dark
eyes wide with horror.

Outside the circle, wolves were closing in. They stepped forward on padded feet, their eyes glowing with power. In the trees, owls, sparrows, and hawks perched, waiting. Behind the wolves, farther back in the trees, stood the commanding forms of the red deer, their sweeping antlers gleaming in the firelight like spears; the great hulking threat of the bears; the wild boars, foxes and badgers and even mice.

And then, out from the trees and up from the ground came the forms of creatures like men, and yet like nature itself —a giant form, translucent and yet marred like bark, with long hair like ropes of vine; a slender creature whose lines moved and faded in and out with the wind; a wild man with long hair and clothes made of fur, arrows on his back made with teeth, and fierce joy and gladness in his eyes.

Virginia heard the woman scream with rage and fear. Then everything was blackness again, and the smell of the coming of spring overpowered the stench of smoke.

* * *

Huss swept into the house with the commanding power of a man long known and respected in the courts of the city. Libuse lived in a rich house near Pravik Castle. In the open foyer, a dozen High Police stood guard, looking uncomfortable as Huss berated their leader.

"This is an outrage!" Huss said, waving his long finger in the Police captain's face.

"I follow orders," the mustached captain defended staunchly, his powerful arms folded across his chest. "I don't question them. We received word of a planned attack on the princess's life and were commanded to place her under house arrest. For her own protection."

"I have never heard of anything so ridiculous," Huss snapped. "The princess is a reasonable woman. It is hardly necessary to arrest her in order to keep her safe."

"Orders are orders," the captain said. "It's not my job to question them."

"Then tell me who gave the orders," Huss raged, "and *I* will question them!"

"No need for that, my friend," said a voice, interrupting the discussion. Every head in the room turned to see Libuse descending the staircase, her long blue dress trailing behind her. The officers at the bottom of the stairs stepped back respectfully as Libuse approached Huss and the captain. She held out her hands to the professor. He took them and held them for just a moment.

"It is good of you to come," she said. "But there is no need for anger. I am being treated well enough."

It was Jerome who spoke then, from his place beside Maggie. "You should not be kept like a common prisoner against your will, my lady," he said. Libuse favoured him with a gracious smile.

"I trust my imprisonment will be over soon enough," she said. Then she turned and addressed the captain, who snapped to attention at her voice. "Captain," she said, "Surely you will not object if my old friends accompany me to my drawing room. I wish to speak with them in private."

The captain's eyes narrowed, but he nodded. Libuse turned and led the way to a small, finely furnished room off the foyer. She closed the doors behind them. When she turned back, Maggie was shocked at the change in her face. Her guard down, the princess was pale and afraid.

"Libuse," Huss said quietly, "do they suspect you?"

She nodded unhappily. "Almost certainly. I do not know how much they know. But if they are investigating me, then it will not be long until they find out far too much. I have covered my tracks carefully, my old friend. But an experienced hunter will find them."

"Do you know who gave the command for your arrest?" Jerome asked.

"Zarras," Libuse said.

"Antonin Zarras," Jerome said for Maggie's benefit. "The Overlord of the Eastern Lands."

Huss seemed to be choosing his words carefully. His voice was low to ensure that no one outside the room could hear. "I have never wanted to know the extent of your involvement with the Ploughman and his rebellion," he said. "I felt it was wise to stay ignorant. But now I feel that it may be best to know."

Libuse nodded. "What can I say?" she said. "My personal fortune is nearly gone. I have given every penny I could spare to the Ploughman. And I have returned the stolen goods of the people to the people whenever I could."

Huss's eyebrows shot up. "You have raided the Overlord's treasury?"

"The money in it stank of blood," Libuse said sharply. "Taxes taken from starving people. It was never Zarras's to take, so I gave it back."

"You will be removed from the Governing Council," Huss said.

"Worse than that," Jerome said, his handsome face raging. "She will be charged with treason and executed. Do you doubt it, Master Huss?"

"For theft, I doubt they would be so harsh. The people would not take kindly to the execution of their princess," Huss said. "But I think that you are in great danger, are you not, Libuse? Unless I miss my guess, your ties to the country militia are more than just financial." His voice became gentler, and he stepped closer to the woman. "I have seen your promise on the finger of the Ploughman, have I not? The ruby he wears did not come from any country woman's treasure."

Libuse hung her head. When she looked back up, her eyes were filled with tears. "I love him with my life," she said. "If the Governing Council ever finds out . . ."

Her voice trailed away, and she looked at Huss pleadingly. He nodded, his face grim. "They will never let you leave this place," he said. "That is certain. Yet if you stay here, you are waiting for the blade to fall."

"Help me," Libuse said quietly.

"Of course we will," Huss said. "I will go to the Overlord. I will . . ."

"No, Master Huss," Jerome said. "You must not become involved. If the princess is forced to leave the Governing Council it will be a great enough loss to the Eastern Lands. We cannot afford to lose both of you."

He looked at Libuse. "I will come for you tonight, my lady. Be ready to flee through the tunnels at midnight."

Libuse nodded, her face grave. There was a sharp knock on the drawing room door. Huss looked at the heavy oak.. "It seems they grow tired of having the princess out of their sight," he said. "So we must return her to them for a time."

* * *

The three left Libuse's house in silence. Huss's brow was wrinkled with worry. Jerome was deep in thought, planning out the rescue. Maggie walked beside them, distraught at her inability to offer even a word of comfort. Everything was happening so fast, and she was still struggling to put together Huss's earlier revelations with what was happening now. Struggling—and yet a clarity was beginning to emerge. She felt a strange strength and a sense that her feet had found their old path at last.

"They want the Ploughman to come for her," Jerome said.

"And he will," Huss answered. "He knows what will happen when they find out what she has done. Make no mistake, he will not abandon her to them."

"But if he comes here," Maggie said, shyly, "what then?"

"Then they will be waiting," Huss said. "They will kill him."

"No," Jerome said. "No, they won't have the chance. The Ploughman will not come here. Libuse will join him in the country before word reaches him of the arrest."

"Have a care, Jerome," said Huss. "This is no easy task you take upon yourself."

"Nothing worth doing is ever easy," Jerome answered, a slight smile playing on his face. "I believe it was you who taught me that."

Huss nodded. "I suppose you will be dragging more of my pupils into this."

"Is it also you who says, 'He is a fool who does with one hand what he could do with two'? I am not such a fool as to think I can do this alone."

"And among the students of Huss you are likely to find many willing to help you," Huss said, with a deep sigh. "When I was a student of the secret, I and my classmates kept our knowledge safe, deep in our hearts. Why do my students insist on wielding knowledge as a sword?"

The two men fell silent for a long moment, and each face betrayed such conflict that it hurt Maggie to see it. At last Huss smiled a thin smile and said, "Go, Jerome. You have very little time."

Jerome nodded and left the courtyard. Huss and Maggie were left looking after him.

Huss turned after a while and started for the house. Maggie fell in stride beside him.

"Jerome risks a great deal for Libuse," she said.

"Yes," Huss answered. "He risks more than you know. But I am afraid he does not have much of a choice."

They were about to enter the door when Maggie asked quietly, "Does he love her?"

Huss stopped and gave Maggie a long look. He smiled slightly and said, "Yes. He loves her, as any subject loves a sovereign who thinks only of her people and would give her life for them. The Empire will never recognize Libuse as a queen, but her people have never seen her as anything else. And Jerome is very much a son of his people." Almost as an afterthought, he added, "In that sense Jerome loves her. But not in any other way."

* * *

The forest pulsed with power as Virginia felt the creatures of the wood draw near. In their footsteps a wild drumbeat echoed. The wind played around Virginia's head like a living thing. She heard voices in it: exulting, laughing, swirling and dancing on the eddies of the air.

"Free!" an ethereal voice cried. The wind danced and shivered as the voice coursed through it.

"The hold of the Blackness is broken," said another, one that spoke with a voice timeless and strong and deep: the sort of voice an ancient tree might have, if it could speak.

"Where has the witch gone?" roared another voice, the voice of youth and battle and tooth and claw; the voice of wolves and hawks and bounding deer. "Let me at her!"

"Gone for now, is she," whispered the voice in the wind, trailing silver tendrils through the air.

"We have defeated her purpose," said the tree-voice. "Rest content."

"I have rested for five hundred years!" roared the animal-voice. "It is time that I act again!"

"Peace," said the tree-voice. "The time to vanquish our enemies will come when it comes."

"What have we been loosed for, if not to fight?" demanded the animal-voice.

"We have been loosed to prepare. And to help this one, as we have done," said the tree-voice. Virginia was suddenly aware of eyes on her. A warm breeze blew through her clothes and hair gently, kindly.

"Sees much, the blind one," whispered the wind-voice.

"She has set us free."

They fell silent. They were waiting for Virginia to speak.

"No," she faltered. "I did nothing. It was you who rescued me."

She heard a sound like the near-silent laughter of a wolf.

"Your need loosed our chains," rumbled the animal-voice. "We feel the power in you . . . the life in you. We have waited five hundred years in darkness, bound and blind, for you to call us out."

"But I didn't call," Virginia said, her voice full of wonder.

A voice spoke in her memory: *Through you I will wake the world.* She shivered, as one shivers at the touch of delight.

Again they waited. Virginia said, "Who are you?"

The wind-voice rushed past her ears. "We are the Children of the Burning Light!"

"We are the Brotherhood of the Earth," said the tree-voice. "We are the living spirits of the forest, of the beasts, and of the wind."

"What happened to you?" Virginia asked.

The animal-voice growled. "We were banished by the traitor Morning Star, held in darkness that we might not rip out the throat of his Empire."

"We fought in the Great War, gloriously," said the tree-voice. "With all of our Brethren and the righteous children of men."

"So few," whispered the wind. "Few men in our ranks."

Virginia felt as though sharp eyes were piercing through her. "Have you children of men forgotten so soon how it was?" the animal-voice asked. "How the teeth and the claws and the antlers of the beasts ran red with the blood of traitors, how the trees sent their roots and branches to block off the roads, how the wind beat on the gates of the city? Do you no more tell how the River-Daughter and the Sea-Father swamped the ships of the enemy?"

Virginia hung her head. "I am afraid we have forgotten everything we ought to have remembered."

She thought she heard the wind sigh, and the tree-voice said, "But the race of men was always short of memory. Or have *you* forgotten, Gwyrion?"

The animal-voice grunted in reply, like the grunt of a boar.

"Forgotten," repeated the ethereal wind-voice. "What else have you forgotten, daughter of men?"

Virginia held her head up again, and her face was wet with tears. "We have forgotten the King himself," she said. "We have forgotten that there was ever a world of beauty before the Empire."

"The Empire!" the voice of Gwyrion, the animal spirit, spat. "Unholy offspring of Men and Blackness! Spawn of death and rebellion!"

The tree-voice spoke then. A note of heart-breaking sorrow strained its words. "Have you truly forgotten the King? Can there be any hope for a world that has forgotten him?"

It was the wind spirit that whispered, "*She* has not forgotten."

"I have seen the King," Virginia said. "He came to me on a hillside near my home."

"Far away, your home," said the wind.

"There!" roared Gwyrion in a voice full of triumph. "The King's feet have walked our earth again! Hope lost? How could

197

you say such a thing, Tyrentyllith?"

The tree-voice answered, "You are right, my brother. Of course you are right. He will come soon if in this generation human eyes have seen him."

"He will come soon!" Gwyrion roared. "We, the Children of the Burning Light, will prepare the way for him! We will fight, as we did in the Great War, and this time we shall see who will rise the victor!"

"In good time, proud one," said Tyrentyllith, the tree spirit. "Many, many of our Brethren still sleep, bound by the Blackness. Their silent dreams creep into the roots of the earth, even now. And do not forget what the prophets have foretold. It is the children of men who must prepare the way for the King."

"I don't understand," Virginia said. "If you are a small part of the King's forces, you must have been a far greater army than men could raise up. How were you ever defeated?"

A palpable silence came over the glen, and Tyrentyllith answered. "We did not only fight men, but the Black Ones as well."

"They would have fallen beneath our strength!" Gwyrion said.

"Lost were we when our heart was taken," the wind whispered sadly.

"It is true," the tree spirit said. "It was not force of strength that won the day against us. We lost the battle when our heart was broken."

"I'm not sure I understand," Virginia whispered.

"Traitors! Traitors are men!" the wind said in a sudden cold blast.

"The children of men are loved above all else by our King," said Tyrentyllith. "When they broke his heart, they broke us. He left the Seventh World of his own choice. For this reason, it is men who must usher in his return. Those who sent the King into exile must open their arms to him again."

"It has begun," the wind said, quiet once more.

"It has begun in you, daughter of men," said the tree spirit. "And there are others. It was the life in you that awakened us, and will awaken the rest of our Brethren. The end of the Blackness is coming."

"Seeks you, does the Blackness," whispered the wind. "It desires to use your power."

"I will never help them," Virginia said.

"We must be gone," said the tree spirit. His voice was gentle in response to her words, though he neither confirmed nor denied what she had said. "We have work of our own to do. The earth has lived long without us. It is time the trees felt spirit at work in them again. But I have a gift to give you, daughter of men."

Virginia felt a small pouch pressed into her hand by a smooth hand large enough to enfold hers entirely. The pouch was woven of rough fibers.

"Seeds," Tyrentyllith said. "Life itself is in your hands. Use it wisely."

Suddenly Virginia felt that the tree spirit was gone, though how she knew she could not say. Before she had time to think more on it, Gwyrion's deep voice was speaking. "The wild calls to me, and my soul rises up to meet the call. I must gather my creatures and teach them again what it means to have a beating heart to guide them! To you, little cousin, I give the strength and eyes of a hawk to watch over you. Heed its call at all times."

Virginia felt and heard the beating of huge wings lifting high above her, and then she knew that Gwyrion, too, was gone. Far off in the forest she heard a wolf's howl, long and wild and free.

Last, she felt the wind begin to play around her once more, and the spirit voice whispered to her.

"My name is the gift I give to you," said the wind. "Llycharath is the name of the wind. In greatest need, call out for me. To ride the skies and hear what I may, I go."

There was a sound like leaves blowing in the trees, and then, though the breeze continued to blow, Virginia knew that Llycharath also was gone.

Virginia rubbed her fingers over the pouch in her hand, and raised her head up high.

"Farewell, Children of the Burning Light," she called. When the echo of her voice had died away, exhaustion fell over her. She lay down in the clearing, and with the far-off keening of a hawk in her ears, she fell asleep.

* * *

Late that night, Maggie rose from her bed and dressed quickly. Huss had supplied her with clean clothes, but she shunned them and dressed instead in the worn, stained clothing from the journey. Her coat seemed lighter without the heavy weight of the scroll tucked inside it. It seemed years since she had left the shelter of Mrs. Cook's home to embark on the journey that had led her so far from everything she had ever known.

A strange joy burned in her, untainted by the gravity and sorrow of the circumstances around her. She had found her path. She knew her enemy now; knew it by name. In the hours of the night she had come to believe it all: in the King, in the Veil, everything. And without fully realizing it, she had committed herself to fighting against Morning Star and his earthly stewards. Thread by thread, she was beginning to see a picture.

Quietly as a cat, Maggie moved down the stairs and into the courtyard. She stayed in the shadows and watched as men began to gather. They wore black and carried swords. Jerome stood in the courtyard near the trapdoor. Each new arrival presented himself by laying his hand on Jerome's shoulder. Jerome touched each of them and spoke words in a low voice.

At last they were all together, fifteen young men with strong arms and a steady fire in their eyes. Maggie watched as Jerome approached the trapdoor and beat out a rhythm upon it. It swung open and the men began their descent.

As the last man's cloak disappeared below the ground, Maggie darted out from the shadows and slipped under the trapdoor even as it began to close. It shut behind her with a musty thud, plunging her into deep blackness. Just ahead of her she could see the faint lantern light of the men. She followed as quietly as she could.

The men wound their way through the underground passages, turning at the door where the rebels had gathered only a night before. The new corridor branched off in several directions, with no markings of any kind that Maggie could see to indicate where they would lead. From one, Maggie heard a distant roar. The men paused for a moment, and she heard Jerome's voice.

"That way leads to the river," he said. "It is a dangerous escape, especially now, when the river is low. It leads out onto a thin ledge, and from there it is a thirty foot drop to the water."

They moved on in silence. After a short while they reached a steep stone staircase like the one that descended from Huss's courtyard, seeming to end in a ceiling of rock. Maggie hung back as the men began the ascent. Jerome put his shoulder to the rock and pushed. It lifted easily. A faint, dusty light came down from the opening. The men extinguished their lanterns and left them in the tunnel as they climbed into the house above.

Maggie waited a while, her heart pounding. At last she bit her lip and climbed the crumbling staircase. She emerged in a wine cellar. The thick cellar door was slightly ajar. She approached it softly and pushed it until she could see outside. The cellar opened into a kitchen, empty but for Jerome and his men. They were creeping silently toward the kitchen door, beyond which a bright light shone. The sound of coarse laughter could be heard from the house.

Maggie waited and watched as the men whispered to one another. In the next instant they burst through the door to the light beyond, and the house filled with shouts and the sounds of clashing steel.

Lightly, Maggie ran to the door and looked out. Jerome's men were evenly matched. There were at least ten guards in the foyer, guarding the stairs, and more were appearing every minute from rooms above and around. Maggie's eyes flitted up the stairs to where she knew Libuse's room must be.

They'll never make it, Maggie thought. *There are too many guards. They'll never defeat them in time to help Libuse.*

The thought was barely gone from her mind before Maggie acted. Fixing her eyes on the staircase, she left the safety of the kitchen and ran into the melee. She darted through the fight and reached the stairs without any trouble. No one even seemed to see her.

As fast as she could, she ran up the stairs. At the top she paused for a moment and looked wildly around her. At the far end of the hall was a door, and someone was pounding on it from the inside.

Libuse.

Maggie raced toward the door, and let out a startled scream when a man in black armour seemed to appear out of nowhere. Her heart pounding wildly, she laughed slightly when she realized that the suit of armour was empty—a piece of art to adorn the hall. But her eyes lighted on the axe in the empty, gloved hand, and she wrested it free and charged at the door.

"Get back!" she shouted, and drove the axe into the door. She hacked around the lock, sending wooden splinters in every direction, and kicked it. It swung open.

Libuse was inside, a spear in her hand raised and pointed at the door. She lowered the spear without a word when she saw Maggie. The princess was dressed like a man in dark clothes. Her long brown hair was twisted into a knot at the nape of her neck.

"We haven't much time," Maggie said. An idea occurred

to her. "Do you have a cloak with a hood?" she asked. "Anything to cover my hair?"

"Yes," Libuse said, and flung open a wardrobe. She pulled out a blue cloak and handed it to Maggie. "Will this do?" she asked.

"Perfectly," Maggie said as she tied the cape around her shoulders and pulled the hood up over her hair.

"Why . . . ?" Libuse asked.

Maggie smiled. "Because Libuse is not a redhead."

Together the two women cautiously made their way to the top of the stairs. Below, the men were still fighting. A few men, both guards and students, lay wounded or dying on the stairs and the floor, but for the most part little progress seemed to have been made. Both sides were succeeding only in frustrating the other.

"We came up through the cellar," Maggie said. "Do you know the way?"

"Yes," Libuse said.

"Then go to the professor," Maggie said. "Go as fast as you can. No one will follow you." She put her hand on the princess's shoulder and pushed her gently. "Go," she said.

Libuse looked deeply into Maggie's eyes for only a moment, but Maggie read volumes in the look. Then the princess turned and ran down the stairs, swift as a gazelle, gracefully leaping the steps. Near the bottom she changed course and vaulted over the banister, landing on the ground where no one was fighting. Maggie watched the princess disappear through the kitchen door and breathed a sigh of relief.

Quietly, Maggie descended the stairs, still clutching the

old axe in her hands. She followed Libuse's example and vaulted the banister so that no one saw her land. Softly she made her way to the kitchen, and stepped inside the door to witness a sight that made her heart stop.

A guard stood in front of the cellar doors, pointing a crossbow at Libuse's throat. The princess held her head high, her whole bearing regal. She was staring death in the face, and she did not look away.

Before Maggie could do anything, the man lowered his crossbow and stepped away from the cellar door. He bowed low as Libuse regarded him.

"Go, my lady," Maggie heard him say. "May the stars give you speed."

Tears filled Maggie's eyes as Libuse entered the cellar and passed beyond vision. A moment later, a shout arose from the foyer.

"The princess is escaped!" a voice bellowed.

Maggie swallowed hard and ran back into the foyer where the guards could see her. Her blood froze as they caught sight of her. She whirled on her heel and ran back into the kitchen, through the cellar doors.

The men were right behind her as Maggie dropped through the trapdoor and raced down the steps into the darkness. She could see nothing—the tunnels were black as midnight, and she had no time to light a lantern. Muttering a prayer under her breath, she stumbled down the black corridor, listening to the echo of footsteps behind her as the guards gave chase. The axe in her hands scraped against the rock walls. She dropped it without regret.

The bobbing light of lanterns danced off the walls behind

her and glinted off the water that ran down the tunnel walls, illuminating flecks of gold in the stone. Maggie's mouth was dry as she ran, and her fingers brushed against the cold, slimy rock.

They were gaining.

She picked up speed, knowing that she had to stay where they could see her; and knowing, too, that she could not afford to be caught. They were shouting for her to stop, and she heard one of them curse as one of his fellows shoved by him, forcing him into the rock wall.

A roaring sound met her ears.

She swerved down the new tunnel. Libuse's cloak caught on the stone. The men were almost upon her as her cold fingers worked to untie the cloak. At last it came free, and she left it behind her without a moment to spare.

Not far ahead, the river roared.

Someone shouted, "This way!" Lantern light filled the tunnel behind her. Ahead, another sort of light was filtering its way into the darkness. Moonlight.

Maggie's legs felt as though they would give way beneath her, but she gritted her teeth and forced herself to give it one last burst of energy. She closed her eyes and ran.

She nearly fell over the ledge.

She caught her breath in great gasps as she looked over her toes at the raging water below, storming at the base of a steep drop. Above her to the right, a great bridge cast its shadow over the river. The lights of other bridges illuminated the river in both directions, and waves crashed up against a dark island downstream. The air was piercingly fresh and cold, and the moon shone high above.

The men were coming.

The ledge was just wide enough to stand on, and slippery with spray. Maggie shut her eyes and moved to the right, her back pressed tight against the rock wall. Her hands clutched for something to steady her, but they found only smooth stone. Breathing hard, she inched along the ledge toward the shadow of the bridge.

She looked down at the river and nearly swooned with dizziness. Closing her eyes once more, she forced herself to keep moving. When again she opened her eyes, she focused them on the shadowy bridge overhead.

She heard a scream as someone burst out of the tunnel and stumbled over the edge, plummeting down to the water. The sound was nearly drowned out by the roar of the black river. She thought she could hear voices shouting above the sound of the water, but she couldn't be sure if they were real or imaginary.

She kept moving along the ledge and did not look back. Her foot nearly slipped on a patch of moss, and she stood against the rock and sobbed through her teeth. As she fought to gain control of herself, she realized that the rock behind her had grown craggy. The bridge was just ahead.

In a few more steps, she reached the shadow of the bridge. She ran her hands along the rock behind her and found that it was pocked enough to scale. The ledge had grown wider, and with a deep, shuddering breath, she began to turn around.

Soon she was facing the wall, and she found hand-holds. Moving slowly, she began the ascent up the rock face toward the bridge.

One step, then another. Her weight pulled at her; her feet

moved only with great effort. Once her hand slipped, and she could not move for a moment. She looked down.

The men were directly beneath her, still facing the river. Maggie watched in fearful fascination as the men looked around them, pointing and shouting to each other.

They didn't know where she was.

She held her breath, afraid that they would hear her over the sound of the crashing river. The helmet of one of the men nearly brushed the bottom of her foot. She clung to the rock with all her strength, the cold and damp of it creeping into her like an illness.

At last they moved on, back to the tunnels. A fog had risen, and it swallowed the guards in grey. Maggie felt numb, chained to the rock without hope of moving again. She was in limbo, lost in the fog and in the darkness, and no one would ever find her. No one.

A voice forced itself through her mind, her own voice. *The worst is over . . . you've only got to get to the bridge now. It isn't much farther. Move!*

She obeyed. She lifted one foot and found a new grip for it. In moments she was climbing again, and then she was directly under the bridge.

She caught hold of the iron bridge and climbed slowly up over the side, aware of the long emptiness beneath her that ended in the churning river. She did not look down.   At last she stood on solid ground again. The bridge glowed with street lamps that burned all down its length, even in the fog. She looked over the side and saw nothing but grey. When she looked up, she saw that even the moon had disappeared in the thickness.

Slowly, wearily, she began to walk along the bridge. It was the first time she had been alone since Nicolas had first joined her in Calai, and now the loneliness was nearly overwhelming. The fog had swallowed up the whole world and left her the only person in it.

No, she thought, *Libuse is out there somewhere. And she's safe, because of you, Maggie Sheffield.*

Thoughts of Londren, Mrs. Cook, and Pat filled her thoughts as she stepped off the bridge and began the weary walk to the professor's house. But soon, other faces began to fill her mind. She saw Libuse, and Huss, and Jerome. She saw Nicolas, and she remembered the face of the Ploughman. And she remembered the terror and exhilaration of leading the guards after her, away from the princess, down through the tunnels to the river. The terror was already fading into memory, one more thing to look back on and remember in days to come. It almost seemed as if it hadn't happened.

She wanted Jerome. She wanted him very badly, and she was afraid that something had happened to him. He had gone to war with the High Police to rescue the princess, and who could say if he had survived? She swallowed a lump of fear and kept going.

Deep inside her, an unrest was growing. An unfamiliarity —she thought of the night's adventures and it seemed that she did not know herself anymore. The old Maggie Sheffield had been lost somewhere on the road to Pravik. It was not likely she would ever come back.

It was for the best, and Maggie knew it. Still, somehow, it hurt.

10

An Unfamiliar Soul

MAGGIE FOUND HER WAY BACK to Jarin Huss's house. The courtyard gates were locked. She rattled them and twisted the lock futilely before exhaustion crept over her and she sank down on the cobblestones and slept.

She awoke to see a tall, dark figure coming through the thinning fog, his broad shoulders stooped with weariness. She struggled to her feet, and her eyes looked up and met his. She started to cry.

Jerome reached out for Maggie. She was wet and her clothes were torn from climbing the rocks. She was shivering with cold, and he drew her close to him. His black cloak folded in around her and enveloped her with warmth. He held her tightly for a long time, and then he stepped back and studied her face again.

"The guards chased a woman out," he said. "You?"

Maggie nodded.

"That was very foolish," he said, his voice low and choked.

"Libuse escaped," Maggie defended herself. She hung her head and looked away from him. His hand touched her chin and brought her eyes back to him.

"You are the bravest person I have ever known," he said.

"No," she said, shaking her head. "I am a coward, just like you."

Maggie's resolve crumbled, and she put her head on his chest and cried. He held her again and buried his face in her hair.

Through her sobs, Maggie asked, "What happened to you?"

"I lost nine good men," Jerome said. "Good friends."

They fell silent. Jerome said, "It is cold and late. The house is warm and waiting for us."

He took a key from his cloak and opened the gates. As they stepped into the courtyard, Maggie lifted her head at a strange smell.

"Do you smell something?" she asked.

Jerome looked around him, his dark eyes full of fear.

"Smoke," he said.

Glass shattered. Flames were everywhere, licking out the windows of the house and consuming the ivy trellises that ran up its sides. Fear gripped Maggie and tightened around her heart. From a corner of the courtyard she saw a figure step forward, dragging a black robe on the ground with a sound like chains rustling through dry leaves.

"Run, Maggie!" Jerome shouted. She obeyed. She ran out of the courtyard and into the street, and turned just in time to see a soldier in black and green bring a heavy club down on Jerome's head. He crumpled to the ground as soldiers poured into the courtyard from every shadow and corner.

Maggie sank back into the shadows and watched the High

Police drag him away.

* * *

Lord Robert buried his face in his hands as the train hurtled uncaringly down the tracks. The compartment door opened and shut. His head snapped up. It was Pat.

"The conductor is as worthless as the rest of them. He knows nothing," she said. The train swayed and Pat sat down unsteadily beside Mrs. Cook. The elderly woman was staring out the window, her face still red and streaked with tears. The sunlit world outside was golden and beautiful, even through the faint serpentine images on the glass, but it offered no comfort. The sun had risen on a nightmare.

As soon as they realized that Virginia was gone, Lord Robert, Mrs. Cook, and Pat had swept the train from one end to the other. They questioned passengers and workers and searched for any sign of the young woman. It was as though she had vanished through the Veil into the Otherworld. The thought occurred to both Lord Robert and Mrs. Cook, though neither voiced it.

They had searched for hours and returned, defeated, to the compartment. Now they sat in grim silence, and the question beat relentlessly on Lord Robert's mind.

What now?

They couldn't continue on without Virginia. To go back seemed insane. The engine driver said that during the night they had passed through towns and a great expanse of forest. They had no idea what time Virginia had left the train.

Lord Robert stood abruptly. Mrs. Cook moved her vacant

stare from the window to the laird's face. She and Pat waited in silence.

"I am going after her," he said. "I don't know how long it will take. But I'm not going to stop until I find her, or until I know for sure that . . . that she can't be found."

He stopped and met the eyes of his listeners deliberately. "She was under my care. I pledged to protect her long ago, and I will not fail her now. But you need not stay. Go home. By now the High Police won't be so hard on our trail. You will be safe."

Mrs. Cook answered first, and she sounded weary. "No, Lord Robert," she said. "I knew when Dan Seaton came stumbling into my house that my life wasn't going to be the same again. I can't go home any more than you can. I have my Maggie to find now, besides."

She turned to Pat and rested a matronly hand on the young woman's knee. "You make your own choice, dear. You have a future in the Isle to pursue."

Pat cleared her throat. "Actually," she said slowly, "I'm afraid I don't have much of a future in Bryllan now." Her voice grew very quiet. "I've never been very honest about my work in Cryneth. And I can't tell you about it now, but . . . well, I have my own reasons for avoiding the police. Besides, I'm not going to let you go off on your own. Of course I'll help you find Maggie."

"Then this is good-bye," Lord Robert said. He raised a hand to silence Mrs. Cook's protests. "I will go alone. I told you, I don't know how long it will take to find Virginia. And I think it will be easier for me to find her on my own. You'll stay on this train until it takes you to Pravik. I am getting off here."

His grey eyes went to the window that framed a deeply forested, tangled world. Mrs. Cook's voice seemed to come from far away.

"How close is the nearest town?" she asked.

"I am getting off *here*," he said.

"There is nothing out there!" Mrs. Cook protested.

"Virginia is out there," Lord Robert answered.

He left the compartment then, saying something about questioning the conductor. When Pat went to look for him twenty minutes later, he was gone.

* * *

The whole horrible truth broke over Maggie slowly, carried on waves of gossip and whispers. At a loss for what to do, she had left the street where Huss lived and wandered through Pravik until the sun began to dilute the blackness of the night. When morning had fully arrived, she haunted the marketplace and fed on penny loaves and rumours.

News of the arrest had spread quickly. On its heels came speculations, which hardened into full-blown facts before the sun had risen to the middle of the sky. Jarin Huss, Pravik's oldest and most respected scholar and professor, had been charged with subversive activities against the Empire. His apprentice, ostensibly acting on his master's orders, had been charged with the murder of Princess Libuse.

Maggie's blood ran hot, then cold, as the lie settled in. She could publicly refute it, of course—and be arrested and charged along with Huss and Jerome. Unconfirmed rumours were already saying that a woman had been involved. There were no physical descriptions abroad yet, but Maggie knew it wouldn't be long. Her choices were despairingly clear: stay and wait for the police to find her, or get out of Pravik. A part of her wanted to stay, to be near them—near Huss, near Jerome. They had become a part of her—the new her—and she a part of them, and it comforted her to know that they were physically close. But another truth beat in her heart and kept her from giving up: that if Huss and Jerome had a living hope, she just might be it.

As she wandered through the city, a plan of sorts formed itself in her mind. Huss and Jerome needed Libuse. If she was to reappear in Pravik, very much alive, then the professor and his apprentice could hardly be charged with her murder. Maggie would have to find her. Libuse had gone to the tall man in a cloak, the one they called the Ploughman; Maggie would follow.

Maggie closed her eyes as a cold premonition took her. This was a very serious thing she would do. There would be consequences she could not even imagine. She could feel it. Jerome's words came back to her mind.

Peace is a dreadful thing to break, Maggie.

It seemed to Maggie that she was balanced precariously on a heap of dead branches, holding a flame in her hands that would ignite the whole thing if she just let it go. She didn't want to be responsible for that, not really.

It didn't matter. Something had to be done.

Only one thing stopped her from leaving the city immediately. The scroll could not be given back to the Order.

A weapon more powerful than any sword, Huss had said. *The truth . . .*

She would leave the city of Pravik and try to find the Ploughman. But not until she had the scroll tucked safely inside her coat again.

* * *

It was an overcast, foggy day. Maggie was glad for the greyness that closed around her like a blanket. She made her way cautiously through the streets of the plateau, where Pravik Castle stood watch over the slopes. Somewhere in the depths of the castle's cold stone, Huss and Jerome awaited death. Maggie thought of them as she passed the towering walls and whispered a prayer to the stars to remember them.

Not far from the castle lay the smoldering ruins of Jarin Huss's house. The gates were open, swinging slightly in the cold wind. The walls were black and crumbling, and silence shrouded the yard.

The scroll might well have burned in the fire, Maggie thought. Perhaps this whole thing was a waste of time. Even so, her feet carried her into the courtyard and through the front door of the house.

Maggie drew her coat up around her face, blinking painfully as the acrid air assaulted her eyes. The house was dark, darker even than it had been in better days. Everything was black. She touched the remains of a coat rack and its ashes crumbled away beneath her fingers.

The scars on her hands were throbbing.

She walked up the stairs gingerly. The air was even worse on the second floor of the house. One of the stairs gave way beneath her foot, and she nearly screamed. She jumped up a step and struggled to calm herself before going on.

Somewhere in the deep recesses of her mind, she thought she heard laughter.

No! No, they're not dead! No! Why does no one help me find them? They are here still, alive, waiting for me to find them . . .

Maggie shook her head, as though she could physically dislodge the memories. She remembered it all now, all of the things she had never been able to recall: the ashes and burning embers that were all that remained of the cottage; the barking of the sheepdog as she ran to the place where all of her hopes had burned to the ground. She remembered standing in the ashes, digging, digging, while her hands and feet burned and the villagers called to her to come away.

She remembered laughter. Then she jumped, and looked around her wildly. For only a moment, the laughter had seemed to come from somewhere close by. Surely it was not just a memory. Surely she had just heard the same laugh echoing down the black hallways of the house she now walked in . . .

Her heart stopped as something moved in the hall. She breathed out a sigh of relief as the cat rubbed around her legs and mewed plaintively. She bent down and lifted the animal in her arms, cradling its warmth against her body.

"How did you get here, eh?" she murmured, as the cat rubbed its head against her face. "It's good to see you, too."

The cat climbed up on Maggie's shoulders, and she was content to let it stay there. Its presence comforted her; its big grey eyes searched the way for danger. She moved down the hallway and gently pushed against what was left of the door to

Huss's study.

She stopped short at the sight that greeted her eyes.

The fire had destroyed everything. All of the old professor's books, all of his papers, everything he had worked for forty years to collect. His notes had burned; his bed and desk were gone. There were gaping holes in the floor. From the looks of things, the fire had been lit in this room.

But the scroll was untouched.

It lay on the table where Huss had been studying. Maggie reached out tentatively and touched it. Even the layer of soot and ash that covered everything else had left the scroll alone. It was as whole as when Maggie had first laid eyes on it, the day that Old Dan had entrusted it to her keeping.

She shivered at the presence of great evil in the room. A desire rose up inside of her to destroy it herself; to light it on fire or tear it to pieces, and to make sure that not a shred of it could be read or used by anyone ever again. She forced the desire back, reached forward, and picked up the scroll. She rolled it up quickly and tucked it inside her coat, fighting against the abhorrence toward the thing that still swept over her.

She heard the laughter again.

The cat's claws dug into her shoulder and its whole body stiffened as Maggie slowly turned around.

The black-robed figure stood in the doorway, one hand stretched out toward Maggie. She recoiled as the stranger stepped forward, seeming to glide over the floor. She could not see a face below the hood, but she could feel the malevolence of the stare that was fixed on her. The cat screamed and leapt from Maggie's shoulder at the intruder. Maggie's eyes opened wide as the cat's body passed through the black robes and landed, crying piteously, on the floor beyond.

And then Maggie heard music.

It was harp music, and a voice was singing with it. She knew that voice as well as she knew the shape of the scars on her own hands. It was Mary.

The music swelled and filled Maggie's heart and ears. With it came strength. The black-robed figure began to move back, its whole shape bowed in cowardly posture, even as Maggie opened her mouth and started to sing the song that she heard so clearly.

Maggie stepped forward as the sound of her voice swept through the room. As she moved, the floorboards around her became solid and clean, the soot melting away. The ashes of books and paper slowly began to transform, coming together and becoming smooth and formed and coloured; becoming books and paper once more. The song became a mighty river, filling the room and rising above the little house; rising and flowing out to the farthest reaches of the world.

And the black-robed figure was gone. It disappeared without a trace. The second it disappeared, the song stopped. Maggie was not conscious of stopping it; it was simply not there anymore. The cat was laying on the floor, and Maggie picked it up just in time to feel the little animal's last breath leave its body. She buried her face in its fur and whispered her thanks to the valiant creature, and then she laid it down and ran from the house.

* * *

Lord Robert Sinclair stepped into the glen and felt his heart leap to his throat. Virginia lay on ground lately scorched by fire. Her clothing was singed and black with soot. She lay so still that the laird could not move for a moment for fear of what he would find. His only link—she could not be dead.

He forced himself to take a step closer, his foot falling without his notice into the track of a large wolf. Before he moved another agonized inch, Virginia stirred. He ran to her, falling to his knees in the scorched earth.

"Is it you, laird?" Virginia asked.

"Yes, yes, it's me," Lord Robert said, taking the girl in his arms and resting her head on his shoulder. "It's me. You're safe now."

Virginia stiffened and pushed back from the laird. She sat on her knees and looked in his direction, listening to the sound of his breathing. His breath quickened as he looked at her. She was the same Virginia as ever. One wrist was still bandaged, though the bandages were torn and shabby; her face was scratched and her clothes were blackened from heat and smoke. Yet something was different. A fire seemed to blaze in her green eyes, the red in her dark hair seemed more pronounced—yet it wasn't physical change that made his heart beat faster.

He could not begin to point to the change in a tangible way, but she had changed. She had always been a girl before, a pretty blind girl from the Highlands. And now a woman sat before him: a woman shining with the glory of another world.

"By the stars, Virginia," Lord Robert whispered. "What happened to you?"

"Much," she said at last. "So much has happened. I don't

know . . ." She broke off and looked up, as if she was seeking guidance from the sky.

"Why did you leave the train?" Lord Robert asked. His words seemed to wrench her back, to force her into conversation she did not want to have.

"Someone was after me," Virginia said. "She would have killed you all if she'd found me with you."

"Someone?" Lord Robert asked.

"I don't know who she was," Virginia said.

"Did she find you here?" the laird pressed. "The earth is burned black all around you."

"Yes, she found me," Virginia said. "But I—I defeated her . . . and *they* came."

"They?" Lord Robert's voice was shaking with excitement. Only now was he noticing the tracks that scuffed the dirt all around the clearing: wolf and bear and fox and badger, deer and squirrel and mouse.

"The spirits of the forest," Virginia said in a low voice.

"Tell me," he said, urgently. "Who were they—these spirits?"

"The spirits of animals, and trees, and wind," Virginia said. "They have been bound since the exile of the King. Laird, I . . . please, don't ask me any more."

"The King?" Lord Robert said. His voice was taut. "What are you talking about?"

Virginia began to cry silent tears. "I have seen the King myself," she said. "He came to me in Angslie. He is—he is spring, and light, and goodness—I can't describe him. He is peace. He is beautiful."

Lord Robert fell silent at last. He had long known that

Virginia held much back from him, that she did not trust him, but he felt it now more keenly than ever. She was a stranger to him, this woman-girl with the fire of another world in her unseeing eyes. She had finished speaking, he knew, and yet if he could have wrested more from her with his hands, he would have done it. He looked at her, and something in him twisted until he felt as though it would break. He needed understanding. Needed it desperately. For the first time Virginia, with her closely-held secrets, seemed to him like an enemy.

"We are far from any shelter," Lord Robert said, and stood abruptly. He reached down and helped Virginia to her feet. "Let's go. I don't want you spend a night out here. Your attacker could come back."

"She would not dare," Virginia said, almost to herself. But the laird heard, and frowned.

His thoughts waged war with each other until he and Virginia reached the railroad tracks, and on until they had followed the rails to a small town with an inn. He did not speak to Virginia again until he bade her goodnight and retired to a room of his own.

* * *

Maggie did not stop running until Pravik was behind her and she was standing on the side of a great slope that swept away to farmland and miles of country roads. The slope was wooded with small, friendly trees, and Maggie threw herself into the damp warmth of dead leaves beneath the branches and cried.

She did not understand anything that had just happened, but she was acutely aware of several things. For one thing, she was alone. There was no Nicolas with her to poke fun at her and tell her which way to go and keep her from getting lost in this strange territory, or to find her a Gypsy wagon with feather pillows to sleep in. Huss had given her something terrifying and incredible in the truth which he had revealed to her, and now he was gone. Nor was Mrs. Cook there to pat her hand and assure her that everything would be fine after a cup of tea, and Pat was not there to look bold and ferocious and more than a match for anything that came along. Mary was not there to sing to her, and somehow Mary's song had hurt her. Its strains had gone deeply into her and come up as something wild, something she couldn't control, something that was at once beautiful and so foreign it frightened her.

And Jerome—she loved him. She knew that now, just as she was sure that he loved her. She could not say how or when it had happened, much less why. She wanted him so badly, and he was separated from her by thick, cold stone and the unforgiving eyes of the High Police. All of her aloneness washed over her in waves, dragging her heart out bit by bit to drown in the deep.

The worst of it was that she no longer knew herself. She could not take comfort in the familiarity of her feelings and reactions. The old Maggie, predictable and timid, had disappeared, piece by piece, on the roads of the continent. She was someone else now—someone who fought battles and roamed with Gypsies and knew ancient secrets; someone who knew what it meant to love fiercely and to sing miracles. Mary's song had completed the change in her. Maggie did not even know what she had sung; the words and the melody had left her without so much as a memory of their form. She was left with the bitter loneliness of a young woman who did not know her own soul.

In time the thought of Jerome and Huss brought Maggie back to herself. She stood unsteadily, lightheaded from crying. With miserable clarity she realized that she had no idea how to find the Ploughman. The High Police would be on her trail soon—and in their shadow, the black-robed Order of the Spider would follow. The scroll inside her coat felt heavy.

Maggie drew a deep breath and staggered down the hill to the farms and country roads below. Perhaps a rebel who went by the name of the Ploughman could be found among the farmers of the Eastern Lands. She wandered down the road about a mile, past recently harvested fields where flocks of birds gleaned from the remaining stubble. Now and then the birds would rise up together, calling and cackling, and swoop down over the road on their way to a new picking field. Maggie would stop and watch the birds diving and soaring all around her, and would stand still until every last little straggler went fleeting past.

The road was rough and worn with deep wagon ruts. Maggie's feet slipped on the dry earth and the sun beat down on her head. Still she walked, until the bright world around her had become something of a blur. Fragmented thoughts drifted through her mind.

After a mile or two the farmland gave way to wooded hills. The trees sent sparsely-clothed branches out to offer the road what shade they could. The shadows cooled Maggie's eyes, and she lifted her head as her mind troubled over the problem of where the road was taking her and what she was going to do when she got there.

The road narrowed and Maggie became faintly aware of the distant sound of a train—then, suddenly, there was a noise of metal grinding against metal, a dreadful squeal and whine, and a cloud of birds burst from the trees a small distance away. Distinctly human sounds followed the flutter of birds' wings on the wind.

Maggie stood undecided for a moment, and dashed into the woods, trusting her ears to lead her to the source of the noise. The sounds of confusion came closer and she slowed instinctively in case danger lay beyond the forest tangle. She could see the place where bright sunlight lit a clearing just beyond a row of trees.

As she neared the clearing, a sound like the call of an owl fell on her ears. She stopped and looked all around her. There was something afoot in the woods, she could feel it. Every shadow seemed to be hiding something. But no, there was nothing there—she looked again, and again her eyes found nothing. Maggie tore her eyes away from the surrounding forest and looked back out to the place where the trees ended.

Low, yellow-leafed branches blocked her path, and she ducked and pushed her way through until she stepped abruptly out onto the edge of a ridge. Below it lay the scene of a train wreck. The iron serpent was long, its cars stretching out of sight around a bend. Its first ten cars had been derailed, and it lay twisted in the hollow.

Men, rail workers from the look of their uniforms, walked the length of the train inspecting the damage. Most of them stood in front of the dragon's head engine, where an enormous man-made wall of brush had caused the train to go off of its tracks.

Maggie began to pick her way gingerly down the slope when one of the figures standing in the clearing turned and looked straight at her, and she found herself looking into the face of Patricia Black. Pat's face was surprised, then elated, and she shouted Maggie's name and ran to her.

Maggie was nearly at the bottom of the slope when Pat reached her, but she was not smiling. She knew it, and was sorry for it, especially as Pat's face clouded. But if she could not smile—not in the face of all that had happened and all she was trying to do—she could yet look, with eyes that shone welcome and need.

Pat shook off whatever had clouded her face. She beamed and caught Maggie in an embrace. Maggie held her friend as if she would never let her go. Fierce gladness burned in her heart.

She did let go at last, and Pat stepped back and looked Maggie over with thinly veiled curiosity.

"You're not in Pravik," Pat said, and laughed slightly. "Bless this wreck, then. Without it we would have gone all the way to Pravik in search of you and been cheated at the last." Maggie finally managed a weak smile as she sought words, and Pat continued, "Mrs. Cook is with me. And we've got so much to tell you!"

She linked her arm with Maggie and dragged her off to a train car where Mrs. Cook anxiously awaited Pat's return.

"You go in first," Pat said. "Mrs. Cook won't know what to do with herself!"

Pat shoved Maggie gently. Maggie smiled at her and went

through the door of the compartment. She did not see the way Pat watched her go, with her dark eyebrows knotted in perplexity. Maggie was different, Pat thought—she looked as though she'd been living too close to the stars, and now all their light and solemnity was shining through her eyes.

"Oh!" Mrs. Cook said when Maggie entered the little room, and her hand flew to her mouth. Then her arms opened wide and Maggie stepped into the warmth of the elderly woman's love. Mrs. Cook burst promptly and sobbingly into tears.

"My dear girl," she cried, while Pat hovered over them both, grinning like a child who has played a clever trick. When Maggie stepped back, her face was flushed and her eyes were bright with very deep love, and even Mrs. Cook noticed that there was something deeper there than she had seen in Maggie before.

"It is so good to see you," Maggie said, feeling suddenly as though words could flow out of her in an unending torrent, but before she could say anything more she was cut off by the call of a bugle. The sound wavered in the air and slowly died. Maggie moved to the window. Her eyes opened wide as she caught sight of something dark moving in the trees.

Then they appeared, out from the darkness of the forest, spilling down the hill to the train. It seemed as though there were hundreds of them, men in dark clothing, brandishing swords and clubs and whooping like boys on a holiday. They descended on the men of the train, whose courage failed them at the sight. Almost as one the men turned and ran for the safety of the train cars. Pat's long knife was drawn in a flash, and she was nearly out the door when Maggie reached out and

227

caught her arm.

"Wait," she commanded. Pat put up the knife even as she stared at Maggie in surprise.

Maggie's eyes were drawn to one lone figure, who was even now emerging from the woods. He was on horseback, unlike the others, and he wore a long, navy blue cloak with a hood that had fallen back from a dark, handsome face. His hair was black and thick, and even on horseback he looked tall. Maggie recognized him almost instantly.

The Ploughman.

He shouted orders to his men and they swarmed around the train, boarding the cars with wild shouts. From their compartment, Maggie and Pat could see them begin to stream back out, carrying crates and rolling barrels ahead of them.

"What sort of cargo was on this train?" Maggie asked.

"Food," Pat answered. "Bound for the Overlord's storehouses. And weapons."

"I need to talk to that man," Maggie said, pointing to the Ploughman.

"All in good time," Pat said, one eyebrow raised. "I'm sure they'll drag out the hostages sooner or later."

"They don't want prisoners," Maggie said. "These men aren't bandits."

"Oh no?" Pat asked. "It looks to me as though we're being robbed."

"They're farmers," Maggie said. "I left Pravik to find them."

"Oh," Pat said, "I see. We're being robbed by friends of yours."

"Come with me," Maggie said. Pat and Mrs. Cook

crowded out of the compartment behind her. They picked their way to the door of the car and lowered themselves down to the ground. The rebels were everywhere. One man saw them and shouted.

"You there!" he said, pointing a thick finger. "Back on the train!"

"I wish to speak with the Ploughman!" Maggie called back as the man moved in front of them. "I am a friend of his."

The man looked at her incredulously. "Come along, then, miss," he said. "We'll see if your friend the Ploughman recognizes you!"

There was laughter from the surrounding rebels, and the men formed a wall of bodies around and behind them, escorting them to their leader. Maggie approached the tall man on his horse and dropped to one knee.

"I am a friend of Libuse," she said. "And of Jarin Huss."

"Stand up, then," the Ploughman said. His deep voice sounded amused. When Maggie looked up into his face she saw that he was smiling slightly. "You look familiar," he continued. "I have seen you somewhere, though I don't know your name."

"Maggie Sheffield," she told him. "Professor Huss and Jerome need your help."

The Ploughman silenced her with a wave of his hand. "I see by your face that you do not bring good news," he said. His eyes left Maggie, going to the train and his men at work emptying it. "We will speak later, after this carcass has been cleaned and we are away. Stay here." He pointed to the place next to his horse. "My men will be your escort."

So saying, the Ploughman rode away. His men moved in closer to the three women.

"He's a well-spoken bandit, that friend of yours," Pat said in a low voice.

"Are we really going to go with them?" Mrs. Cook asked nervously.

"I am," said Maggie. She put her hand on Mrs. Cook's arm suddenly. "You should go home. Get back on the train. Help will come soon and take you to the city. You shouldn't be here."

Mrs. Cook drew herself up to her full, plump height. "My girl," she said, "you are here, and I will not leave you alone again. Something has happened to you, that's plain enough, but I won't have you making a stranger of me."

She smiled, and her tone of voice changed. Her eyes twinkled as she spoke. "I've been through some adventures of my own, Maggie. I'm not afraid of them."

When the rebels were finished they loaded every last parcel from the train onto their backs and the few horses and pack animals that were hidden in the woods. The bugle sounded, and the company melted back into the woods from whence it had come, bearing Maggie, Pat, and Mrs. Cook away with it.

11

Dreams and War

"Hear the call of the Huntsman's horn;
"The stars all sing when the chase is on;
"Over the sky fields and cross the moon;
"The darkness meets its downfall soon."

"Heed the song of the Huntsman's soul;
"He sings of battles fought and won;
"He sings of love and stars aglow;
"Of a King, a Heart, that all hearts know.

"Hear the call of the Huntsman's horn;
"Dawn will come though night is long;
"Sing with triumph, sons of men,
"Know your King will come again."

IN ANCIENT DAYS BEFORE THE WORLD WAS BORN, the King spoke
the Huntsman's name; and in that moment, he came into
being. The Horn of the Huntsman has ever sent fear into the
hearts of all things black; it is the sound of righteousness at
war. The Great Star-Rider was born to persecute the Blackness,

and though he has gone from this world along with the King, his wrath echoes still in the heavens.

I, the Poet, have heard the call of the Huntsman. This night it rang in the tops of the trees and shimmered among the stars. No, he has not yet returned—not for many long years of the moon will the Huntsman return to sound his call. But I have heard the spirit of that call echoing back from a future day, and I have felt the Blackness quiver.

* * *

The Ploughman and his men rode up into the woods, following hidden paths through the forest. They rode through the falling of darkness and into the night, and the band of men slowly thinned out as individuals broke away and took much of the plunder with them. When at last they left the forest and began to ride through a stubbled field toward a small farmhouse that glowed in welcome, the band had dwindled to five men, the Ploughman, and the three women.

The men dismounted onto the hard packed earth outside the little house, leading their horses and that of the Ploughman away to the nearby outbuildings. Maggie, Pat, and Mrs. Cook swung down from their saddles, and young boys appeared from the farmyard shadows to take their mounts away. A shadow momentarily blocked the golden light that spilled from the door, and Maggie recognized Libuse standing in the doorway, dressed in peasant clothes.

The princess went to the Ploughman and they whispered together for a moment. Libuse turned and approached Maggie.

"It is good to see you here," the princess said, smiling. She

Worlds Unseen

was breathtakingly beautiful as the light of the house played on her face and drew all the gold out of her hair. She caught Maggie's hand tightly. "Your friends are welcome as well. Come! There is supper waiting."

The princess led the eight newcomers inside, where a long wooden table had been set with bread and soup, cheese and butter. The men sat at one end and dove into the food. Maggie, Pat, and Mrs. Cook sat with the Ploughman and the princess at the other end.

A large farmwife with a permanently fixed scowl set a steaming bowl of soup in front of Maggie. She picked up a spoon and stirred the broth in circles, watching flecks of spice whirl into the center around chunks of potato. The others were waiting for her. She set the spoon down and looked up at Libuse.

"Professor Huss has been arrested," she said. Her voice caught. "And Jerome."

Libuse looked at her in stunned silence. She cleared her throat and asked, "Why?"

"They say the professor murdered you," Maggie said.

The Ploughman placed his hand on Libuse's arm, but she pulled away. She stood, her face flushed. "How could they?" she said. "How dare they?"

"There will be a trial," the Ploughman said.

"I don't know when," Maggie said.

"Soon," the Ploughman said. His face was stern, almost angry. "Why did you come here?"

Maggie did not look at his face. Instead, she looked up at Libuse again, her face pleading. "I thought if you went back, they would have to release them."

"No!" the Ploughman said. He stood, towering head and shoulders above his lady. He took her shoulders. "They want you back. They'll find a way to kill you and not spare the professor for it. You can't go."

"I must," Libuse said. Her face was pale, but she slipped away from the Ploughman and sat back down. She picked up her spoon and took a swallow of soup, though her hand shook as she raised it to her mouth. She looked up at the Ploughman. "I will go back," she said.

"I don't understand," Maggie said. "If Libuse comes back to Pravik alive, it will prove that the professor is innocent!"

"They already know that he's innocent," the Ploughman said. "If he really had killed Libuse they'd congratulate him for it. It's not murder they're concerned with."

"Then . . ." Maggie said.

The Ploughman sighed heavily. "Zarras wishes to stamp out resistance to himself. He suspected Libuse's connection to us; that's why she was arrested. When she disappeared it provided a good excuse to go after those responsible for unrest in the university."

"Professor Huss and Jerome," Maggie said.

"No matter," Libuse said. "Professor Huss is like a father to me. I can stop his execution. If I go back they will have to let him go, if only for a little while—but it will be time enough for him to leave Pravik."

"No!" the Ploughman said again, thumping the table. "You are not going back."

"I can't leave them to die," Libuse said.

"If you go back, I will come for you," the Ploughman said. "I will ride into the city and free you myself."

They looked at each other in silence, their faces golden in the warm firelight. Something seemed to shift in the air between them, filling the room with a strange sense of power and danger. The men at the other end of the table had stopped eating and were staring down at their leader and his lady. Pat and Mrs. Cook looked at each other uneasily. Maggie kept her eyes on Libuse.

The princess shifted in her seat, picked up her spoon, and took another sip of the steaming broth. "Well," she said, and the men at the other end strained forward to hear her. "Why don't you?"

The Ploughman dropped into his seat. "How can I?"

"Your men would follow you to the gates of death, you know that."

"That doesn't give me the right to lead them there! It is too soon, and Pravik too dangerous a place."

Libuse set her spoon down and turned so that she was facing the Ploughman. "If you are right, and Zarras is moving against us, what choice do you have? Betray your own cause, leave the Eastern Lands, or fight back."

"That is only one choice."

"Then why not make the first move?"

"Libuse," the Ploughman said, smiling gently, "you are not talking like a general. You are talking like a child who wishes to convince her parent that what is bad for her is really good."

Libuse laid her head on his chest. He brought his hand up to stroke her hair, his ring shining scarlet in the light of the fire.

"I can't let him die without trying to help him," Libuse

said. She lifted her head and her face was tearstained. "Can you?"

The Ploughman looked into her eyes for a long moment. He stood abruptly and waved his men out of the room. "Leave us," he said. "Maggie, stay. Your friends also."

The men left with a clatter, nearly knocking the table over in their haste. The Ploughman stood and began to pace by the fire. He reached for a quarterstaff near the door and feinted with it as he talked. Once again Maggie felt as though some power was in the room with them, golden power, glowing in the Plowman's eyes, stirring with his movements. There was heat in his words; heat like burnished gold.

"I will not let the professor be killed as a murderer," he said. "I will not let his student be slandered as an assassin. They are brave men. They have stood against corruption all their lives. They have inspired others to do the same. They have been father and brother and loyal subjects to the woman I love."

He whirled around to face the others. "That is what my heart tells me. But what about my men? I can risk my own life; can I risk theirs?"

"Their lives have always been at risk," Libuse said. "Since the day they determined to stand against Zarras."

"But they made that decision to defend their children," the Ploughman said. "Their wives, their mothers, their liberty. Not the liberty of an old man they do not know, though in his own way he has fought for them."

He stood still, back to the fire, the quarterstaff glowing. "It had to come to this, sooner or later," he said. "Me against Zarras. My men against the High Police. But never did I

236

anticipate making the first move."

He sat down at the table and bowed his head so that it rested against the staff. "How can I lead them into this?"

"Ask them," Maggie said.

Libuse and the Ploughman both turned to look at her. She looked down but continued to speak. "You and Professor Huss have fought to give the people a voice. To give them the freedom to choose their own destinies. So ask them. Let them decide if they will march on the castle or not."

The Ploughman stood again, slowly. "If they refuse, then I will go to Pravik myself. I will force Zarras to listen . . . somehow. And if we fight, and we win, then how shall we answer when the forces of Athrom march on us? To defend ourselves is one thing, to attack an Overlord quite another. The Emperor will not look kindly on us. But if we lose, or if we don't go at all . . ."

Libuse stood and took his hand in her own. "Let history write the story, my love," she said. "It is your task to make it."

The Ploughman's men were crouched outside the door where their leader had sent them. He threw it open and smiled to see them there, so close that they nearly fell inside when he opened the door.

"Light the beacon fires," he said. "We hold council in the morning."

* * *

The scowling farmwife, whose name was Mrs. Korak, cleared away the remnants of supper. Libuse lit a candle and led the visitors out the back of the house to a low-roofed outbuilding full of empty bunks.

"I'm sorry there isn't anywhere nicer for you to sleep," she said, ducking through the doorway of the long, dry shack. "The hired men sleep here during the harvest. It's nothing special, but it's warm."

"It's plenty good enough for us," Mrs. Cook said. Libuse smiled and set her candle down on top of a rough, low shelf.

"I'll leave you, then," the princess said. "I hope you sleep well. If you need anything, I sleep in the kitchen—knock on the back door and I'll hear you."

"Well, she's a rare one," Pat said when Libuse had left. "What did you say she is?"

"A princess," Maggie said. "Of Pravik's ancient ruling family."

"And she sleeps in the kitchen," Mrs. Cook said, shaking her head. "She's lovely, Maggie, just lovely. And to think you saved her life!"

"I didn't do it alone," Maggie said, lowering herself down on the cot next to Mrs. Cook. "Good men gave their lives for her." The thought of Jerome came to her, waiting to give his life, and she shut her eyes tightly. She leaned her head against Mrs. Cook's shoulder. In a moment she found herself burrowed in the older woman's arms.

Mrs. Cook patted Maggie's shoulder, a gesture meant to ease trouble as much as it could. "I'm here now, dear," she said, "and Pat, too. Why, you're practically home!"

"It's good to be home," Maggie said. Pat chuckled.

Mrs. Cook's arms tightened around Maggie. After a while Maggie sat up and said, "Tell me why you left Londren. You didn't come just to find me—I'm sure you didn't. I want to know everything."

Pat and Mrs. Cook looked at each other. The whole story came out—of Lord Robert's unexpected arrival, of Virginia and her strange gift, of the High Police, and of their escape over the Salt Channel to the continent.

"And you, Maggie?" Pat probed when they had finished. "You're not the same person who left us. What has happened to you?"

So Maggie told her own story. It seemed incredible that so much had happened in such a short time. Her life in Londren seemed very far removed from this life of rebels and Gypsies and evil shadows that lived and breathed. When she talked about Jerome, her throat tightened and her heart burned, but she told them only that he was Huss's apprentice and a brave man.

When she had finished her story, she drew the scroll out from her coat and unrolled it gingerly. The candle burned slowly down to the brass holder while Maggie told her friends everything that Jarin Huss had told her; of the King and the Order of the Spider and the Gifted.

"So," Mrs. Cook said when Maggie had finished, "it would seem my life has come full circle at last. I never wanted anything more to do with the council, and now here I am."

"What are you going to do with the scroll, Maggie?" Pat asked. "If those shadow creatures were after it, isn't it a dangerous thing to have laying around?"

"Huss thought it would be a help to us somehow," Maggie said. "He said the truth was a weapon. I just wish I knew how to use it."

"Weapon or no," Pat insisted, "what are you going to do if

the baddies come after it again?"

Maggie shuddered. "I don't know. I don't want it. Giving it to the professor was like getting rid of a fifty-pound weight. But I can't just let the Order have it again."

"Give it to the Ploughman," Mrs. Cook suggested. "He can protect it, if nothing else."

Maggie rolled the scroll back up and ran her fingers along its surface. "You may be right," she said. "Tomorrow."

"Well, of course," Mrs. Cook said. She laid down on her bunk with a sigh. "There can't be much danger in keeping it for one night longer."

Maggie curled up on the bunk next to Mrs. Cook. She fell silent listening to the familiar rhythm of the older woman's breathing. Oh, how she had missed the presence of these two! In their company, she almost knew herself again—but then the thoughts and feelings of her new life crowded in. Only now, Pat and Mrs. Cook had entered her new life, and they loved the new Maggie just as they had loved the old. She was comforted by the thought.

After a few minutes, Maggie heard Pat's footfalls on the wooden floor, and through closed eyes she felt the darkness deepen as Pat snuffed out the candle.

Maggie lay awake a little longer. From her bunk she could see out the window, where far over the brown fields a beacon flared to life.

"Look at that, would you?" Pat asked, her voice drowsy.

"Go to sleep," Mrs. Cook said. "I've no wish to look at anything but the backs of my own eyelids."

Maggie smiled and rolled over so that she faced away from the blazing signal.

She slept as a child; content.

* * *

The laird's sleep was dream-plagued that night. He awoke
more than once feeling as though he was wrestling with
something; as though he struggled with a shapeless enemy.
Every trace of the actual dreams vanished when he opened his
eyes, and nothing would recall them. Once or twice he went to
check on Virginia, and always she was sleeping soundly. Even
in sleep a strange light seemed to emanate from her face, and
he felt hunger as he looked at her. Deep hunger, gnawing at
him.

A dream woke him for the last time when the sun was
just beginning to fill the world with its rays. The air was cold
and crisp and smelled like winter. The laird lay in bed and
thought of Pravik. He made his plans before stirring from the
bed. They would catch an early train and reach the city just as
the sun was setting. Then it would be a simple matter of
finding Jarin Huss. Perhaps the Easterner could shed some light
on what had happened to Virginia. Perhaps he could make her
trust them and tell them more.

An hour had passed when Lord Robert swung his long
legs out of bed, pulled on his clothes, and headed down the
hallway in search of Virginia. He rapped lightly on her door.
She called to him to come in. He began to open the door, then
paused as a sound like the beating of heavy wings came from
inside. Shaking off a feeling of foreboding, he opened the door.
Virginia was sitting in a rocking chair next to her bed, waiting.
There was no one else in the room, man or bird.

241

Still, the foreboding grew stronger. Virginia was sitting straight, her back stiff, her hands folded in her lap. She did not even turn her head to acknowledge the laird's presence. The sight of her called to mind a hundred visits to the side of the mountain in Angslie, where Virginia's strangeness had always followed a vision.

The laird swallowed his desire to know. "The next train for Pravik should come through in about half an hour," he said. "I would have come for you sooner, but the train station is not far."

Virginia bowed her head and spoke so quietly that Lord Robert could hardly hear her. "Laird," she said, "must we go to Pravik?"

It was such a strange question that Lord Robert was taken aback by it. Then annoyance flared up in him, and he said, "Of course. What would you rather do, go back to the High Police?"

Virginia's head remained bowed. She did not respond.

"I'm sorry," Lord Robert said, suddenly weary—far too weary for first thing in the morning. "Of course we must go to Pravik. I need the help of Jarin Huss."

"I have seen," Virginia said. "Last night."

"What was it?" he asked. The foreboding still hung over him; contesting now with his curiosity.

"I saw you," she said. When she looked up, her face was pale. "You were falling into darkness, and I could not reach you to stop your fall."

Her voice broke. Lord Robert could see that she was struggling not to cry.

"If we stay away from Pravik, it may not happen,"

Virginia said. "Please, let us go anywhere but there."

Lord Robert looked out Virginia's open window at the town that spread below them. He could see the train station just down the street, and the black smoke of the iron serpent waiting to leave. As he looked away from the view, his eyes rested on something on the windowsill. A feather.

With a suddenness that took him by surprise, he turned to Virginia and said, "No. We are going to Pravik. I have traveled too far to turn back now!" His voice gentled, and he knelt down by Virginia's chair. "It will be all right," he said. "You'll see."

He took her arm. They left the room and the inn behind.

* * *

Across the countryside, beacon fires called the Ploughman's men to him. They arrived with the dawn, filling the barnyard with the sounds of hooves and creaking wooden wheels. Maggie awoke to see pale sunlight filtering over the low windowsills.

Pat was still snoring, and Mrs. Cook breathing deeply, as Maggie slid out of bed and pulled her shoes on. Outside, someone poured water into troughs for the horses. The choir of birds on their way south for the winter was just beginning to sing.

Maggie pulled her coat around her and stepped out of the bunkhouse. A low mist blanketed the ground, blurring the fields and the yard in watercolour shades of grey and green. Young boys, thirteen or fourteen years old, tended to the horses. Men stood in small groups, talking in low voices. No one seemed to notice Maggie.

There were about thirty men crowded in the barnyard. Some of them had perhaps been at Pravik Castle, but they were a different set entirely than the university students who had led them there. These were men with the creases of hardship drawn deep across greying brows. Their shoulders were broad; their hands rough; their faces coarse. They wore hand-sewn clothing, many times patched, mud-spattered from the early morning ride. They filled the barnyard with the smells of pipe smoke and soil and the singed smell of too many nights spent inches from the hearth. At first glance Maggie thought them all old enough to be her father, but as she looked closer she realized that they represented many generations. Here were young men, not much older than herself, with hands as rough and weathered as those of their grandfathers, men stooped and grey but still strong.

Lamplight cut a path through the mist from the farmhouse door, and the Ploughman and Libuse, warmly dressed in woolen cloaks, stepped into the barnyard. Mrs. Korak stood behind them with a ladle in her meaty hand, scowling, watching as the Ploughman greeted his visitors. Libuse, too, walked among the men and greeted many by name. They bowed their heads in deference as she approached. They held respect for her as did the people of the city—but not, Maggie noticed, more than they held for the Ploughman.

A young boy led two horses into the yard and stood near the Ploughman, silently holding the reins. The Ploughman turned and took hold of his tall black horse. He mounted, and Libuse mounted the sorrel beside him. The boy jogged back to the barns.

The Ploughman galloped over the field, and the men mounted up and followed. A flock of geese burst up from the field before the horses, filling the early morning with their cries.

Maggie turned to see Mrs. Korak still standing in the doorway. The woman's eyes looked to Maggie.

"You'll be wanting breakfast, I suppose?" she asked.

"I'm not hungry," Maggie said. "Can I help you with anything?"

"Not unless you have ears to hear a meeting five miles away."

Maggie looked at the elderly woman with a new appreciation. "I wish I knew what was happening, too," she said.

"Well," Mrs. Korak said, "there's a horse in the barn."

"Do you mean it?" Maggie said.

"Boy'll show you the way."

"I shouldn't," Maggie said. "They didn't invite me."

Mrs. Korak snorted. "They should have. Get going now. You might hear a thing or two."

Maggie lost no time in mounting a bay mare. One of the farm boys—by now Maggie had counted six or seven youngsters doing chores around the yard—sat behind her in the saddle and pointed the way.

"You see that hill yonder?" he said, pointing over her shoulder.

"I see it."

"Under the hill is a great meeting room. Just below the oak tree."

Maggie squinted as she looked across the misty fields. The

hill was shadowed.

"Go," the boy said. "You'll see it as we draw near."

The horse made good time across the fields, but when Maggie arrived at the base of the hill, there was no sign of human life except for the tracks of horses, mysteriously ending at the base of the hill—which Maggie realized was really more of a mound, man-made many long years ago. She took a deep breath of cold air and looked up at the tangled branches of an ancient oak that grew up at the top.

The boy slid off the horse and cautiously approached a thicket at the base. He crouched low and listened, then, finding things to his satisfaction, he pulled back a thick curtain of brush, opening a dark space wide and tall enough for Maggie to walk through. She dismounted and approached the hole. Just before ducking inside, she looked at the longing face of the boy.

"Can I come with you?" he said. "The horse'll be all right."

"No," Maggie said. "How would I protect you from Mrs. Korak when we got back?"

The flushed look on the boy's face told her she had hit on a sore note. She grinned. "Thank you," she said, and disappeared into the darkness.

Maggie found herself in an earthen room with roots growing through the ceiling and walls. The smell of horses was strong, and as Maggie's eyes adjusted, she saw that she was standing in a stable full of animals. The room stretched to either side and disappeared around what Maggie thought was the curve of a circle. Across the stable was a wall, and in it, a door.

It was standing partially open, and Maggie could hear voices. She made her way past the horses, who ignored her, and slipped through the door into a circular room orange with lantern light on earthen walls. It was a large room, wide enough to seat two or three hundred men, and it was full to the bursting.

The old men sat on rough-hewn benches; the younger men cross-legged on the floor. In the center of the room the Ploughman stood, quarterstaff in hand, his face solemn. He had only just stopped speaking, and now his eyes swept the faces of his men. He saw Maggie and his eyes rested on her for a moment, but he said nothing. Libuse was standing on the far side of the room, against the wall.

An old grey farmer with a hump in his back and strong arms spoke. "We will follow you," was all he said.

"You risk everything," the Ploughman said.

The old man smiled, an ironic smile. "We have nothing to risk," he said.

"Your lives," the Ploughman said. "Your families."

"We live in slavery," the old man said. "Yearly taxes will starve our lives; the Man Tax will take our families. Fight them then or fight them now, we will fight."

The Ploughman motioned toward a group of thirty or so men: those who had gathered with him in the farmyard. "These at least have an obligation to fight with me, though I would not force them," he said. "They are my tenants. I am their lord. The rest of you own Zarras as your landlord."

"He has our lands," a younger man said. "You have our loyalty. You have fought for us. We will fight for you."

"If we win," said the changing voice of a boy who was

barely a man, "perhaps the Emperor will listen to us."

"Perhaps he will kill you," the Ploughman said.

There was silence.

Libuse moved from the wall and came to stand by the Ploughman. "Enough now," she said. "You have your army."

"And there is much to do," the Ploughman finished.

* * *

Pat and Mrs. Cook were in Mrs. Korak's kitchen when Maggie returned, picking at bowls of porridge. Maggie and the farm boy had left the mound ahead of the Ploughman, slipping away while the rebel leader spoke with a few of his men.

Maggie pushed open the wooden kitchen door. The warmth of the hearth and the smell of food wrapped around her and she yawned.

"Tiring morning, was it?" Pat asked. Maggie ignored her and glanced at Mrs. Korak, who was eagle-eyeing her. The farmwife looked down and pounded a lump of dough as Maggie brushed past her.

"They're going to Pravik," Maggie whispered. Mrs. Korak nodded and pounded harder.

Maggie sat down next to Pat. Mrs. Cook shoved a bowl of porridge in her direction. Pat had stopped eating, and was looking at Maggie with one eyebrow raised.

Maggie stirred her porridge. "I don't know how much I should tell you," she said, finally. "I followed the Ploughman to council this morning."

She was interrupted by the clatter of hooves in the yard. A boy poked his head in the door and said, "Ploughman's back!

Twenty men with him."

"Good boy," Mrs. Korak said. "Go take the horses. On with you!"

The boy darted back outside. "Twenty," Mrs. Korak said. "His leaders. There'll be more talking today. And eating." She grimaced. "There's porridge enough for all, anyway."

Maggie, Pat, and Mrs. Cook sat quietly while boots stamped and voices filled the next room where the Ploughman and his men gathered around the long table. Libuse entered the kitchen after a few minutes.

"Twenty-three, Mrs. Korak," she said.

The farmwife shook a spoon threateningly. "I'll teach that boy to count one way or another. Twenty-three. Do their lordships require porridge with or without milk?"

Libuse smiled. "Without is fine, I'm sure. We mustn't overtax the cow."

"If my kitchen's going to feed them, they'll eat milk," Mrs. Korak said. "I'm not stingy."

"Of course not." Libuse laughed.

Mrs. Korak laid out two dozen wooden bowls on the counter and began ladling porridge into them. Mrs. Cook jumped to her feet to help, following Mrs. Korak's lead as she added milk to each bowl.

"Double in that one," Mrs. Korak said as Mrs. Cook added milk to the largest of the bowls. The farmwife picked up the bowl after Mrs. Cook had filled it and handed it to Libuse.

"For the master," she said.

Maggie and Pat stood to help carry the bowls into the rough dining room, leaving their own breakfasts half-eaten on the kitchen table. The Ploughman had a roll of paper spread out in front of him, and on it he had drawn a map. Maggie's eyes fell on it as she set breakfast down before two of the men.

Surprised, she saw the intricate layout of Pravik Castle and the area around it. Even for one as new to the Eastern Lands as she, the castle and the streets at the head of the plateau were clearly recognizable. The question leaped into her head, though it didn't come out her mouth—how long had the Ploughman been preparing to attack Pravik? He had fought the suggestion that he do so, yet he owned detailed maps of the city.

Self-consciously Maggie began to leave the room, but the Ploughman held up his hand. "Please," he said. "Stay. All of you."

Pat, Mrs. Cook, and Libuse lingered near the door.

"We have made the decision to rescue the professor, no matter what it cost us," the Ploughman said. "But we need someone in the city. Someone to keep their finger on what is happening. We need to know dates and times, how the trial goes. Maggie, as you have spent time in the city, I thought perhaps . . ."

"I'll go." It was Pat. She stepped forward. "Maggie helped rescue Libuse. The police could be looking for her."

"I don't think they saw me clearly enough to know what they're looking for," Maggie argued.

"They've never seen me at all. I'll get a job with a theater, as a seamstress. I've done it before. And if it's gossip you want, there's no better place to get it."

The Ploughman looked across the room to Libuse, then nodded. "You'll leave today," he said.

Pat tried to smile and did not entirely succeed. "Good,"

she said.

* * *

The council dispersed later that afternoon. The early morning chill had given way to sunny warmth, and Pat and Maggie grew tired of hanging around the house. Mrs. Cook had rolled up her sleeves and charged into the kitchen to foist her help upon Mrs. Korak an hour before, and Libuse had disappeared after the Ploughman and his men rode away.

"I've no right to hanker after excitement, I know," Pat said. "I'll have plenty of it soon enough. But if I don't find something to do I'm going to shrivel up. Let's go for a walk."

So they did: out over the brown fields behind the barns. Crows and small birds disdained to pay them any mind as they wandered through the remains of the harvest. They had nearly reached a small, lonely tree on the far side of the fields when Pat shaded her eyes.

"I think that's Libuse under that tree," Pat said. "Do you think we'd better leave her alone?"

Maggie didn't answer. Something about the lone figure drew her. Libuse was kneeling on a carpet of fallen leaves with the tree's thin branches spread out over her head. Pat saw Maggie's intent and touched her shoulder, then stopped to wait for her.

Maggie approached Libuse quietly and soon saw that she was kneeling before a grave. There were tears on the princess's face, and all at once Maggie regretted intruding. But she did not have time to leave before Libuse spoke to her, without looking.

"You remember the wounded boy from the riot?" Libuse asked. Maggie knelt down beside her and nodded.

"He was the Ploughman's brother," Libuse said. "I did all I could to keep him alive, but . . ." She struggled to regain control of herself. "When the Ploughman was very young, his parents were killed in an outbreak of disease. They might have pulled through, but the winter was cold, and the taxes had taken more than they could afford to give. There was an older brother as well, and this one—" She indicated the grave. "This one was a baby. One day the soldiers came to collect the Man Tax. The older brother was thirteen, and they took him.

"The Ploughman was left to take care of his brother. The tenant farmers on his land helped however they could. As he grew older, the Ploughman vowed to repay them by treating them as brothers and not as slaves. They grew to love him. His own people, and the tenants of Antonin Zarras, look to him as their voice. As their defender."

"Are there no other landholders here?" Maggie asked.

"Not in this part of the world," Libuse said. "Zarras's father bullied and stole and plundered until he held titles for all the Eastern Lands except the Ploughman's little plot of ground. Antonin Zarras is not much older than the Ploughman, you know. They knew each other once."

She grew quiet, and with her fingers she touched the gravestone. "But it was for this one he fought, most of all," she said. "To make a better world for him. And now we may make a better world, but he will never see it."

Maggie knelt down beside the princess. A biting wind whirled through the tree branches, out of place under the warm sun. "What sort of better world will the Ploughman make?" she asked.

"A world where the people have a voice," Libuse said.

"Is that all?" Maggie pressed. "In the university . . ."

"In the university they have time and luxury to make great plans and dream great dreams. Out here people are too busy surviving." Libuse smiled grimly. "The university students would like to see the Empire itself brought down. But they can't do it. Not with their talk. The Ploughman cares nothing for all that, yet he strikes the first blow. And who knows where it will end?"

Maggie fingered the scroll inside her coat. "I know we're only trying to rescue an old man," she said. "And maybe the storm will blow over. So why do I feel like we're about to change the world? To shatter peace forever?"

"It is the peace of death we break," Libuse said. The tone of her voice told Maggie she was quoting someone. "The people cannot continue to live in slavery."

Libuse grew quiet and distant, and said, "I suppose I'm a university revolutionary at heart. If I could have my way there would be no Empire. The Ploughman speaks of a world where the people rule themselves, but I fear that too. I long for a ruler. One who will be merciful and just. Who will be good, truly good. Life would be so small if we were all we had. We need something—someone—to make us look up."

"To take us beyond ourselves," Maggie said, understanding completely.

Libuse smiled, and for a moment her eyes shone. "To make us believe in beauty and wonder and goodness. To fill us with awe. How long since I have been filled with anything close."

"How wonderful it would be to have a king like that!"

"I am not sure that any such person exists," Libuse said, and sighed. "In the ancient days, my family ruled a kingdom very different from the Empire. Sometimes I wish I could have seen it—I think it must have been a paradise, where kings and queens were different from the overlords of our day. But then, sometimes, I am glad that I can't."

"Why?" Maggie asked.

"Because I'm afraid it would not be any different than it is now," Libuse said. "I am afraid that people would be just as selfish and cruel and power mad as they are today."

Maggie looked down and felt the scroll again, and with her eyes dancing she said, "Perhaps the King of the Worlds Unseen will come."

Libuse looked partly amused, partly disturbed. "Jarin Huss's exiled lord of the ancient days? He is a myth."

"How do you know?" Maggie pressed.

Libuse threw up her hands. "I don't know! How can I? That is just the trouble. I would dearly love to believe in him. But I have no reason to. Even if he did exist, he has been away so long . . . why would he come back?"

Maggie had no answers, but she suddenly pulled out the scroll from her coat.

"What is that?" Libuse asked.

"A very old document," Maggie said. "Huss says it is five hundred years old. As old as the Empire."

"Can you read it?" Libuse said. Maggie passed it to her. The princess unrolled it carefully and looked at the strange characters with a furrowed brow.

"I can't," Maggie said, "but Huss can. He says it is signed

by Lucius Morel himself."

Libuse looked up and met Maggie's eyes. "Tell me the significance of it," she said.

"It is a covenant," Maggie said. "Binding the evil powers of the Otherworld to the Empire. It says that the Empire will rule the world by the power of the Otherworld until the leaders of that world's evil come to claim it. The forces of the Otherworld work through the Order of the Spider."

"Huss has spoken of them," Libuse said. "He has always said that they hold great power, and that somehow they hold sway over the Empire itself. He has long spoken of them as our true enemy. But I am not sure that they exist, either . . . even Huss has never seen such a person face to face, except for one woman who he thinks belonged to the Order."

"I have seen them," Maggie said. "I have seen more of the Otherworld than I want to. And all of it has been so black."

No, Maggie realized even as she spoke the words, it had not. Huss's tale of the King—Marja's words of one who shone like all the heavenly lights together—those things had not been black. They had filled her with the "awe of beauty and wonder and goodness" that Libuse longed for and could not believe in. She thought of the black-robed stranger who had met her in Huss's burned out house. A fiery thrill coursed through her as she recalled the power of the song that had flowed through her then. Above all, Mary's song had not been black. Wild and free and powerful, but not black. Suddenly she thought that she could sing again, that she wanted to sing again. She could weave such a song that all of the glory and beauty of the ancient days would wash through the farmyard like a tide, and no one could stand in its wake and not believe.

Behind them, Pat cleared her throat. They turned to see her pointing to the farmhouse, far over the fields. "Looks like the Ploughman has returned," she said.

Libuse gathered her skirts and stood. There was nothing more to say. Together they walked back to the farmhouse.

* * *

"You will arrive after dark, but the gates of the city will still be open. The men will take you to an inn where the service is reasonable." The Ploughman reached into his cloak and drew out a small leather pouch full of coins. "This should keep you till you find work. I'm sorry there isn't more."

Pat took the pouch and thanked him. "I am ready to leave," she told him.

"Then say your good-byes," the Ploughman commanded gently. "You ride in ten minutes."

Maggie reached out and put her hand on Pat's shoulder. Across from her, Mrs. Cook did the same. For a minute they stood in silence. "Oh, for goodness' sake, say something," Pat burst out. "I can't stand to have all this emotion hanging over my head."

Mrs. Cook said, "Are you sure this is a good idea?"

"Yes," Pat said. She hugged Mrs. Cook tightly. Mrs. Cook sniffled and wiped her eyes when Pat let her go.

"Doesn't really seem fair, does it?" Maggie said softly. "We've only just come together again, and now you're leaving."

"I won't be away long," Pat said. "Anyway, I volunteered. I want to do this."

The two young women hugged each other tightly. Maggie

whispered, "Be careful. And send us back only good news."

"Take care of yourself, too," Pat answered. "No more disappearing. Stay by Mrs. Cook. She'd die of loneliness without you."

"Enough of that," Mrs. Cook interjected. "I can handle myself with or without a couple of scamps like you. My life would certainly be quieter without you."

Two men arrived in the courtyard. Pat was swept up in the bustle of preparing to ride. Before either Maggie or Mrs. Cook had a chance to say anything more, Pat was riding across the fields in a flurry of dust.

Maggie slipped her arm through Mrs. Cook's. Just before she disappeared into the tree line, Pat turned around and saluted farewell. Maggie and Mrs. Cook returned the salute, and Mrs. Cook smiled.

"She never could stay in one place for long," she said.

"Did you worry about me terribly when I was gone?" Maggie asked.

"Oh, yes," Mrs. Cook said. "Would I have come after you if I hadn't?"

"I don't know," Maggie said. "I thought perhaps you had some other reason for coming here."

"What other reason would I have?" Mrs. Cook said. "Besides the fact that Pat was going, and I couldn't bear to be alone again."

"Well . . ." Maggie faltered and continued. "You were a member of the council. I can't help wondering—did seeing Old Dan and Lord Robert again make you miss the old days?"

Mrs. Cook became suddenly very quiet, and she waited a long while before answering. "I don't really know. Worlds unseen—well, who wouldn't be fascinated with such an idea? To tell you the truth, Maggie, maybe I did start to miss the council days. But if I did, it wasn't on account of Old Dan, or Lord Robert either."

"Then what did it?" Maggie asked.

"The girl," Mrs. Cook replied. "Virginia Ramsey. The minute I laid eyes on her, with her wrists bound and her face so deathly pale as to drain the blood from your own face, I thought to myself, 'That girl is hope. And someone is trying to kill hope.' I suppose that's a very odd thing to think, but there you are. If you hadn't been missing still, Maggie, I would have gone after Virginia myself."

"Hope," Maggie repeated. Into her mind flashed a phrase that Jarin Huss had read to her: *When they see beyond the sky . . . take these Gifts of My Outstretched Hand; Weave them together; I shall come.*

"She sees beyond the sky," Maggie said. It took her a moment to realize that Mrs. Cook was looking at her strangely.

"What did you say?" Mrs. Cook asked.

"'When they see beyond the sky,'" Maggie said. "It's a line from an old prophecy. Jarin Huss read it to me."

"I remember," Mrs. Cook said abruptly. "Lord Robert thinks like you do. He said Virginia was Gifted."

Mrs. Cook stopped and wiped her eyes ferociously, and Maggie waited for her to continue. But the elderly woman was done speaking, and she wandered off to the kitchen saying something about Mrs. Korak needing help with supper. Maggie watched her go with troubled eyes, but she did not go after her. Somehow she knew that she ought not to pry.

* * *

Maggie awoke that night to the sound of horse hooves in the yard. A faint blue light was coming in one of the windows —the moon, Maggie thought, and remembered that there was no moon on this night. But no, she must be mistaken. Moonlight was undoubtedly shining through the window.

She climbed softly out of bed and tip-toed to the window, expecting to see one of the Ploughman's riders in the yard. It was late, and for a moment she wondered if there was trouble.

When she reached the window, her eyes opened wide. Her fingers reached up and lightly brushed the window pane as though she would touch the being outside.

It was a man on a horse, but both rider and animal were larger than any Maggie had ever seen. The horse's eyes glowed with white fire. Its mane and tail were blue-white against a body the colour of the night sky. The man wore a long, dark blue cloak with stars woven all through it,and the stars were shining—the source of the light that fell on Maggie's face and lit the farmyard with magic. The man wore a tunic and leggings and knee-high boots. Around his neck was a silver band, and he held a silver horn in his hand. On his back was slung a bow and a quiver full of arrows that shone like the stars in the cloak. The man's face was unlike any Maggie had ever seen. It was a beautiful face, both fine and rugged, and framed by long black hair. The man's eyes were white and blazing, much like the horse's.

As Maggie watched, the horse reared up on its hind legs. The man raised the silver horn to his lips and sounded a long, deep blast. Before the sound had faded away, the horse and

259

rider had disappeared.

Maggie's heart burned inside of her, and a phrase she had never heard before was suddenly playing through her mind.

"*Hear the call of the Huntsman's horn;*
"*The stars all sing when the chase is on;*
"*Over the sky fields and cross the moon;*
"*The darkness meets its downfall soon.*"

As the words began to beat a rhythm inside of her, Maggie ran out of the bunkhouse and into the yard. There were no hoofprints, no marks to show that anyone had been here. Only . . . Maggie crouched down to the hard-packed earth where a faint light was glowing. She picked up the shining thing carefully and found that it was a thread. It must have come from the Huntsman's cloak, for its slender length shone with the blue-white light of the stars. In her cupped hands it shone all the brighter.

Maggie stood in the center of the empty farmyard and let the light of the thread dance on the earth and the sides of the buildings, recalling the mystical moment when the whole yard was as full of the light as if one of the stars had come down to earth.

With her heart full to the bursting, Maggie sat down cross-legged in the dirt and tilted her head up to the night sky.

She fell asleep there.

12

Betrayal

MAGGIE AWOKE, vaguely aware that she was stiff and sore and a little cold. Someone was shaking her gently. Her eyes fluttered open to see Libuse looking down at her with a face full of concern.

Libuse sat back and let out a relieved breath when Maggie's eyes opened. "You're all right," she said. "I was afraid something had happened."

"Something did," Maggie said, sitting up. Her mind was cloudy and she was not entirely sure why she was sleeping in a farmyard. An image of a horse and rider flashed through her mind.

"I dreamed . . ." Maggie began. Her hand tightened around the silver thread. She held it up in front of her face with awe-filled eyes. "No," she said. "It wasn't a dream."

"What is it, Maggie?" Libuse asked. "What happened?"

"I saw a man from the Otherworld," Maggie said. "If I could call him a man, though I feel sure he's not one. Not really."

Libuse looked skeptical, but she was listening.

"He was a hunter," Maggie said. "The Huntsman—he

blew his horn. It was a signal." She smiled. The thread felt like a precious secret in her hands, throbbing with hope. "Things aren't only stirring here. The Otherworld is preparing for battle, too."

"Maggie, I—" Libuse started to say. Maggie took her hand and pressed the thread into it.

"Keep this," Maggie said. "It's a sign. We're not alone."

Libuse cupped the thread in her hands. Her eyes widened as she realized that it was shining.

A minute later, Mrs. Korak ordered them inside for breakfast. There was work to be done, and Libuse and Maggie did not speak again that day.

* * *

Virginia and Lord Robert had not yet settled into their rooms at a Pravik inn before the name of Jarin Huss reached their ears: the venerable old professor had been charged with insurrection against the Empire and the murder of an Eastern princess. His trial—and doubtless his execution—was less than a fortnight away.

Lord Robert paled at the news, but Virginia only sank deeper into silence. She had not spoken once since they had set out for the city.

The next morning Lord Robert left the inn in search of news—alone. It seemed wise to leave Virginia behind closed doors. The city was swarming with High Police.

* * *

Two days later a rebel carrier brought news from Pat. She had a job, not, unfortunately for her tastes, with the theatre. She was working in a dress shop, but enough gossip passed through every day to make the long hours more than worth her while.

The date for the public trial and sure execution of Jarin Huss and Jerome was still unknown, but old women with uncanny instincts for such things put it at less than two weeks.

The Ploughman sat in long silence when he read the letter, his fist crumpling around the paper. It was not enough time. Libuse stood behind him and whispered in his ear. He reached up his hand, the one with the ruby ring, to take hers and hold it tightly. Watching them made Maggie's throat ache. She thought of Jerome, and immediately wished she hadn't.

That day, Maggie followed some of the farmers into the barn. They carried heavy sacks, collected from every smithy in the region. They moved aside straw and dirt and pulled up four long floorboards to reveal case after case of swords, spears, bows, and arrows. The contents of the sacks went in along with them.

The next few days passed in a blur. Hundreds of men arrived at the farm every morning before the sun came up, farmers and peasants, boys as young as thirteen and men as old as sixty. They pulled bows, clashed swords, and marched in rows as the Ploughman gave orders.

Practice.

Mrs. Cook, Mrs. Korak, Libuse, and Maggie worked for hours in the kitchen, struggling to keep up with the appetites of the peasant men. Most brought some food with them for the women to prepare. They knew better than to expect the

263

Ploughman to pull food out of thin air.

Another letter from Pat. The trial would take place in four days.

The Ploughman clenched his fist again and went back to work.

"Three days from now the Tax Gathering begins," Libuse told Maggie in the bunkhouse, over the light of a candle. "Many will come to Pravik from all over the province. Zarras wants this trial public."

More weapons arrived. More men came to march and shoot and fence in the fields.

One evening, the men took their weapons home with them. A few stayed, and they sat with the Ploughman at Mrs. Korak's long table and argued and pounded the wood and pored over maps, planning and planning well into the night.

Maggie went out into the yard sometime after four o'clock in the morning. The sky was cloudy, but here and there breaks in the grey allowed stars to shine through. The moon was wreathed by thin, ghostly wisps of cloud.

The moonbeams shone straight into Maggie's soul. She opened her mouth and sang softly.

Hear the call of the Huntsman's horn . . .

* * *

Lord Robert wandered through the city, listening. He heard nothing new: Huss and his apprentice were imprisoned in Pravik Castle under heavy guard; the apprentice, acting under Jarin Huss's orders, had murdered the last living heir of the ancient royal family of Sloczka.

Lord Robert had not seen his old friend in forty years, but it had not felt like such a long time until now. The murderer who awaited trial in Pravik Castle could hardly be the same man who had sat at the council table in Angslie and opened up the ancient writings for his companions. Yet it was the same man. Time had taken its strange toll, and Lord Robert felt utterly alone.

The worst of it was, he could not shake a feeling of responsibility. Had he somehow brought his old friend to this? The rumours on the streets spoke of Huss as an odd man. There were whispers of a strange and mysterious branch of science and history that had led the old professor into madness. Was it true? Had the study of the Otherworld led to this?

If it had . . . what did it matter?

Lord Robert clenched his jaw as he walked. There was power in the Otherworld. Enough to rescue a friend, to change the course of things. If only he could touch it.

His head hurt.

He was walking along a cobbled path beside the dark river. Young trees lined his way. Their yellow leaves crunched beneath his feet, and the breeze from over the river was cold.

He lifted his eyes and saw her.

Evelyn.

She was leaning on the wrought iron fence overlooking the river. A rain of yellow leaves drifted to the ground all around her. She wore a dress of burgundy and gold, and her black hair was shining. She looked unchanged, as young as the day they had met: young and breathtakingly beautiful, and full of power. His heart caught in his throat. She turned, and their eyes met.

No dream, this.

She turned away and began to run.

His heart pounding, tears rushing to his eyes, he ran after her.

Through the streets they ran, Evelyn always just ahead, running like a deer. There was no one else anywhere; it was only the two of them in the world. Weaving through the alleys and the streets, now by the river and now in the city, Lord Robert did not know how far they went. But suddenly they were standing on the Guardian Bridge and all of the white marble statues were stretching their hands out toward them, and Evelyn stopped, leaning against the side of the bridge. Lord Robert was there, and she was in his arms, and she was kissing him.

Forty years had not passed; it had only been weeks since he had seen her last. Surely, surely, it had only been weeks. He wanted to ask why she had left him, where she had gone. He had suspected her of so much! But he had been wrong; he knew now that he had been wrong.

She moved away from him, just a little, so that they could look into each other's eyes. Her eyes were so black, black like her hair, and beguiling. "You doubted me, my love," she said.

He hung his head. "I did not know," he faltered. "Where —where did you go?"

"I had to leave," she whispered. "My enemies were at work. They would have killed me if I had not gone."

"I would have gone with you," he said.

"I would not put you in danger," she said.

"You broke my heart," he told her.

"But I am here now," she replied.

It did not occur to him to wonder how it was, why it was, that she was here now. She was, and that was enough. He was lost in her presence, a man in love with a mist that blinded his eyes and closed his ears, with a being of power that made his heart ache with longing.

She began to move away from him, and he held her hands to keep her from running away. "Will you leave me again?" he asked, his voice breaking.

"No, my love," she said. "But our enemies are once more at work. I need your help. You have something we need— something that will take us deeper into the worlds unseen."

He could not answer before she was in his arms again, kissing him again, and for a long time he could see and hear and feel nothing but her. When she had moved back, her arms around his neck, he said, "I will do anything you ask of me."

Her deep red lips curled in a smile. "I know you will, dear one. I know."

* * *

Lord Robert did not return to the inn that night, and Virginia did not sleep. She sat in a rocking chair in the corner of her room and listened to the creak of the floorboards. She had found her way to the window and opened it, so that the hawk could sit on the sill. Its presence comforted her. Once she nearly fell asleep, and she imagined herself back on the mountainside with her fingers entwined in the wiry fur of her hound. His whole body rose and fell as he breathed, deep breathing . . . but no, she awoke, and the hound was gone. The hawk stirred and ruffled its feathers.

Visions visited her throughout the night. She saw Pat, working in a dress shop, listening intently to the gossip of dozens of housewives and maidservants who passed through. She saw the streets below her window filled with the clash of swords and the shouts of battle. She saw scenes she had seen before: a tall man on horseback, shouting orders, the air twisting and warping in golden waves around him; a young woman with auburn hair running along the ramparts of the city wall.

Virginia wept that night, because she saw another vision as well: that of the laird falling into darkness, while she tried to reach him and found that she could not.

His long absence did not surprise her. When he left she had felt, deep inside, that he would not be back. His fall had begun already.

Near morning, the vision came again. Only it was different now, for when Virginia reached out to stop the laird's fall, he pulled her down with him.

So she waited.

* * *

The year's first frost was on the ground when Maggie awoke. She rolled over with a groan—her journey through Galce had not taught her to love sleeping on the ground. All around her, the Ploughman's soldiers were already packing up camp.

Maggie jumped to her feet, embarrassed to be sleeping still when the others were already at work. She expected a reprimand, but the men said nothing.

They had slept outside the walls of Pravik, surrounded by wagons full of crops and goods—taxes. They would enter the city in less than an hour. Maggie rubbed her stiff arms and yawned, picking up the wooden crutch she had brought from the house of the Ploughman. She had ridden a horse most of the way here, but she would be walking into the city.

She looked around at the little group of six men who were readying themselves for the day. They were a harmless looking crew, farmers all. One man wore a wide-brimmed hat over bushy gray hair that stuck out at the bottom; another rubbed a lucky coin given him by his sweetheart. There were other groups like them camped throughout the woods, none farther than an hour away from Pravik. Throughout the day they would drift in, one and two at a time, until the city was full of self-made soldiers. Under their clothes the men carried swords and long knives, quivers full of arrows, and bows. Some wore carefully patched leather armour.

The Empire had a strict limit on how much weaponry peasants were permitted to own and carry, and the rebels were smashing the limit to little bits. Maggie knew it, as well as she knew how much trouble she would be in if anyone discovered that the cause of her limp was a sword strapped to her leg beneath her skirt. She sat down on a fallen log and strapped the sword on while the men finished their own preparations, then stood and practiced hobbling around on her crutch. No one would bother to search a cripple, or at least, that was the official hope of the rebels. An inordinate number of cripples would enter Pravik throughout the day and evening.

One of the men finished loading a bad-tempered, foul-smelling donkey with long bundles of straw, in which was hidden a liberal number of arrows and a long bow. The donkey brayed loudly, and the farmer-soldier smiled. Hopefully no gatekeeper would be in a mood to meddle with the beast.

Dirt was kicked over the fire, and the sorry-looking company headed down the road. They were mostly on foot now, their horses acting as pack animals. One horse pulled a wagon full of corn. The bottom of the wagon was false. Row after row of swords rested just beneath it. They were well-made swords, forged by blacksmiths who could have been jailed for the trouble. Strapped to the sides of the wagon, hidden beneath the corn, were heavy oak quarterstaves.

They walked together for a while. Soon some pulled ahead while others lagged behind. The roads soon became crowded with tenant farmers and tradesmen. All of the Eastern Lands seemed to be coming to the Tax Gathering. Maggie hobbled along and kept her eyes cast down. The sword chafed against her leg, and she winced. At least she did not have to fake the discomfort of walking.

In about an hour, she had reached the outskirts of Pravik. Maggie avoided looking around to see how many men she recognized. She knew there were about two hundred militia men seeking entrance into the city, and a hundred more still to come with the Ploughman. The thought made her heart beat faster. She imagined Mrs. Cook worrying about her back at the farm.

"There's nothing to worry about," she said under her breath as she hobbled into the city.

By the time she located Pat's dress shop, her leg was raw from the rubbing of leather and metal, and the tears of pain in her eyes were real. She pulled herself up the steps to the shop and entered with a grimace. A bell rang to announce her arrival. Before she could properly take in her surroundings, she heard Pat call.

"Maggie! Maggie, what's happened?" Pat rushed up, all concern on her face. She linked her arm through Maggie's and turned to a large woman behind the counter.

"This is my friend," Pat explained. "I'll just take her back to my sewing room, out of your way."

Without waiting for permission, Pat hustled Maggie to the back of the shop and through a door into a snug, well-lit room. Before the door shut behind them, they heard the woman's voice bellowing, "Don't let it interfere with your work!"

Pat stuck her tongue out at the door and then turned to Maggie again. "What has . . ." she began to say, and broke off when Maggie lifted her skirt to reveal the end of a leather scabbard. Pat's jaw dropped for only a moment.

"Is he here?" she asked, her voice dropped to a barely audible whisper.

"He comes tomorrow," Maggie answered. "But our men are filling the city."

"How many?" Pat asked.

"Two hundred," Maggie told her. "Another hundred or so with the Ploughman."

Pat frowned. "I haven't been able to get a message out to warn you. This city is crawling with soldiers. They suspect trouble, I think."

"How are the people of Pravik going to react?" Maggie asked. "Libuse says she hopes for support from them."

"I don't think we'll get much help from the upper class,"

said Pat. "They don't like what's happening, but they're too busy courting the favour of Athrom to oppose Zarras openly. But the poor people are sick of being taxed out of health and home, and they're tired of the High Police. We might have their help. They're not well armed, of course."

"No," Maggie said. "Of course not."

"Did you all bring weapons with you?" Pat asked.

"Most of us," Maggie told her.

Pat sat down in her sewing chair and picked up a half-embroidered cloth with a sigh. "You realize that all of this is complete insanity," she said. "And I still haven't figured out why I'm on the rebels' side and not keeping the peace."

Maggie sat down gingerly, careful to keep the sword in place. "You've been on the rebels' side for a long time, haven't you?" she asked.

Pat looked up, but her eyes did not meet Maggie's. "Pravik is not the only place where revolution is stirring, in some form or another," she said quietly. "There are movements like the Ploughman's in Cryneth, and Londren and Cranburgh as well. But none are so foolhardy or so desperate as to try something like this."

Pat looked up from her stitching suddenly. She met Maggie's eyes this time. "Do you think we're actually going to win?" she asked.

Maggie thought of the Huntsman. "Yes."

"All I know is that all my life I've been chafing against the Empire," Pat said, "and now for the first time I may be able to hit it where it hurts."

She stood up and moved to a window overlooking the street. "On the other hand," her voice came, "this might be my chance to die."

She turned around and smiled wryly. "I don't think I'll bother telling the boss I won't be coming in tomorrow."

She sat down with a thump and picked up her sewing again, stitching furiously. "Forgive me if I ignore you for a while," Pat said. "The old battleaxe'll kill me if I don't finish this today, and it'd be a shame for me to die before the battle. Where's Mrs. Cook?"

"Back on the farm," Maggie said. "She and Mrs. Korak have vowed to protect the old homestead with their lives."

"Good, good," Pat said. "I pity the soldier who will brave their rolling pins and frying pans, don't you?" She grinned and then suddenly became serious. "I'm really glad she's not going to be here for the battle. If it comes to a battle."

"So am I," Maggie said, and her eyes wandered to the window. Rising above the rooftops of the city, the towering height of Pravik Castle was plainly in sight. Her pulse quickened. Jerome was in there, and Huss. For the two of them, hundreds of men would risk their lives and their dreams. "So am I."

* * *

Lord Robert walked with his head bowed. He rubbed his eyes with his fingers. He felt as though a fire was burning behind his eyes, low and hot and threatening. Evelyn stepped closer to his side, and she put her hand through his arm and walked with her fingers resting in the crook of his elbow. Her touch made the fire cool, and he lifted his head higher.

The inn was just ahead, its high roof silhouetted against

the darkening sky. The moon was shining and stars were just beginning to come out, but from the silence in the streets, it might have been midnight. It was a deep, foreboding silence; portent of approaching evil. Lord Robert thought of all Evelyn had revealed to him, and he shivered—and felt his heart become colder, steeled, ready to do what he had agreed to do.

With his next step the silence was shattered by a blood-chilling cry. A dark form hurtled out of the sky toward Lord Robert and Evelyn. Evelyn cried out, and Lord Robert threw up his hands to protect her. The hawk sunk its claws into his arm, drawing blood, and knocked the laird to the ground with its great weight. He struggled against it, desperate to keep the bird's beak and claws away from his face. Evelyn came up behind the bird with a knife in her hands, and he heard the hawk's cry as the knife plunged down. With a scream, the bird lifted high into the air again.

"Get up!" Evelyn commanded. Lord Robert scrambled to his feet. He crouched defensively, watching the black sky for a sign of attack. For a long moment there was nothing. He saw the movement of black shadow against black sky—the bird was diving toward them again. Lord Robert had pulled out a knife, and he slashed at the hawk as it bore down on him. Once again man and bird fell, but the hawk was twice wounded now. It flopped to the ground and began to dance, lashing out with its beak, its wings spread low over the cobblestones.

The hawk slashed at Lord Robert's legs, tearing the tall man's trousers and drawing blood. A movement from behind caused the hawk to swing around, but not fast enough. Evelyn brought a heavy stick down on the creature's head, and with a piteous cry the bird lay still.

"Let's go," Evelyn said, her voice ragged. Despite her command, she stood for a moment watching the dead hawk. Moonlight glinted off the bird's beautiful red-gold feathers, and for an instant Lord Robert thought he saw fear in Evelyn's face.

"What's wrong?" he asked, drawing close to her.

"It is nothing," she said. "Only—what makes a hawk dive out of the sky in the night, when it cannot see? The enemy is at work. Where is the girl?"

Lord Robert led Evelyn into the inn and through the half-lit dining room where a few stragglers were still picking at their suppers. Lord Robert's bloody arms and legs drew looks and whispered comments, but Evelyn waved her hand and the room fell silent. The people turned back to their dinners, disinterested in the intruders.

Up the stairs they went, and down the hall until they had reached Virginia's room. Lord Robert opened the door and stepped inside, leaving Evelyn in the door frame with his back to her, where he could not see the smile that disfigured her face.

The blind girl was standing at the open window, her hands in front of her. At the sound of the opening door her back grew rigid, but she said nothing.

"Virginia," the laird said, approaching her slowly. "I've come for you."

Slowly Virginia turned. Lord Robert saw a long feather in her hands, red and gold like the hawk whose life was bleeding away on the street below. Her unseeing eyes seemed to look through him, to the figure in the doorway. Something like recognition passed over Virginia's face.

Before the laird could move or say anything else, Virginia

275

took a step toward him and reached up with one hand. Her fingers touched Lord Robert's face gently and fell back to her side.

"Is it too late for you?" she asked softly. Lord Robert felt a pang in his heart. Evelyn stepped closer to him. His coldness returned. Cold strength. He could not let his emotions get in the way.

"Take me if you can," Virginia said, but Lord Robert could not tell if she was speaking to him or to Evelyn. "But I will not go willingly."

Lord Robert felt Evelyn's hand on his shoulder and heard her rasp, "Do it!"

He reached inside his coat and pulled the needle out slowly, almost reluctantly. He lifted it slowly and then jabbed it into Virginia's neck. She gasped and fell against him, momentarily struggling to stay on her feet. Then he felt her grip on his arms loosen, and she slipped to the floor with a long exhalation.

Evelyn made a sound a little like laughter, and said, "Get her up! We're running out of time."

Lord Robert knelt and gently lifted Virginia in his arms. It seemed like only yesterday that he had carried her just this way, away from Angslie to Londren, and then to the continent. Evelyn was already rushing out of the room, and he hastened to follow her.

In the dining room not one person looked up to see what was happening. A spell seemed to have settled over the room, enclosing every person in his own private cares and thoughts. They left the inn without molestation and walked hurriedly through the streets toward the outskirts of the city, stepping around the body of the hawk on their way out.

Just outside the city, three men in black masks waited for them. They had two extra horses with them, and Evelyn mounted one with graceful ease. One of the men silently took Virginia from Lord Robert and threw her across his saddle, mounting behind her. Lord Robert started to protest that he would keep her with him, but a word from Evelyn silenced him. The laird mounted the last horse, and the silent company rode away.

They quickly left the road, heading into deep forest. Their path angled up sharply. The horses picked their way through the foliage, almost fearful in their steps. At last the company stopped and dismounted. Tethering the horses, they continued on foot. The man whose horse had borne Virginia now carried her as they pushed deeper and deeper through the trees.

At last they stepped out onto a bare hilltop. The ground sloped fiercely down on the other side, covered with trees. Down the slope and over the trees, the city of Pravik gleamed.

But it was the hilltop that called all of Lord Robert's attention now. In the center of the clearing burned a great bonfire, but its flames were an eerie blue, and the smoke that rose from the fire moved like a living thing. A figure in black stood with his back to the fire. His robes fell over his hands and feet and shadowed his face. At the edge of the clearing, armed men stood in silence.

The black-robed man stepped away from the fire and came toward the new arrivals. Their escort had slipped away, leaving Lord Robert, Evelyn, and the man who still held Virginia. The man stepped closer and made a sign in the air. Lord Robert could see the tip of a white beard and two piercing grey eyes beneath the black hood.

The man came close and held out his hand, the sleeve falling back to reveal a white, bony hand with purple veins that stood out like cords. Evelyn gracefully bowed on one knee and kissed the extended hand. The man nodded and Evelyn rose.

"My Lord Skraetock," she said, "I have brought you a new ally. Lord Robert Sinclair."

Lord Robert bowed. The sight of the man both repulsed him and drew him. There was power in him. It made the air around him vibrate like a thousand insects' wings.

"Welcome, Lord of Angslie," Skraetock said in a voice that was low and rich.

Lord Skraetock lifted a hand and motioned to the guards who waited around the edge of the clearing. Two men stepped forward and began to bind Lord Robert's hands behind his back before he could move to stop them. He opened his mouth to protest, but the rich voice interrupted him.

"I am sorry, Lord Robert," he said. "I trust that in the future we will have no need of such manners. But for now your bonds are necessary. You are not ready to stand in the presence of the Covenant Fire unprotected. Without restraint you might find yourself acting against your own best interest."

When Lord Robert's hands had been securely bound, the men led him to a place at the edge of the clearing where he could see the bonfire. Guards stood on either side of him.

"Now, faithful one," said Lord Skraetock to Evelyn, his voice deepening, "what *else* have you brought me?"

"The seer," Evelyn said with a cruel smile. She jerked her head to motion the man forward, and he stepped forward so that the light of the bonfire fell on Virginia's face.

"Stand her on her feet," Lord Skraetock commanded, and the man obeyed, holding Virginia up.

The pale, bony hand reached out and a cruel light blazed in the grey eyes. "Awake, Gifted One," said the deep, rich voice.

Virginia drew in a deep, shuddering breath, and Lord Robert saw her stand on her own. Evelyn stepped closer.

"Bow down before your master," Evelyn commanded.

Virginia lifted her face and said, "I serve only one master: I serve the King."

Lord Skraetock drew back his hand as though he would strike Virginia, but instead he brought his hand down lightly and ran his fingers along the side of her face. She shrank back from his touch, and he laughed, a low, rippling, mocking laugh.

"You kneel within the protection of the Covenant Flame," he said. "Your exiled king has no power here. Here is only the power of fire and darkness, *my* power! I am the lord here, and no other."

"The King will return from exile," Virginia said. She seemed to be struggling to get the words out. "I have seen him, and I have seen the awakening of his army." Quietly, terribly quietly, she whispered, "*I remember.*"

"You have seen lies and foolishness!" Skraetock hissed. "What good has trust in the king done you? Only a blind woman could fail to see that we have won."

He stepped closer and cocked his head. "But you are not so blind, are you? If I wish to see I must sacrifice for the power. A power you were born with. Yes, you have seen many things. Tonight you will see for me."

"I cannot control what I see," Virginia said.

"I can," Skraetock said. His eyes drank in the sight of the girl. "You have no idea what you are, do you? But I know. I know the power in you."

"I will not help you," Virginia said, pulling one arm away from the man who held her.

Skraetock's voice grew thin. "We shall see," he said. "Evelyn?"

Evelyn motioned the guard away and stood behind Virginia herself. She began to trace patterns in the air, and Virginia gasped for air. Her knees buckled and she fell to the ground, her breath trembling with pain.

"Evelyn brought you here to make atonement," Skraetock said, speaking to the blind girl who lifted her face in defiance. Her unseeing eyes shone with the effort.

"You see, a few months back she misplaced something important to me," Skraetock said. "I want to find it. You will find it for me."

Virginia opened her mouth to speak and cried out in pain instead. She had raised herself to her knees, and now she fell again. Evelyn continued to trace patterns in the air behind her.

"More," Skraetock said. "Zarras the Incompetent has been whining for my help. He thinks he is losing control of his lands. He is. So you will help us find the rebels and destroy them. Do you understand?"

He raised his hands swiftly, palms up, and iron bars formed of the dust of the ground and surrounded Virginia. In moments a cage surrounded her, and it rose until it hung above the fire.

Skraetock and Evelyn turned and faced the fire. As the

heat beat on their upraised hands, the dark stain of a tattoo appeared on the palm of each one's hand: a spider.

* * *

Maggie had brought the scroll with her. She sat with it spread out before her in the little room Pat had rented. Candlelight illuminated the ink scratchings in such a way as to make the writing seem alive, dancing with the motion of the flickering flame.

A movement in the shadows made Maggie jump. She laughed a little with embarrassment when Pat sat down beside her.

"I thought you were going to give that thing to the Ploughman," Pat said.

"I meant to," Maggie said. "It just . . . never was the right time."

Pat reached out as if to touch the parchment, and drew her hand back just before she did. "The light makes those signatures on the bottom look new, somehow," she said. "Still wet. As though it has just been signed."

"It has never looked quite so evil before," Maggie said. The signatures shone red-black and seemed to run on the parchment, spreading their stain.

"It's not the parchment at all," Pat said suddenly. "It's the light . . . look!"

Maggie turned to see what Pat was talking about.

The candle flame had turned blue.

* * *

The Ploughman sat by the fire, his eyes scanning the heavens. The stars were shining brightly across the sky, ornamented by the sickle moon.

Who am I? he asked.

A man, his voice replied.

More than a man, a deeper voice inside him said. He felt a warmth brush past his face and heard the faintest echo of clanking armour. He closed his eyes and took a deep breath to rid himself of the delusions. Childhood delusions. *Something with me,* he had said as a child. *There is something with me. I am never alone.*

He opened his eyes again and searched the stars more intently. A gold mist passed before him and disappeared.

"What are you looking for?" Libuse asked. She was dressed like a soldier, in tunic and trousers, with leather armour and a sword hanging from her hip. On her back was slung a spear.

"A sign," the Ploughman said, turning to look on his love. Her hair was shimmering in the moonlight, and her eyes glowed as warmly as any star. She had braided a silver thread into her hair, and it seemed to shine in the darkness.

"Tell me," he said. "Do you believe that the stars hear us, as some say they do? Is there help for us out there?"

Libuse looked to the sky. Her fingers played with the glowing thread in her hair. "I think there must be, my love. Surely the power that has given us courage for the fight will not abandon us in the middle of it."

"We need more than courage now," the Ploughman said. "We need victory."

"And we shall have it," Libuse said. "I do not think it is the stars themselves that help us," she said. A smile began to play at her mouth. "Not the stars, but the One the stars themselves serve."

"If there is such a One," the Ploughman said, "I would give anything to have him riding beside me now."

"Perhaps he is," Libuse said.

The Ploughman reached out and took his lady's hand. In the moonlight he kissed it gently. "If not," he said, "it is enough for me that you are here. You are my courage, my heart."

13

The End Begins

THE SMOKE RISING AROUND VIRGINIA DRUGGED HER SENSES. She heard cries as though they were very far away—men's cries, death cries. The guards? She smelled blood and heard the hiss of liquid and fire, and beneath it chanting.

She heard rippling laughter inside her head. He was inside her head.

"Find the scroll!" Skraetock commanded, his voice ringing through her mind like the painful sound of a bell in a closed space. She clenched her fists and thought back.

No.

Pain washed through her, and she cried out. In a moment it was gone. It left her panting for breath. Still fighting.

"Find the scroll," commanded the voice again.

I will not.

Once again pain coursed through her, wave after wave, unceasing. She curled up on the floor of the cage, trying to shut it out, to stop the agony. The pain sharpened in her eyes and she covered them with the heels of her hands, skin wet with tears of agony. She fought for control: the control to speak—to call out for help. She could not. Skraetock would not leave her alone long enough. The pain ceased suddenly and left her trembling. She tried again to form a word, but still she could not.

Something was happening inside her mind now. Her head was an instrument and someone was trying to play it. It was a warm feeling, warm and enveloping, and it called to her to let go: relax, release her control. She nearly gave in when a deeper part of her fought its way to the top.

No!

He was tearing her apart. Her eyes hurt so badly. It would never stop, she thought, until she was dead.

But something in her mind was letting go. She was losing control, no matter how hard she tried to hang on. Light played through her mind, stabbing her. The visions came, though tears ran down her face as she wished them away. Away where he could not see them.

She saw the auburn haired young woman she had seen before. She was sitting in a room in Pravik with a scroll opened before her. Pat was with her, looking over her shoulder. They seemed uneasy.

The room they were in was nondescript, a little rented flat just like a hundred others in the city, and yet Virginia knew exactly where they were. From the laughter in her head, she knew that *he* knew, too. In the same way, Virginia knew the young woman's name and how she had come to have the scroll. Through the searing pain and the sound of chanting voices that dragged her down deeper into darkness, Virginia at last managed to cry out:

"Run, Maggie! They're coming!"

Far back in her mind, amidst the tearing visions, she saw

another face—a boy's face. She sent the message to him as well, though it took more strength than she had and left her feeling as though something inside was shattering.

"Yes," hissed the voice of Lord Skraetock. "We're coming! They can't run anymore!"

Virginia felt as though claws were digging into her neck. She choked for air. Laughter flowed all around her, mingling with the chanting and the smoke, and the claws released her.

"Now, where are the rebels?" Skraetock's voice asked.

Virginia could not stop the visions. It was the future she saw. Men, brave men, golden men inside with tawny lion's manes and true hearts, though outside they were common and plain. They stood up to the Empire and its black ways. They won.

Until the creatures came into Pravik, howling and shrieking and tearing and killing, and Skraetock was laughing.

Everything went black. The pain was gone. Virginia closed her eyes and tears slipped out as despair slowly overtook her. She had betrayed the people and the purposes of the King.

She let go, and slipped away into utter blackness.

* * *

Maggie rolled up the scroll abruptly and stuffed it back inside her coat. She laughed uneasily. "Funny how a piece of paper can make me so nervous."

Pat was still staring at the candle. "It's gone back to its normal colour now," she said. "If you hadn't seen it too, I would have said I'd imagined it."

There was a sound outside like a door slamming, and

Maggie jumped. "What was that?" she said.

"Just the neighbour's dog, playing with the gate again," Pat said. "Are you all right, Maggie?"

Maggie's heart was pounding, but she nodded. "Just a little jumpy. I'm sorry."

Pat stood up and stretched, yawning. "Never thought I'd say this, but since Mrs. Cook isn't here to offer you some tea, how about I make some? It's good for the nerves, you know."

Maggie laughed and nodded. "I know. Thank you, Pat."

* * *

Nicolas's feet hit the cobblestones as he flew over the bridge. He was running blindly, following only instinct . . . and praying, praying to the stars that he was not too late. He had come back to look for her. Something within had driven him to look for her. Now urgency propelled him forward.

His fingers reached for the slender sword that hung from his waist. He skidded to a stop. The bridge was behind him and a webwork of streets lay before him. His pounding heart sent him off in one direction, and he ran again.

Nicolas Fisher did not know what he would find; he only knew what he had heard, and the fear it had wakened in him. A voice he did not know, crying out in deep pain:

"*Run, Maggie! They're coming!*"

* * *

The kettle had just begun its high-pitched whine when a knock pounded at the door. Pat frowned.

"Who in the world?" she said. She rose and called out,"What do you want?"

"High Police," came the answer. "Open the door."

Maggie and Pat exchanged anxious glances. Maggie pulled Pat's long knife down from its resting place on the fireplace mantle and handed it to her. She drew her own sword out of its sheath and stood back from the door, nodding slightly.

Pat flung the door open and drove her knife into the surprised officer. There were others in the hall. They lifted a shout and pushed their way into the flat.

* * *

Nicolas tore up the stairs, the clash of steel meeting his ears. His sword was ready. He rounded the corner and slashed into the first black and green uniform he saw. The man fell with a cry and Nicolas whirled into the fight, unable to think, or see, or hear anything but the steel and the shouts of his opponents.

When four men lay on the ground, Nicolas looked up from his last opponent to see recognition in Maggie's eyes. "Nicolas!" she cried, and threw herself into his arms like a sister whose long-lost brother has just come home.

"You were in danger," he said, embarrassed by Maggie's enthusiastic greeting. "I heard someone trying to warn you," Nicolas continued. "And I knew where you were so I—I ran."

"You may have saved our lives," Maggie said.

"Don't speak too soon," Pat said. She had moved to the window. "Black-and-Greens in the street. They're on their way up."

"Then let's not wait for them!" Nicolas said. He joined Pat and threw open the window. A latticework covered with creeping vines, yellow with the turning of the seasons, formed a shaky ladder to the ground. The High Police had left the street and were coming up the stairs.

Nicolas started his careful climb to the ground. Pat and Maggie looked at each other, nodded, and followed him out.

* * *

The second day of the Tax Gathering dawned bright. The peasantry picked themselves up from the alleys and doorsteps where they had slept, outside inns crowded to the bursting point. Almost as one, the people of the city crossed the bridges and climbed the streets of the plateau to Pravik Castle.

There would be a trial today.

Maggie, Pat, and Nicolas joined the curious who flocked to the castle. Maggie recognized others in the crowd. Some limped as she did. Here and there an old farmer smiled at her, a smile of encouragement.

It would work.

It had to work.

They were among the first to reach Pravik Castle. Maggie reached into her coat pocket and fingered a small map the Ploughman had given her. She lagged behind as Nicolas and Pat passed through the gates into the huge courtyard where the trial would be held. Maggie shivered, for she could see through the gates where a massive gallows waited.

She pulled the map out of her pocket and studied it quickly, darting into the crowd as quickly as her leg would allow. She moved through the gates and around the castle wall away from the courtyard until she reached a low door where castle servants went in and out.

Her heart was pounding as she went through the small entrance. No one stopped her with so much as a word, though guards stood all around.

They will hire extra help for the Tax Gathering and the trial, Libuse had said. *Chances are no one will notice you.*

Or the others, Maggie hoped. She could not do this alone. She had entered a low-ceilinged room with stone walls dark with soot and floors stained with mud. There were many servants in the room, and merchants delivering special wares, and others on other errands. She raised her eyes and looked around her quickly—there. She knew the face of the hump-backed old man near an inside door.

She limped to his side. He acknowledged her with a slight nod. "You're late," he said. He started off through the door, and Maggie followed him. Three others were waiting on the other side.

Together they moved through the castle corridors, consulting the Ploughman's maps when they had need of them.

"You there!" a guard shouted. Maggie kept going, her heart pounding. Footsteps hurried down the hall behind them —and passed them. The guard was calling someone else.

They climbed a twisting flight of stairs.

"Shouldn't we be going down?" whispered one of the men. "To the dungeon?"

"Ploughman says they'll keep the prisoners here," the hump-backed old man said. "We do what he told us."

You shouldn't do this, Libuse had said. *The men can do it alone. Stay where it's safer.*

I have to see him, Maggie had answered. *If we—fail—I may never have another chance.*

Libuse had smiled. *I understand completely.*

They rounded a corner and a guard looked up in surprise. His face was red and he held a flask in his hand.

"What the—" he started to say.

He had no opportunity to finish.

As they pushed through the halls, fighting nearly every step of the way, Maggie felt exulted at the ease with which the High Police fell. They were drunk to the last man.

Nobody makes wine like my grandmother makes wine, the farmer had said in a late-night meeting with the Ploughman. *And nobody drinks it like the High Police. A present, perhaps, might be in order . . .*

Maggie heard Jerome call her name before she saw him. For a fleeting instant she was afraid—afraid of him, afraid of herself, afraid she had dreamed everything. She lifted her eyes and saw him through the fight, behind crossed iron bars. One side of his face was bruised and swollen, and his clothes were torn and filthy.

She pushed through the fight, the cries of the High Police and of her fellow rebels like distant memories in her ears. He reached for her through the bars. She took his hands and looked into his eyes and he kissed her.

The moment was fleeting. Maggie's sword struck at the lock on the cell until it was finally broken and Jerome was free. She pressed the sword into his hand as he moved by her. He did not pause to talk to her, or even to look at her, but hurried down the long corridor, deeper into the dungeon.

"The master is this way," he called over his shoulder. Maggie followed him.

* * *

Drums beat in the courtyard. Antonin Zarras, Overlord of the Eastern Lands, stepped onto the platform next to the gallows. He was a short, dark man; handsome though his physique evidenced that he habitually ate better than any dozen of his tenants. The crowd murmured as he appeared, flanked on all sides by High Police.

"We have gathered here for the annual bringing in of taxes," Zarras said. "Always a happy occasion. I welcome you, my people, many of my tenants. I commend you. For you are here to show your loyalty in a time when our lives are threatened."

His dark eyes glinted. "In this city, there have been threats. Men have risen who wish to destroy us all. To take over, to plunder you, my people, and to ravish all you hold sacred." He leaned over the top of his pulpit and swept the crowd with his eyes. "Many years ago a royal family ruled this land. Its descendants have served on the Overlord's council for centuries. A short time ago, Professor Jarin Huss and his apprentice murdered the last scion of that family. Today we bring them to justice."

Shouts and rumbles came from the crowd, and Zarras smiled. "Bring them out," he commanded.

There was a shout from the castle gates, and the crowd turned almost as a man. Many gasped. Others cheered.

Libuse was walking through the crowd, straight toward

292

the platform where Zarras stood. A column of armed men marched behind her, and the Ploughman stood at her side. Many in the crowd bowed as their princess moved past, but her eyes were only on Zarras.

Stunned High Police parted for her as she climbed the steps of the platform and came face to face with the Overlord. The Ploughman and his men pushed past the soldiers. The High Police said nothing, did nothing. They had been caught completely off guard, and now the threatening looks of the crowd and the weaponry of the Ploughman's men kept them still.

"What is the meaning of this?" Antonin Zarras stuttered. His eyes went from Libuse to the Ploughman and back again, as though he wasn't sure which was worse.

"I should ask you that, Zarras," Libuse said. "Is this not a trial to avenge my death? It seems to me that all is not as it seems."

Zarras licked his lips. "I cannot say how glad I am to see you alive," he began.

"Perhaps we should not tell the people—" Libuse took in all the crowd with a sweep of her arm, "—how you had me arrested. How you intended to kill me. How you are now trying to murder two more of your enemies, enemies only because they work on behalf of this very crowd."

A young man in the crowd, a university student from his dress, shouted something in agreement.

"You are in trouble, Zarras," Libuse said quietly.

The Ploughman stepped close to the Overlord. He towered over Zarras, and the Overlord shook as the Ploughman drew his sword.

"There will be a trial today," the Ploughman said, raising his voice so all the crowd could hear. "You, Antonin Zarras— you are on trial."

The Overlord was white. He stood in silence for a long moment, facing the man he had known as a friend in his youth. "You always hated me," he said.

"No," the Ploughman said. "The only one guilty of hate here is you."

The Overlord's lip curled. "You are outnumbered."

"We are well trained."

"Who trained them?" the Overlord pressed. "Farmers trained by farmers. Boys trained by old men. You cannot fight High Police."

"I trained them," the Ploughman said.

"Trained by a madman," the Overlord said, so quiet that no one heard him but the Ploughman. "Even as a child you were delusional."

The Ploughman bowed his head and hefted his sword. "Let the professor and his apprentice go," he said. "And we will leave you with your life."

"I will never let them go," Antonin Zarras said. "If you kill me they will die instantly, and so will you."

"I think not," a new voice said. Antonin Zarras whirled around, his face livid. It was Jerome who had called out. He stood at the end of the platform with a sword in his hand and the professor behind him.

For a moment Zarras stood in speechless rage. "Kill them!" he screamed. "Kill them all!"

He drew his own sword with one swift motion and lunged forward, straight at Libuse. The Ploughman's staff knocked the sword away and the Overlord fell back. He looked up at the Ploughman in terror.

"You should have tried to kill me," the Ploughman said, his face golden with rage. "That I would have accepted. But do not touch the ones I love."

"Kill them all!" the Overlord screamed again. The High Police sprang into action.

And Antonin Zarras died.

* * *

Virginia's skin crawled as the smoke drifted across her. She heard the voice of Evelyn, hoarse and ragged with excitement, shouting commands over the chanting. The smoke was hot with more than fire, and it burned Virginia's skin.

A smell like brimstone filled the air and made her sick. She saw.

The smoke was billowing up in great, black clouds. Wisps of green and blue smoke played through the blackness. Here and there a wisp of smoke took on the likeness of something else: a claw, a gaping mouth, a burning eye.

She saw the strength draining out of the black-robed men of the Order, their energy leeched to feed the churning cloud of smoke. She watched as the guards in black fell to the ground, crying out for help, until their voices were silenced in a hissing roar.

And then she saw the creatures rising up all around her, stepping out of the clouds. There was a great black hound, breathing tendrils of green smoke; ravens with burning eyes; creatures like horses with goat's feet and lion's teeth. Most horrible of all were beings in the shape of winged men, twelve feet tall, who carried swords and maces, and laughed as they rose up from the flames.

* * *

Libuse ran across the platform to Professor Huss and the others. "Come quickly," she said, motioning for them to follow her.

They leapt from the platform into the crowd. Jerome carried his master. The crowd parted for them and the Ploughman's soldiers beat back the High Police. They ran out of the gates and into the streets until they entered the blackened courtyard where Maggie and Nicolas had first met Huss and Jerome. Libuse hurriedly beat out a rhythm on the stones, and the trapdoor opened for them.

Together they descended into the dark tunnel. Libuse lit the candle that waited at the top of the stairs. Through the damp, dark tunnels they wound their way, taking corridors that Maggie had never seen before.

At last they reached a place where the ground sloped up. There were no stairs, only ruts carved into the stone to make footholds and handholds. The way grew steeper as they went, and the roof of the corridor came closer and closer. For the last stretch they were forced to crawl on their hands and knees, and Maggie feared that Huss would not make it. He set his jaw and climbed.

When they reached a dead end, Libuse pushed against the roof with all her might, and it gave way before her. A faint light filtered in from the small opening and was blocked as

Libuse led the way out.

Maggie was last to emerge from the tunnel, and she looked around to see a part of the city she had never imagined existed. They seemed to be inside a very old hall, one that had fallen into ruin over many years. It was built of white stone. Much of the roof was missing. All that remained of the walls were rows of white pillars that held up the roof on either side.

At first Maggie thought that the hall must once have been a place where nobles gathered to eat and drink, but the more she looked, the more the gloomy atmosphere of the place convinced her that this was not so. It was then that she noticed the white stones, laying on their sides, that filled it.

"What is this place?" she asked, her voice filled with wonder.

"This is the Hall of Kings, burial place of my ancestors," Libuse said. She spread out her hands to indicate the stones. "Here lie the ancient rulers of Sloczka. At one time this was a place of pilgrimage, but the Empire discouraged pilgrims and allowed the hall to fall into ruin."

"Why have you brought us here?" Jerome asked.

"Because you are in no condition to fight," Libuse said, "and the Ploughman wished that you both be kept safe until the battle was over."

"And you are to stay, no doubt?" Huss asked. Libuse lowered her eyes.

"The Ploughman wishes it," she said.

"What if the battle turns against us, and even this place is lost?" Jerome asked.

"Then it seems to me that there is no more fitting place for me to die," Libuse said.

297

"We could escape back through the tunnels," Maggie said. "The tunnel leads out to the river."

Libuse nodded, and said, "Yes, and if the enemy should come here then you all must try to escape."

"What about you?" Maggie asked.

"If the battle is lost," Libuse said, "it means that the Ploughman is lost. If that happens, I will not run from death."

"Yet you would send us away like cowards?" Jerome asked.

"For the good of all," Libuse said. "Someone must survive to continue the fight. You possess such belief—belief in a holy king, in a final end to tyranny. That hope cannot die here."

"You can say such things, and yet you do not yourself believe?" Huss asked.

Libuse looked away. "I am not sure what I believe. Only what I wish I could."

From somewhere close by, the sounds of battle reached the ruin. Jerome's fingers opened and closed on the hilt of the sword Maggie had given him. "I should not be here. It is a shame to hide while the battle rages," he said.

"Is it a shame to protect someone you love?" Maggie asked, turning to face him. He looked deeply at her for a moment, and said,

"No."

"The master needs your protection," Maggie said. "And as you are holding my sword, so do I."

Jerome chuckled, a deep, throaty chuckle, and he seemed to stand a little straighter. "You are right," he said. "Of course you are right."

They stopped talking at the sound of a shout, and they

turned to see a figure entering the ruins.

"Get out of sight," Jerome said. Huss and Libuse obeyed. Jerome stood behind a pillar with his sword drawn, waiting for the figure to come close enough to be identified. He didn't look like a soldier, but even so, there was no telling whether he was friend or enemy.

Maggie broke the stillness. "Nicolas!" she called. With a barely noticeable sigh of relief, Jerome sheathed his sword.

Huss stretched out his hands in welcome, rising from his hiding place near one of the tombstones. "It is good to see you again, boy."

"And you, sir," Nicolas said. He looked embarrassed and Huss chuckled.

"No need to be nervous," he said. "We won't make you explain your disappearance, or anything else you don't feel like talking about."

"What are you doing here?" Maggie asked.

"Haven't you heard the shouts?" Nicolas asked. "I came looking for you to tell you—we've won! The Ploughman has driven the High Police from the castle. They flee the city even now. The battle is over."

Their exclamations of delight died suddenly as a strange sound made its way through the pillars of the burial hall. It was the sound of drums beating in the distance . . . a slow, ominous beating. A death march.

Jerome pulled his sword out and held it ready, his brow knitted in concern. Libuse held her spear, her head high, listening. And Nicolas crouched slightly, his own slim sword in his hand. They waited.

A shadow fell slowly over the hall, covering it in darkness

as though dusk had come—hours and hours too early. Maggie felt her heart beating harder with fear, and her eyes strayed to meet Nicolas's. They had felt this shadow before, this creeping, numbing fear. The ravens and the hound both had carried it with them.

* * *

The victory celebration had ended as abruptly as it had begun. The people of the city stood outside the gates of Pravik Castle, their eyes fixed on the horizon where clouds gathered. The rebel soldiers had fallen completely silent. They watched the darkening skies with drawn, bloody swords.

Evil was coming, and every man and animal among them could feel it.

The drums beat louder.

A shadow, deeper than the already dark sky, fell on the street just below them. There was a blinding flash, not of light but of darkness, and for the first time the Ploughman beheld his new enemies.

He was facing a giant, a creature in the shape of a man with bull's horns and eyes that burned, and a mouth that grinned hideously. The man-thing held a black mace and an equally black sword, almost invisible against quivering black wings. He roared as he stepped inside the walls of Pravik.

Behind him came the bone-chilling howl of a hound. The shadows of winged creatures flew over the walls, screaming with hatred and glee.

Once again, the battle was joined.

14

The Peace of Death We Break

IT IS ONLY A FOOL WHO WRITES WHILE HE IS DYING. Yet I must . . . I must. This pen is my only friend, and I do not wish to die alone.

There is so much pain in dying. I did not know it would feel as it does.

I am Aneryn. I am the Poet. I am the Prophet. I alone remember . . .

The Blackness whispers through the Veil. It threatens such terrible things. But now there are other voices. Is it truly the Shearim I hear? They comfort. But their voices are so faded.

Gone now.

The trees are very green. The ground on which I lie is very black, and it is tangled with white roots. It is hard and smells like a thousand days gone by. It smells like my childhood.

Have I ever been a child?

I am Aneryn. The Poet. The Prophet. I wish . . .

Birds are flying overhead . . . great white flocks. Perhaps in the end they will take me away with them. But I do not want to leave. I do not want to go.

It hurts to die.

I can see a light, very far away. It is opening in the sky and its rays fall on me. They have just touched my fingertips, and now they move toward my face. Perhaps I will not die after all, for everywhere the light touches I am healed.

I am strong. I am peaceful.

I am Aneryn, the Poet; I am Aneryn, the Prophet; I am Aneryn, the Strong . . .

I have no ink left with which to write. My chronicle is over.

And I see him now. He is coming.

* * *

The Ploughman thought of Libuse as he fought. *My courage.* His spear made little dent in the armour of the horned warrior, and his horse bucked and threw him to the ground. He rose to his feet with his sword drawn and jumped out of the way of the creature's crashing mace. He heard shouts. His men were joining him. He watched as the black warrior drove into them and brought them down as if they had been children. The Ploughman watched and gripped his sword more fiercely. Fury boiled in him and he attacked.

The horned warrior was stronger, but the Ploughman was fast. He ducked and thrust, weaving in and out, moving constantly, a fly annoying a man. All around him his people were falling; the battle was failing and he knew it. But for him, in this moment, there was only one adversary and one fight, one death to meet if he should fail and one victory to gain if he should win.

At last he stood with his feet firmly planted on the ground and lifted his sword to meet that of the enemy. The impact of the horned warrior's blade shattered the Ploughman's sword, and he threw the useless hilt aside and plucked his fallen spear from the ground. As his hand tightened around the smooth wood of the shaft, the flat of the black warrior's blade caught him in the stomach and sent him flying through the air. He landed on his back on the ground and struggled to breathe, to move, to do anything. The enemy's sword slashed down. The Ploughman rolled so that the blade caught his arm. The wound burned, but it was not deep . . . the horned warrior was playing with him.

A huge clawed hand closed around the Ploughman's throat and lifted him off the ground like a doll. The horned warrior drew back his sword, preparing to plunge it into his enemy's limp body.

As blackness rushed in on him and pain threatened to overwhelm his senses, the Ploughman lifted his spear desperately and aimed blindly for the monster's head.

And a strength not his took him.

A battle cry rang in his ears—his own voice, but in the echoes of it there were other voices—stronger, golden voices. It was not his strength that aimed his spear, not his strength that threw it; yet it worked through him.

Childhood delusions.

The horned warrior roared with pain and dropped the Ploughman. He landed in a crouch on the ground, fingers brushing the bloody earth. He looked up to see what had happened.

His spear had pierced through the eye of the horned warrior. With one last infuriated cry of pain, the creature staggered and fell. It was dead.

The Ploughman pulled his spear free and raised it high, screaming his battle cry over the streets of the city. He ran into the thick of the battle, and the earth shuddered at his footsteps.

* * *

They felt the hound's presence before they saw it. They could hear the sound of it breathing, sniffing the wind, and they felt the deepening of the darkness as it drew near. Maggie and Libuse huddled closer to Huss, all three of them crouching behind a white stone while Jerome and Nicolas stood in the open, waiting. The sound of the creature's approach filled the ruined hall with dread.

In the blackness of the shadow, the white pillars of the hall seemed to glow with a light of their own, like ghostly moons in a starless sky. A howling rose up from somewhere close. Libuse rose slightly from her crouch, clutching her spear. The thread she had braided into her hair shone silver-white as star fire.

Nicolas saw it first. He ran forward, screaming defiance to the death that waited to meet him, and drove his sword deep into the hound's foreleg before it could react to his attack. The hound growled deep and lunged forward without warning. Its teeth sank into Nicolas's shoulder, and it shook him like a rag.

"Nicolas!" Maggie cried. Libuse had gone pale. Huss was sitting on the ground between them, his eyes closed and his face drawn.

Jerome leapt to Nicolas's aid, swinging his sword powerfully at the hound's side, He opened a long wound over the creature's rib cage. Snarling, the hound dropped Nicolas and swung on Jerome, who sprang away from the animal's snapping jaws.

Libuse jumped up and ran from their hiding place. She grabbed Nicolas and started to drag him away from the fight, when the hound caught sight of her. Its eyes flashed in anger at the sight of the princess of ancient days in whose hair the star fire dared to shine, and it turned from Jerome. He ran desperately after it, trying to draw it away from Libuse and Nicolas.

It seemed to Maggie that she beheld it all as in a dream, even as she left her place from behind the white rock and ran to her companions. She could hear herself shouting and yet did not know what words she used; she could feel the tears on her face but could not feel herself crying.

She saw Libuse throw her spear. She saw the hound shrug it away as though it had been a matchstick. She saw Libuse step over Nicolas and stand tall, the thread in her hair burning with light so pure and bright that it seemed to drive back the darkness where the princess stood. She saw the hound's teeth glistening, she heard it roar, and she saw it leap forward . . .

And then she saw Jerome, though she did not know how he had come to be there, driving and twisting his sword deep into the hound's neck while the creature was still in the air, and she saw the blood that evaporated into green steam and heard the sounds of the hound's death throes.

As the hound's writhing body fell to the ground, she saw its horrible claws bury themselves in Jerome's chest, and she saw him falling under the hound's weight, and she heard a sickening breaking sound.

She was at his side then, and he was reaching for her. The lower half of his body was under the massive bulk of the hound, but his hands were free and she took them and held them to her throat, crying. For a moment she felt his hands tighten around hers, and then they loosened. She bent down and kissed him, and he was gone.

Maggie felt Huss's bony hand on her shoulder, and she felt Libuse slip her arm around her waist. But she stayed on her knees, holding Jerome's hands, and cried soundlessly.

Then she lifted up her voice and sang a lament—an ancient lament, drawn from the depths of her heart where Mary's song played, and in it was all the anguish and loss of five hundred years since the exile of the King, but for her it was all about one man.

* * *

Maggie ran. Around her and below her the city of Pravik was in flames. A battle raged the like of which had never been seen in five hundred years. She ran through the streets, not seeing the battle, not seeing the nightmare. She ran through the castle gates, up and up until she stood on the walls and looked over the boiling turmoil. The song was in her. The song ran through her veins. The song was wild and full of power.

The creatures of Blackness turned their heads to look at her. They began to move toward the castle, to beat their wings, and she saw it all in slow motion. They were coming for her. They were coming for the thing she carried.

"Can you hear me?" she cried. The wind took her words and bore them away to a hilltop where an evil blue light burned. "Your power is breaking," she shouted, her voice strong because of the song. "It is drowned in the blood of those who die in honour!"

Still they were coming—scurrying up the walls, flying through the air. It would take them a million years to arrive, she thought. They moved so slowly.

She reached into her coat and pulled out the scroll. The shadow around her seemed to shiver. She unrolled the parchment—the scroll that had come so far, withstanding fire and water, the ancient testament to treachery. The song in her veins welled high, and with strength that did not come from herself she tore a piece from it and held it over the flaming city.

"For Mary," she said. She released the torn paper and watched as it rose in the ash-filled air, drifting up with the smoke.

She tore another piece and let it go. "For John," she said. The wind swirled and another piece rose on the air. "For Jerome."

The last bit of parchment she held high before releasing it. "For the King!" she shouted. Her voice rushed along the walls of the city, danced up the eddies of the wind, and echoed through the hills and mountains of Sloczka.

When her voice died down, a hunting horn sounded long and clear through the sky. A flash of light like the birth of a star flooded the hills and tore through the darkness. The torn pieces of parchment burst into flames and burned, clear and white, until there was nothing left of them.

In that instant the creatures of darkness were knocked away from the castle. They fell to the streets, screaming in rage and fear. They turned on the soldiers, snarling, clawing. A goat-headed man bared razor teeth, raised its bloody black sword, and charged forward.

Its sword met the Ploughman's. The rebel leader's eyes blazed with fierce golden light. He pressed the goat-man back. He raised his sword to end the creature's life. Around him his enemies closed in, yet it hardly seemed to matter. He was surrounded. The goat-man looked up at him with mocking red eyes, laughing. The Ploughman was outnumbered.

He would fail. He must fall.

His sword was still raised high, the goat-man still lay at his feet. He closed his eyes for a moment and looked up. He could see a single star shining.

He brought the sword down. In its wake a golden arc cut the fabric of the air.

In that instant the city was filled with pounding hooves and flowing manes; with golden armour and great white swords. The golden riders—horses and riders, from over the sea—drove into the forces of the Blackness.

The Ploughman fell to his knees, suddenly exhausted. He raised his eyes and tears flowed down his cheeks.

Here was his strength.

Here was his childhood delusion.

He heard shouts and whoops as his men renewed their strength and fought again, but he could not join them. He could only weep.

* * *

On the hilltop there was nothing but confusion. The feel of it woke Virginia from unconsciousness, even as she felt the fire underneath her grow with a vicious, cruel heat. She could hear Evelyn cursing and screaming with fury. In her mind's eye she saw golden forces in Pravik and knew that the Blackness had lost.

Evelyn was fleeing the hilltop. Virginia saw the laird going with her, and she reached out to him, but he did not turn to look at her.

She saw Skraetock. He stood before the fire with his hands raised and his mouth twisted. He was staring into the flames. As he stared the flames grew hotter and higher, and she knew that he had used her enough and now meant to kill her.

She heard a shrieking as though there were yet spirits in the fire who had not taken form and flown to the city, and now they were dancing all around her. The sound and the searing heat nearly overwhelmed her, but with pain no longer controlling her, with Skraetock no longer binding her strength, she formed a word in her weakness through her cracked, blackened lips.

"Llycharath . . ." she whispered.

An instant later, a wind flung Lord Skraetock aside and cowed the shrieking flames. It tore the bars of the cage and carried Virginia away with it.

* * *

The battle ended with the coming of morning. The golden riders vanished with the first rays of the sun. Of the vanquished shadow creatures there were left only black stains on the cobblestones. Throughout the day the people of Pravik laboured to put out the last of the smoldering fires and salvage what they could of the ruins left in the battle's wake.

Men and women from the surrounding countryside walked and rode into the city throughout the day. Mrs. Cook and Mrs. Korak arrived in the evening, bringing the stores of the farm's cellar on a wagon behind them.

With the sunrise of the next morning, a long procession made its mournful way to the western mountain on which Pravik rested to lay to rest all who had given their lives in the battle. They passed by the reaching hands of the Guardian Bridge and through the gates of the city to the hillside. Maggie walked with one hand on Jerome's coffin, and Huss walked on the other side. The line of coffins stretched far ahead of them, each one carried on a small wagon pulled by farm horses and ponies. It stretched down the high hill to a valley where open graves waited.

At the head of the line the Ploughman walked. His cloak was torn and his face streaked with ashes as a sign of mourning. Libuse walked by his side, a broken spear cradled in her arms. Around the splintered handle was twisted the silver thread of the Huntsman.

Behind them came the widows and mothers and children of the men who had fallen. They wept loudly as they walked. Then came the men, rebel soldiers and villagers and farmers who had come to the new freedom of Pravik. They marched grimly and silently.

Pat was behind them on crutches, and Mrs. Cook walked beside her with one arm around Virginia's waist. Virginia had been found in the road by villagers on their way to the city. Her skin was dark with soot and her lips cracked and bleeding, but there was a power about her that made even her friends a little afraid. She would not say where Lord Robert had gone, but all understood he was not coming back.

Nicolas was missing from the procession. He had left the city unnoticed in the commotion that followed the battle. He had come to Maggie first, while she kept vigilance beside Jerome's open coffin.

"I'm sorry, Maggie," he had said, faltering. "He was a brave man."

Maggie had not answered.

"Anyway, I'll be going," Nicolas had said, his tone deliberately light.

Maggie had turned with tear-filled eyes, but Nicolas was already nearly out the door. At the last minute he had turned and looked at her, and she had heard anguish in his voice.

"He loved you very much," Nicolas told her. "I heard the love in his heart. It was beautiful."

And then he was gone. "He will be back," Huss had said when she told him.

"You sound very sure."

"The world is taking sides," Huss had said. "Soon even the most determined wanderers will have to make a choice. And I am sure I know what side he will choose to take."

The long procession reached the bottom of the hill. The men came and lifted the coffins, laying them on the ground beside the open graves. High on the hill behind them Pravik stood mournful watch, and the wind sighed up and down the sides of the valley.

Maggie stood near Jerome's coffin as the Ploughman stood in the midst of his people and spoke of the battle and the courage of those who had fought. More, he spoke of the future, in which their toils would be rewarded. A future in which Athrom would hear them and they would be free.

Libuse spoke also, of days gone by, and of the faded glory of the Eastern Lands which once more was beginning to shine. "In the Hall of Kings there does not lay one man of more worth than we lay to rest here today," she said. "This day we say farewell to the truest sons of the East."

At the last Huss stood and spoke a blessing over the burial grounds, a blessing pronounced in the name of the King. Maggie stood and sang her lament once more.

Finally the last moment came. Maggie's eyes clouded with tears as the men came and began to lower the coffins into the ground. She stayed near as they took up the body of Jerome, and her eyes widened. A large white seabird flew down and perched on top of the coffin. It smiled at her with knowing eyes and bobbed its head once. Then it spread its wide wings and soared away.

Maggie watched it go, and she called after it. The bird bore her last farewell along with it to the southern sea.

* * *

That night Maggie ate for the first time since the battle had ended. She sat on a cushioned seat near the fire in the house of Libuse and let her eyes trace the outlines of the faces that sat at the table with her. The Ploughman and Libuse; Mrs. Cook and Pat; Huss and Virginia. They were a strange little company, Maggie thought, but a smile came to her as she reflected that they were no stranger than another council that had met, forty years ago, to dream dreams that would lead to this day.

Pravik was taken, but the battle was not over. Athrom would not hear them yet. Even now High Police were marching from Athrom. The Emperor roared in his den, eager to avenge the death of his Overlord and teach the rebels a lesson. In the city, the people were moving underground. The tunnels through which Maggie had run from the guards what seemed like an eternity ago were only one level of a great web of tunnels and caverns that led deep down into the rocky foundations of the city. The High Police would find nothing but mystery when they arrived.

Soon they would go, too, but the little company wished to eat one last meal above the ground. In a way it seemed that they were still sitting in the old Pravik: the Pravik where Libuse had longed for the days of her ancestors; where the Ploughman had lost his brother in a riot sparked by hopelessness; where Huss had battled the Empire by teaching secret truths to all who would listen. It was the Pravik where the old Maggie still lived, the Maggie who had ridden over the Guardian Bridge with Nicolas and shivered at the sight of the pleading statues, before love and truth and song had changed her forever.

But it was not the old Pravik any longer, no matter what illusions and memories the night whispered to them. When Maggie took Huss's arm that night and left the house of Libuse, she stepped into a new world.

Rachel would love to hear from you!

You can visit her and interact online:

Web: **www.rachelstarrthomson.com**
Facebook: **www.facebook.com/RachelStarrThomsonWriter**
Twitter: **@writerstarr**

THE SEVENTH WORLD TRILOGY

Worlds Unseen   **Burning Light**   **Coming Day**

For five hundred years the Seventh World has been ruled by a tyrannical empire—and the mysterious Order of the Spider that hides in its shadow. History and truth are deliberately buried, the beauty and treachery of the past remembered only by wandering Gypsies, persecuted scholars, and a few unusual seekers. But the past matters, as Maggie Sheffield soon finds out. It matters because its forces will soon return and claim lordship over her world, for good or evil.

The Seventh World Trilogy is an epic fantasy, beautiful, terrifying, pointing to the realities just beyond the world we see.

"An excellent read, solidly recommended for fantasy readers."

—Midwest Book Review

"A wonderfully realistic fantasy world. Recommended."

—Jill Williamson, Christy-Award-Winning Author of **By Darkness Hid**

"Epic, beautiful, well-written fantasy that sings of truth."

—Rael, reader

Available everywhere online or special order from your local bookstore.

THE ONENESS CYCLE

Exile   Hive   Attack   Renegade   Rise

The supernatural entity called the Oneness holds the world together.
What happens if it falls apart?

In a world where the Oneness exists, nothing looks the same. Dead men walk. Demons prowl the air. Old friends peel back their mundane masks and prove as supernatural as angels. But after centuries of battling demons and the corrupting powers of the world, the Oneness is under a new threat—its greatest threat. Because this time, the threat comes from within.

Fast-paced contemporary fantasy.

"Plot twists and lots of edge-of-your-seat action,
I had a hard time putting it down!"

—Alexis

"Finally! The kind of fiction I've been waiting for my whole life!"

—Mercy Hope, FaithTalks.com

"I sped through this short, fast-paced novel, pleased by the well-drawn characters and the surprising plot. Thomson has done a great job of portraying difficult emotional journeys . . . Read it!"

—Phyllis Wheeler, The Christian Fantasy Review

Available everywhere online or special order from your local bookstore.

TAERITH

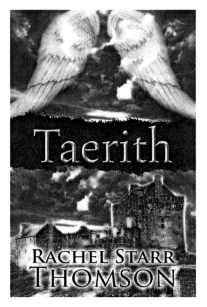

When he rescues a young woman named Lilia from bandits, Taerith Romany is caught in a web of loyalties: Lilia is the future queen of a spoiled king, and though Taerith is not allowed to love her, neither he can bring himself to leave her without a friend. Their lives soon intertwine with the fiercely proud slave girl, Mirian, whose tragic past and wild beauty make her the target of the king's unscrupulous brother.

The king's rule is only a knife's edge from slipping—and when it does, all three will be put to the ultimate test. In a land of fog and fens, unicorns and wild men, Taerith stands at the crossroads of good and evil, where men are vanquished by their own obsessions or saved by faith in higher things.

"Devastatingly beautiful . . . I am amazed at every chapter how deeply you've caused us to care for these characters."

—Gabi

"Deeply satisfying." —Kapezia

"Rachel Starr Thomson is an artist, and every chapter of Taerith is like a painting . . . beautiful."

—Brittany Simmons

Available everywhere online or special order from your local bookstore.

ANGEL IN THE WOODS

Hawk is a would-be hero in search of a giant to kill or a maiden to save. The trouble is, when he finds them, there are forty-some maidens—and they call their giant "the Angel." Before he knows what's happening, Hawk is swept into the heart of a patchwork family and all of its mysteries, carried away by their camaraderie—and falling quickly in love.

But the outside world cannot be kept at bay forever. Suspecting the Giant of hiding a treasure, the wealthy and influential Widow Brawnlyn sets out to tear the family apart and bring the Giant to destruction any way she can. And her two principle weapons are Hawk—and the truth.

Caught between the terrible truths he discovers about the family's past and the unalterable fact that he has come to love them, Hawk must face his fears and overcome his flaws if he is to rescue the Angel in the woods.

*"A beautiful tale of finding oneself, honor and heroism;
a story I will not soon forget."*
— Szoch

*"The more I think about it, the more truth and beauty
I find in the story."*
—H. A. Titus

Available everywhere online or special order from your local bookstore.

LADY MOON

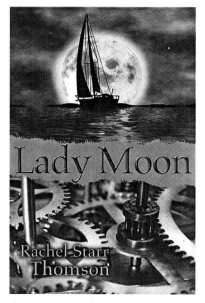

When Celine meets Tomas, they are in a cavern on the moon where she has been languishing for thirty days after being banished by her evil uncle for throwing a scrub brush at his head. Tomas is a charming and eccentric Immortal, hanging out on the moon because he's procrastinating his destiny—meeting, and defeating, Celine's uncle.

A pair of magic rings send them back to earth, where Celine insists on returning home and is promptly thrown into the dungeon. Her uncle, Ignus Umbria, is up to no good, and his latest caper threatens to devour the whole countryside. He doesn't want Celine getting in the way. More than that, he wants to force Tomas into a confrontation—and Tomas, who has fallen in love with Celine, cannot procrastinate any longer.

Lady Moon is a fast-paced, humorous adventure in a world populated by mad magicians, walking rosebushes, thieving scullery maids, and other improbable things. And of course, the most improbable—and magical—thing of all: true love.

"Celine's sarcastic 'languishing' immediately put me in mind of Patricia C. Wrede's Dealing with Dragons series—a fairy tale that gently makes fun of the usual fairy tale tropes. And once again, Rachel Starr Thomson doesn't disappoint."

— H. A. Titus

"Funny and quirky fantasy."

Available everywhere online.

REAP THE WHIRLWIND

Beren is a city in constant unrest: ruled by a ruthless upper class and harried by a band of rebels who want change. Its one certainty is that the two sides do not, and will not, meet.

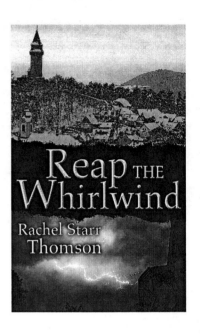

But children know little of sides or politics, and Anna and Kyara— a princess and a peasant girl—let their chance meeting grow into a deep friendship. Until the day Kyara's family is slaughtered by Anna's people, and the friendship comes to an abrupt end.

Years later, Kyara is a rebel—bitter, hard, and violent. Anna's efforts to fight the political system she belongs to avail little. Neither is a child anymore—but neither has ever forgotten the power of their long-ago friendship. When a secret plot brings the rebellion to a fiery head, both young women know it is too late to save the land they love.

But is it too late to save each other?

Available everywhere online.

Short Fiction by Rachel Starr Thomson

BUTTERFLIES DANCING

FALLEN STAR

OF MEN AND BONES

OGRES IS

JOURNEY

MAGDALENE

THE CITY CAME CREEPING

WAYFARER'S DREAM

WAR WITH THE MUSE

SHIELDS OF THE EARTH

And more!

***Available as downloads for
Kindle, Kobo, Nook, iPad, and more!***

CPSIA information can be obtained
at www.ICGtesting.com
Printed in the USA
LVOW12s0023100917

548025LV00001B/9/P